ALIAS THE NIGHT WIND

Frederic V. R. Dey

OTHER BOOKS IN THE ARGOSY LIBRARY:

The Blue Fire Pearl: The Complete Adventures
of Singapore Sammy, Volume 1
BY GEORGE F. WORTS

Clovelly
BY MAX BRAND

Drink We Deep
BY ARTHUR LEO ZAGAT

The Gun-Brand
BY JAMES B. HENDRYX

Jan of the Jungle
BY OTIS ADELBERT KLINE

Minions of the Moon
BY WILLIAM GREY BEYER

The Moon Pool & The Conquest of the Moon Pool
BY ABRAHAM MERRITT

Tarzan and the Jewels of Opar
BY EDGAR RICE BURROUGHS

War Lord of Many Swordsmen:
The Adventures of Norcross, Volume 1
BY W. WIRT

THE ARGOSY LIBRARY

ALIAS THE NIGHT WIND

FREDERICK VAN RENSSELAER DEY
WRITING AS
VARICK VANARDY

ALTUS PRESS
2017

EDITED AND DESIGNED BY
Matthew Moring

PUBLISHING HISTORY
"Alias the Night Wind" originally appeared in the May 10, 17, 24 & 31, 1913 issues
    of *The Cavalier* magazine (Vol. 28, No. 3–Vol. 29, No. 2). Copyright © 1913 by
    The Frank A. Munsey Company.
"About the Author" originally appeared as "How I Wrote a Thousand Nick Carter
    Novels" in the February 1920 issue of *The American Magazine*. Copyright ©
    1920 by The Crowell Publishing Company.

THANKS TO
Doug Ellis

ISBN
978-1-61827-307-9

Visit *altuspress.com* for more books like this.
Printed in the United States of America.

TABLE OF CONTENTS

CHAPTER I

A MIDNIGHT INCIDENT

A TAXICAB OF nondescript character pulled up at the curb twenty feet around the corner from the avenue and a man stepped down from it.

Two uniformed policemen, the peg-post and his relief, who had withdrawn from the intersection of street and avenue prior to their exchange of duties, appeared from behind the corner of the building at the same instant.

An electric arc light shone full upon the face of the man at the cab who was putting some coins into the outstretched hand of the chauffeur.

The cop who was relieving his companion on "peg" saw the face that was so distinctly lighted up, and he halted, straightened, and stiffened where he stood.

"F'r th' love uh Mi—" he gasped, not completing the meaningless expression.

He seized his companion by the arm with a grip that tightened and clung the firmer when the man attempted to wrench himself free from it. For the second officer had seen the direction of his friend's glance, and caught the change of expression, and had sensed rather than heard the exclamation. He also saw the face so distinctly outlined by the glare of the arc light, but unlike his companion he did not recognize it, although he knew by the demeanor of his "side-partner," that the man at the cab door, engaged in paying his fare, was a man "wanted."

When he tried to jerk himself free from the detaining grasp, his companion, in order to detain him, seized him bodily, and held on with both muscular arms.

The man at the cab, having dropped the coins, saw the two officers and he stood quite still, looking toward them with calm scrutiny while the taxicab departed.

The entire time thus occupied may be estimated by counting five slowly. He watched the short struggle that followed between the two officers, impersonally, and somewhat critically, judged by his attitude. Nobody would have suspected that his impulse was to turn and run away from those uniformed officers of the law—they, least of all.

"You gink! Stay where you are! Don't you know what 'ud happen if you tackled that guy?" the first cop breathed hoarsely to his companion while he struggled to maintain his grasp. "It's th' Night Wind."

"Let go uh me, you—"

"It's the Night Wind, I tell you, man alive!"

"All the more reason, then. Let go, will you?" the second one exclaimed, still struggling to free himself. "The Night Wind, is it? Curse him! Let me at him!"

But the first one was bigger and stronger than his companion, and he held on the more tightly, while the man who was the object of their contention drew a step or two nearer, as if the scene interested him.

When they continued their struggles for yet another second or two, one to break loose, the other to prevent it, the solitary spectator shrugged his shoulders, smiled coldly, turned and walked swiftly away.

"D'yeh want a broken wrist,'r an arm,'r a leg,'r mebby a neck, yeh bonehead?" the first cop insisted, hanging on. "Ain't he maimed everything he's touched? Ain't he sent every cop to the hospital who's tried to lay a finger on him? Didn't he break Shuster's arm above the elbow, an' twist Banta's right wrist so outa shape that he'll never in the world get it back again?

"An' ain't Casey down at St. Vincent's right now, and Ragowski up at Mount Sinai, all because uh him an' his devilment? An' you wanta go after him? *You!* You'd be like a week-old chick in the grip of a hawk, so you would. An' ain't Rushton, down at headquarters, that's called the strongest man on the force, got his arm in a sling—his arm that was broke in two places by the grip of him? An' *you* wanta tackle him, do yeh? G'wan, then, and try it."

He released his hold so suddenly that the other, who had been trying to escape, staggered backward to the curb before he could recover himself. But the rapid-fire reminders that officer Myers had shot at him had had their effect. Compton was no longer eager—and, besides, he realized that it was too late.

The Night Wind had disappeared.

But Compton, only now relieved from the peg, nursed his grouch just the same.

Over and over again, ever since the unbelievable performances of the Night Wind had shaken the entire "force" to its foundations and stirred the ambition of every young cop in the city, he had dreamed of such an opportunity as the one which had just nodded to him and passed on.

He had thought out, many times, what he would do when the chance came. He had taken jiu-jitsu before he applied for his police examination, and he had never had occasion to test it. He was husky and strong, and quick as a cat. Fear had never gripped him yet, so he did not know what it was.

He used some impolite language in making his comments upon Myers' conduct when he discovered that the Night Wind had really disappeared. He was still muttering unpleasant things when he started away on his beat.

Myers took the peg, also muttering; but his self-directed remarks were chiefly of personal satisfaction over the fact that he had not been caught in the passing cyclone.

Five minutes later the roundsman appeared, and he stepped to the middle of the street to speak to the peg.

"What's this I'm hearin' about you, Myers?" he demanded in a tone that was not pleasant. He "had it in" for Myers, and wanted nothing better than a chance to "get him right." And a roundsman can make trouble for a patrolman if he has the will to do it. Myers knew perfectly well to what Martin referred, but he replied indifferently:

"You're hearin' so many things about me that nobody else does, that mebby the thing you're referrin' to now ain't got to me yet."

"Ain't it? Well, Compton tells me that the two uh yeh just saw the Night Wind, and that when Compton wanted to tackle him an' take a fall outa him mebby, you hung onto him an' wouldn't let him. What about it?"

Myers chuckled. He had not pounded pavements ten years for nothing, and he knew a thing or two about worming out of difficulties when they arose. It had been his abilities in that line, coupled with a proportionate quality for getting himself into them in the first place, that had kept him a patrolman.

" 'Twasn't th' Night Wind at all, Martin," he lied glibly. " 'Twas a peaceable citizen gittin' outa his cab at th' corner at this unholy hour in the mornin', because mebby he didn't wanta have his wife hear a cab drivin' up to the door. I knew that Compton hadn't ever seen the Night Wind, an' I thought I'd throw a scare into him, so I grabs him by th' arm, an' I says in his ear: 'There he is now. F'r th' love uh Mike, don't go near him 'r you'll git your neck broke sure!' And I'll say this much for Compton, if he *is* a new man—he's game, all right. He'd 'a' gone f'r that guy in a holy minute if I'd 'a' let him, and there'd 'a' been a nice respectable citizen all mussed up, and Compton himself brought up on charges afterward for doin' it; and him new on th' force."

"You're lyin' to me, Myers," the roundsman said, adding to his remarks what he regarded as the appropriate and necessary trimmings. Myers shrugged his shoulders.

"All right," he said. "Have it that way if you like."

"I'll make a report on it, anyhow."

"All right. I'll look up the respectable citizen as soon as I'm off duty, an' ask him to step around and see the cap'n," Myers bluffed—and won.

The roundsman went on his way. Myers grinned after him, but wisely kept silent. Two blocks away the young officer, Compton, turned into a side street and was a third of the distance toward the next avenue, still muttering to himself about the opportunity that had escaped him because of the obstinacy of Myers, when one of those incidents which happen almost nightly in a great city was suddenly called to his attention.

He had seen a man walking rather unsteadily toward him, still two hundred feet or more away. He had been conscious of two other figures approaching more rapidly, behind the man.

Now he saw the two dart forward, and a weapon that might have been a piece of lead pipe, or a blackjack, swung in the air. Then a fourth figure materialized, seemingly out of nothing. The two footpads were tossed, or thrown, or knocked into the street like pins from a bowling alley, and they scrambled to their feet and ran away just as Compton came up on the run, brandishing his night-stick. The mysterious fourth of that scene was in the act of turning away from the befuddled citizen whom he had saved, but who did not seem to know that he had been in danger.

"What's all this, anyhow?" the puzzled Compton demanded. Then he gasped, for the mysterious stranger moved so that the light of a distant arc shone upon him; and Compton recognized him instantly as the man who had paid off the chauffeur of the taxicab only a few moments earlier.

"'Sss'pect it's ss'old-up," mumbled the citizen. But neither the officer nor the Night Wind heard or heeded him.

Compton, at the instant of recognition, acted. He sprang forward to grapple with the man—and found himself in a grasp that he could not shake off or loosen.

He felt himself whirled around so that his back was toward the man he would have fought. His night-stick was torn from his grasp and tossed into the middle of the street, and a sharp pain followed by a pipe-stem snap at the middle joint of the third finger of his right hand maddened and startled him. Then his gun was taken from him, and he was sent spinning after the night-stick; and the gun, broken and emptied, fell upon him an instant later and clattered to the pavement.

Compton felt as if he had been run through a thrashing machine. He was dazed and lamed and half paralyzed, as if all the volts of electricity that his system would withstand and permit him to live had been shot through him. He thought that both shoulders were dislocated—only they were not; nor were any important bones broken, although the sensation was the same as if many of them might be. Only that one finger had paid the actual penalty of his daring.

He groveled for a moment where he fell, then struggled to his feet, cringing nevertheless in expectancy of an impending blow.

But it did not fall, and Compton looked about him, uncertainly at first, then wonderingly—and then in utter amazement.

The Night Wind had disappeared.

Silently, like a shadow; swiftly, like the element whose namesake he was, the Night Wind had passed on. The calm of a dead street at half past two in the morning, void and vacant save for the presence of the alcoholic citizen and himself, obtained.

But Compton had met the Night Wind at last, and he had escaped—with one dislocated finger. He had something to boast about if he chose to boast. He decided on silence, however, while he gathered his property and resumed his normal state as a uniformed and duly armed guardian of the peace.

He approached the belated one who stood swaying uncertainly upon the curb, regarding him with owlish, judicial calm.

"What's th' anshur, off'shur?" was Compton's greeting.

"The answer is that you'd better beat it for bed unless you

want me to give you one that won't be as soft as your own. Where do you live?" he asked, nursing his finger.

"Thas smi house, ri' there—the one over this way so funny. But what I wanta know's if there was eight men, 'r only six men that you tackled, an' saved me from a gory grave. You give me your number, an' I'll have you broke—I mean promoted as a life saver. Th' commishner's pers'nal frien' uh mine. I say! I know that guy that broke into th' game, off'shur. Thas Bing Harvard. Bing ain't 's full name, but it's 'nuff. Used to be down town in a bank. I knew him—sures' thing you know—when the light fell on him. He's a muscular progy—no—podigy. Used t' tie bow-knots in crowbars, 'n' break ball-clubs in two, across his knees. We was college chumps t'gether. Uh-huh. Thank you, off'shur, f'r openin' that door. I'm distinctly 'bliged."

Compton, after assisting the erring citizen into his home, passed on his way through the street, occasionally touching spots upon his person, tentatively. He had paid little or no attention to the prattle of the man with the load. Only the name that had been mentioned had sunk into his memory, for he had heard it before somewhere, although he could not remember when or where.

So, also, the fact that he had mentioned that name clung to the memory of the man with the load, for notwithstanding his befuddled condition that night, he was a gentleman of respectability, responsibility, and position. A class reunion and a banquet had temporarily diverted him from the beaten path.

Nevertheless, the name of Bingham Harvard—Bing, as the young man had been called—recurred to him while he was in his bath the following morning, and it kept on recurring to him at intervals during the day, so that, when three o'clock came and he was free, he walked several blocks in a direction opposite the one he usually took when he left his office. And he entered a prominent bank just before the doors were closed, and passed, without obstruction, into the private office of the president of it.

"I have called upon a subject that isn't business, Mr. Chester," he announced, familiarly, "so go ahead with whatever engages you. I'm in no hurry."

"Nor I," was the reply. "And I'm glad to see you. You're a busy man these days, I suppose, and therefore forgetful of your father's old friends. Eh, Tom? What particular thing brought you here to-day? I'm anxious to hear about it."

"I saw an old acquaintance last night, Mr. Chester, and if I hadn't been on my way home from a banquet where I had taken too much champagne, I would have seized upon the opportunity to renew an almost forgotten friendship. As it was, I didn't recognize him until after he had gone—but I think he must have known me all the time, and realized the condition I was in, too. Anyhow, he followed me, and saved me from being blackjacked and robbed. At least that is the way it looks to me now, although I wasn't very clear about it at the time. I am referring to Bing Harvard."

The banker straightened and stiffened in his chair. His caller continued:

"The last I knew about him, he was employed here, in your bank. If he is here now, I wish you'd send out for him, and have him in. I'd very much like to—What's the matter?"

The banker's jaws had snapped shut and his eyes had become hard and cold and almost expressionless at the mention of that name. It was the change from a genial friend to the practical banker with secrets to keep that Thomas Clancy had noticed.

"He is not with us now. He has been gone—a month. I don't know where he is," the banker announced, shortly.

"You speak—and act—as if the parting between you was not a pleasant one," Clancy said dryly.

"It was not. It was decidedly unpleasant, Tom," was the slow reply.

"You don't mean, do you, that Bing went wrong?"

"Yes. I do mean that."

"Stole?"

"Yes."

"I can't believe it, Mr. Chester."

"Nor could I, at first. But I had to at the end."

"Tell me about it, won't you? I can't believe but that something is amiss, and that you have been misled. Bing Harvard steal? Take what did not belong to him? I'd as soon think—"

"I'll tell you about it, Tom, under a pledge of secrecy—and that is the only way I can tell it."

"You have it. Go ahead, please."

But the telling of that tale is another chapter—or two—the chapters in Bingham Harvard's life that made him an outcast and that caused the police to give him the alias Night Wind.

And so we will hark back a month to the scene of it, and relate it as the banker saw it and experienced it, and as he made Thomas Clancy see it and feel it—and as Bing Harvard lived through it and endured it, until the tension of his restraint snapped and he made use of the wonderful strength and adroitness that God had given him to scatter his accusers around him like chaff in a gale of wind, and to walk out from among them a free man, although a marked one, and a hunted one, an outcast, and an outlaw, and one of the "wanted."

He knew his own innocence. But he also knew that he was doomed, as guilty; and that he could not hope to establish his probity. And so he committed the first illegal act of his life right then: that of resisting an officer.

But he did that in a way that was not soon forgotten, and he left none behind him who were capable of following when he took his departure, the victim of as cold-blooded a "frame-up" as ever was born in the scheming brain of an ambitious, resourceful, and conscienceless headquarters detective.

So, step backward into the past, and look upon the moving picture that made Bingham Harvard into alias the Night Wind.

CHAPTER II

THE FRAME-UP

THIS IS NOT a detective story in any sense of the meaning.

A sum of money, a large one—the precise amount does not matter just here—disappeared, in manner utterly inexplicable, from the cage of the paying teller of the Centropolis Bank some time during the business day of Thursday, June 13. It was a sum that could not be traced, owing to the denomination and character of the bills which comprised it.

It was gone; that was all there was to it. And it went in three packages, or bundles—and so deftly, and with such consummate skill was it made to vanish, that not so much as the suggestion of a trace was left to indicate the method by which it had been taken.

Nor was it missed until the time came for stowing it away in the time-locked vaults for the night. Then the teller reported the loss after a few moments of useless and unfruitful search for it.

Bingham Harvard was that teller. Not a shadow of suspicion was cast in his direction, nor, for that matter, toward the two assistants who occupied the cage with him. Apparently one of the three must have taken it, yet developments showed that twice during that day there had been an interval, one of three minutes and the other of two or three, both approximated, when any clerk in the bank, being so minded, might have slipped inside the cage and out again, unnoticed.

The directors, hastily summoned, decided to make good the

loss, and to permit no mention of it, even to the clerical force. Of course it was generally known *inside* the institution that there had been a loss, but not whether it had been great or small, or of enough importance to stir them unduly.

But the directors did not swallow the loss as calmly as they appeared to do. They called upon the detective agency which regularly handled their business, and the president summoned in addition a man in whom he felt entire confidence. Lieutenant Rodney Rushton of the regular detective bureau; he being also sworn to secrecy. Rushton's side-partner was told about it, naturally, and his superior officers down at headquarters knew about it. Otherwise it remained a bank-secret.

Rushton had made a reputation for himself; how, will be left for you to decide. On several occasions he had performed really splendid service for President Chester of the bank. Hence Chester's confidence in him and in his ability—and therefore, also, as will be seen, alias the Night Wind.

For a few days Rushton worked cheek by jowl with the accredited agency—or appeared to do so. But Rushton was jealous of the "outsiders," and he wanted to "slip one over" in their direction, as well as to enhance his own reputation in doing it.

He did it, too, and beautifully, according to his criterions.

"I've come to wise you up on this little game of grab-all, Mr. Chester," he announced, with easy familiarity, one noonday a week after the theft occurred. "I know the man, but he has proved himself too slick for me to get the goods on him to the extent of convincin' twelve of his peers."

"Do I understand you to say that you already know who the guilty man is, Mr. Rushton?" the banker asked, with a glance over the length and breadth of the establishment, for every last man of them was directly under his eye from the elevation of his private office, which was, itself, secluded.

"I've got it cinched so far as that goes, only I can't prove it on him—yet" was the assured reply. "I've got to force him to a show-down; see? I've got to get his goat. But that'll be easy enough after you an' me get down to cases."

"I don't think I quite understand you, Mr. Rushton," the banker said, with extreme moderation. "You know who the guilty man is, and you cannot prove it. Something is lacking as to that part of it. Thus far I follow you, but—"

Rushton bent forward in his chair and his small, keen eyes bored into the banker's coldly mild ones, so that the latter stopped with the closing sentence of his protest incomplete.

"Listen here, Mr. President. I've got the trap set, laid and covered, and ready to spring. I ain't said that I can't prove this guy's guilt to *you*. What I did say was that I ain't got enough on him to prove it to a *jury*. See? But, *you?* He—m-m-m!" Rushton cleared his throat ostentatiously. *"You'll* see it!"

"Have you found the money, or any part of it?"

"No. But I've found the guy that's got it, 'r knows where it is, and it's up to you an' me, now, to get his goat so's he'll squeal. They all squeal when they're pinched hard enough—and that's what I want you to help me to do; make him yelp."

"But, how?"

"How? Why, it's like takin' candy from a kid. Guys like he is, once you get 'em goin', take the toboggan plumb to the bottom. They'll put up a face that would sweeten sour milk after a thunder shower, up to a certain point, and make you think they was born obedient to the ten commandments, but they're the quickest to weaken, once you get the bulge on 'em good an' plenty. And that's him—that's this guy, all right. You'd think he was senior warden of a church to look at him or hear him talk, but you'll find, when I throw the hooks into him, that his spine ain't got any bones in it at all."

"But of whom are you speaking? Who is the guilty man, Mr. Rushton?"

The headquarters man crossed the space until he stood beside President Chester's chair. He bent forward and pointed with a stubby, flat-ended index finger, toward the big room of the bank—toward one profile that showed clean-cut and strong upon a well-poised head.

"That's him," he said. "One, two, three—the fourth along the line where I'm pointin' my finger. Him with the wavy hair and the white skin. I don't need to mention no name. He's the guy that done it."

The banker flushed, then turned white. The grip of his fingers tightened upon the edge of his desk where one hand rested when he half rose to follow the indicated direction with his eyes. And he discovered at once whom the officer meant.

"Not Bingham Harvard!" he exclaimed breathlessly, relaxing upon his chair. "Not *that* young man, Mr. Rushton. There must be a mistake. You are zealous, I know, and a keen and experienced officer, but—Bingham Harvard? Oh, no, it is impossible—not to be thought of! I can't believe it."

"Ain't I said that I *know*, Mr. Chester?" Rushton demanded with a mingled scowl and grin on his face. "That's the crook, believe *me;* and he's slicker'n wet soap, too."

The banker did not reply. He sat with bowed head, thinking. He was overwhelmed by what had been told him. And the trouble was that he did not doubt, now that it had been told to him. Why? Because he placed implicit confidence in the acumen of the man who had made the charge—and because he was a banker.

Rushton moved back to his former position and waited. He was cunning rather than logical, keen instead of able. He knew the two classes with which he was dealing—the banker's class and the banking-clerk class; one easily led, the other only too quick to take affright. It was only natural that he should have included the young man, against whom he made the charge, among the latter—and that was Lieutenant Rushton's error. He had picked the wrong man for his frame-up. But he did not suspect that—yet.

Also, he had picked the one whom he believed to be the most likely, and (if any degree of justification is due him) the one whom he believed would weaken and confess when the professional gaff was thrown into him. And there simply had to be a victim, and quickly, for otherwise the detested agency would not be "beaten to it" soon enough to satisfy his egotism.

So Rushton watched President Chester with his small eyes, and waited, although the waiting became irksome before the banker at last raised his troubled glance and put the single worded interrogative:

"Well?"

"Have him in here—now. I'll clap the irons onto him and have him cryin' like a baby inside of two minutes."

"Oh, no; not here. I couldn't do that, Rushton—not before all the working staff of the bank. For they would know instantly what was going on."

"Huh! Not much they wouldn't. Not they. It'll all be done so on the dead quiet that the others won't know a word about it until we are out of the bank and aimin' for headquarters."

The banker raised his eyes again, and there was a quiet if mirthless smile in them.

"You don't know the man you are accusing, Rushton."

"Don't I? Well, I know his kind, and that's though."

"He is apt to be dangerous, if his temper gets the upper hand. I have seen him so."

"Dangerous? Rats! They're all alike, Mr. Chester. They'll put up a bluff that works to a charm, up to a certain point, but"—he pulled a pair of steel handcuffs from one of his side pockets and dangled them for an instant before the banker's eyes—"once let 'em feel the cold chill uh these things on their two wrists, and they weaken like a wet dish-rag. That's what. Dangerous? Huh! They ain't got no grit, 'r pluck, 'r sand to show f'r themselves, only when you get 'em in a corner and there's still a livin' show for 'em to get away. Then they'll fight, just like a rat'll fight. But you let me clap these things onto him"—he jingled the handcuffs together in his pocket—"and I'll gamble that he'll get down on his knees an' beg. Him? Dangerous? I'll make him jump through a hoop an' then lay down and roll over for you, before I've had him in here three minutes. Call him in, and let's have it over with."

"No. Not here. I cannot have him arrested here in the bank, Rushton."

"Eh? Why not? Where then, if not here?"

"At my house, perhaps; this evening. But not here. It will be—I won't have it here. That's all."

"Well, your house, to-night, then. Will you have him there? Will he fall for goin' there to-night, if you ask him? Won't he suspect, an' mebby make a getaway of it?"

"He will go to my house if I ask him. But you have forgotten one thing, Mr. Rushton. You have not offered me anything more than a bare statement to satisfy me of Harvard's guilt."

"Well, ain't that enough? Do you suppose that I'd come to you an' lay a charge like that against an innocent man, or against any man at all, unless I *knew* he was guilty?"

"No. I don't believe you would venture to do that," the banker replied calmly; and believed it when he said it. "But, if there is anything more, I wish you would tell me about it. It is a very great shock to me—a terrible blow, really.

"It is almost incredible, even from you; and yet—but you said that you could satisfy *me,* if not a jury. Tell me what it is that has convinced you of Harvard's guilt."

Rushton had not gone there unprepared. He believed that one of the three tellers was guilty, and that Harvard was the most likely one of the three to accuse—and somebody had to get the hook.

And Rushton never doubted that he would get a confession out of one of the three, and probably out of the victim he had selected. And so he was prepared to meet that last request of Mr. Chester's.

"I understand that you ain't doubtin' me," he said in reply, "an' I guess I appreciate just how you feel about the whole thing. That's why I've been so still about it all, until I was dead certain that I had the thing cinched onto him. You see, them guys from the agency, they went around exhonoratin' the three tellers, right off, just because *you* felt that way about it, and let 'em *see* that you did. But not *me*. Not on your hat-check! I says to myself that none of the other clerks in the bank could 'a' slipped into that cage and got away with the dough without bein' seen, and consequently one uh them three tellers must 'a' done it. Then I says, Which one?—and I ain't makin' any choice between 'em, either. Well, I finds out that one of 'em's married an' got a family, an' another one lives up in the Heights section with his mothern' sister; an' *this* guy lives all alone, in a room an' bath at a hotel that comes pretty near to bein' swell. So—"

"Let me interrupt you. Harvard is not without means. He has—

"Excuse *me*. That don't cut no ice. I was just tellin' you why I elected to make a private call at his dommycile first. It was easiest, because he lives alone, and if I did find the goods there— well, there wouldn't be any call to disturb the folks of the other two. See?"

"I understand you, I think, Rushton."

"Well, I goes up there to his rooms. I finds an open grate there with a blower in it that ain't been used since last winter, and that's probably been cleaned out more'n once since then. An' I digs it out and finds a lot uh charred paper behind that blower, an' most of it's been crushed up into little cinders with a poker after it was burned. But I finds some scraps that ain't quite destroyed, and here they are. You just take a squint at 'em yourself an' see if they don't satisfy you down to at when you consider where and when and how I found 'em."

Rushton produced a large envelope from one of his pockets, opened it, and permitted the banker to peer inside. He thrust a thumb and finger into it, and brought forth a scrap of buff-colored paper upon which, although badly scorched, could still be discerned the outlines of machine-stamped ciphers.

In a word they were partly burned bits of the paper strips

that are used in banks containing counted bills, and which are stamped with the amount that each bundle or package holds.

"He ain't carryin' that sort uh thing home with him an' burnin' 'em up, just for the fun of it," Rushton went on rapidly, for he saw the effect that the exhibit impelled upon the banker, "an' if he just happened to have 'em, without any guilty reason for havin' 'em, 'r hidin' the fact that he did have 'em at all, he'd 'a' torn 'em up an' chucked 'em in the waste basket—and it 'ud 'a' been a heap better for him if he had done that, 'cause they'd 'a' been gone before I got there. Well, I poked around some more, and under a pile of magazines, on a chair, I digs out this."

The "this" when he thrust it forward for the banker to see, was just such a paper strip as has been described, unscorched and intact, save that there were pin-holes through it, and creases upon it, which showed that it actually had been sometime wrapped around a package of bills; and it bore the plain imprint, $10,000.

"Didn't one of them three packages have just such a band as this one around it, and didn't it have the same riggers stamped on it? And wasn't that the smallest one of the three? And don't this here scorched scrap show a figure five as plain as day? And didn't one of them three packages have a band around it that contained a figger five with a whole lot of naughts after it? And look a here." He began to delve again into the envelope, but President Chester put out a detaining hand and stopped him.

"It is enough," he said coldly. "Go, now—and do not say another word at present. Come to my home at half past eight to-night. Bingham Harvard shall be there. But, I warn you now, your task will not be an easy one."

CHAPTER III

A LAW UNTO HIMSELF

AT HALF PAST eight precisely, Rushton arrived. Promptness in appointments is a cherished and boasted virtue of many who are "short" on other accomplishments.

A person with smoked glasses and a shade over the eyes could have told he was a plain-clothes man. As a matter of fact he liked to have the fact recognized, for it afforded many opportunities for obtaining by bullying methods what he could not possibly have accomplished by wit or sagacity. Two other men of his own kind accompanied him.

Harvard was late. He was due at a quarter to nine, but it was nearly five minutes after the hour when he was announced.

He entered the room, where the banker received him with a smile and a cheery word or two of greeting. For President Chester was his friend as well as employer—the best friend he had in the world, he would have said.

Harvard loved and honored him above others and had tried to emulate him in many ways. And so, the tragedy about to be enacted in the life of the young paying teller was destined to cut and sear and to destroy much more than it otherwise might have done.

"I am a trifle late," he said, not noticing—or attributing to some minor detail—the constrained manner of the banker. "I was detained by a small matter of common courtesy. There was a young woman passing the corner just below here who was uncertain about the direction she should take, so she asked me.

She seemed ill, or faint, or something of the sort, so I went a block out of my way to put her on a car. But, where are the gentlemen I was to meet? Haven't they got here?"

"They are in the next room, waiting," the banker replied evasively—And in that next room officer Rushton chuckled and whispered to the companion who was nearer to him:

"That was 'Lady Kate,' who lost her way, all right. I told her to get a squint at his nibs, and she done it. It's a wonder that he got here at all, if she threw them lamps uh hers at him just once."

Harvard was visibly chilled by the manner and tone of the banker's reply. He was intensely susceptible to atmosphere. The experience of his youth had made him so. The geniality of his manner went out of him. He felt the intrusion of something out of harmony. But he said nothing while he selected a chair and occupied it. He had not been informed of the object of his call—merely that he was to meet two or three others who had been bidden.

Rushton had given his consent that the banker should be permitted to question Harvard before the officers intruded upon the scene, but it had been no part of Rushton's plan really to allow it.

He much preferred his own bullying methods.

He did not intend that Harvard should get an inkling of what was to happen until the bolt was thrown, and he intended to throw that bolt himself.

So, when Harvard turned toward the chair, and President Chester hesitated for the right words to utter, Rushton thrust aside the portieres and entered the room, closely followed by his two dromios.

It was, perhaps, a fortunate detail that Harvard had selected a chair at the opposite side of the room from the portieres through which the plain-clothes men made their sudden appearance, otherwise Rushton's methods would have carried him to the extent of attempting to lock the handcuffs upon his intended victim's wrists, as a fitting first act of the drama. At is was, there happened to be a large library table between Harvard and the three officers, and Mr. Chester was seated beside it.

Harvard raised his eyes in astonishment when the three men brushed into the room so unceremoniously. But he recognized Rushton instantly, and got upon his feet, although that was the only movement he made. Something of the meaning of the summons to the banker's house was impressed upon him in that instant—but not the tragedy of it.

Still, he could not doubt the intention of the scene when the two men who were with Rushton immediately stationed themselves close to the only exits from the room. Rushton himself covered the third one, by which he had entered; and he came forward to the end of the table near which the banker was seated and stopped.

Whoever has seen the self-confident leer of an incompetent plain-clothes man when he believes he has got a prospective captive "dead to right" will comprehend how the partly under-shot jaw of Lieutenant Rodney Rushton was thrust forward with the menace of a brandished arm, and how his big, heavy, muscular frame seemed to fill all that room with its portentous-ness.

He was called the strongest man on the force; and he had earned the title, and had entire confidence in the wisdom of it. He had no thought of Harvard's daring to oppose him, and that such opposition, even if it were attempted, might succeed would never have occurred to him.

So he stopped at the end of the table, and leered at the lithe, graceful, well-knit figure of the good-looking young chap who had risen to confront him, whose face was pale, and calm, and emotionless, and whose eyes did not waver when they encoun-tered his sneering, insulting gaze.

"What have you done with the swag, Harvard? Where is it?" Rushton blurted out, angrily, and in a loud voice. "You lifted it all right, and you've got it now. But you can't get away with it.

You oughter have known that from the start. Where is it? Hey? What have you done with it?" Rushton's voice kept on rising as he proceeded, until the last question was .a veritable shout.

Harvard was dazed by the suddenness of it.

The language used—some of it cannot be repeated—and the insult of it was lost for the moment in the larger accusation.

He was charged with the theft of that vanished money. He got that much. And Mr. Chester, the president of the bank and his good friend, seemed to be a party to that awful charge. He was beginning to get that, too; but not quite. Not yet.

Slowly he withdrew his eyes from the leering, sneering regard of the burly officer, and turned them upon the banker, meeting the latter's glance for just one instant, whereupon the banker dropped his own to stare at the toes of his shoes where they rested upon the costly Persian rug.

That act was enough. Harvard did not ask the question which had risen from his heart and was so rudely turned back at his lips; and the little tableau, with all that it meant and implied, was not lost upon Rushton. More than that, it was meat to him—food and drink and relish.

"Caught with the goods, eh?" he sneered. "Haven't got a word to say for yourself, have you? Thought the boss would stand for you, didn't you? Well, you lost out, there, 'cause he won't. Come, now, open up that trap of yours an' get the story outa your system. If yeh don't, I'll squeeze it out uh yeh, you dirty sneak."

Only the cords of Harvard's neck as they swelled, and the veins of his forehead as they stood out clearly defined, and the deadly pallor of his skin, told that he heard the epithets that were hurled at him.

He kept his eyes upon the banker, who as steadfastly refused to encounter them. He did not speak. He did not move. He was still crushed by the suddenness of it all—but something inside of him was writhing and smarting, and struggling toward the surface of his comprehension.

He was stunned, but he was coming to. It was, perhaps,

natural that the three plain-clothes men should construe his attitude as one of guilt, and that the banker, who was watching him, should construe his silence in the same manner.

Rushton drew the handcuffs from his side pocket and rattled them. His body swayed forward half an inch as if he meant to clap them upon his prisoner, but for some reason he did not make the step forward that he had intended.

"Come, you! Give up!" he ordered, jingling the irons. "I've got the goods on you. I've got you dead to rights—just where I want you. You've got about as much show as a feather-duster 'ud have in a blast furnace. Come, now, hold out them dainty hands o' yours, that ain't done nothin' but count money, while I clap these little steel ornaments on 'em."

Rushton actually took a step forward, and for one instant Harvard's eyes shot a glance at him. It did not linger even for a fraction of time, but Rushton stopped—and he could not have told why he did so. Harvard spoke one word.

"Wait," he said; then he looked toward his employer again.

"Mr. Chester, do you believe this thing?" he asked, and his voice was calm and low pitched.

The banker raised his eyes as if to speak, caught the intent gaze of the young teller, and lowered them again. He did not reply. Harvard raised his chin in an involuntary gesture, caught his breath once, and shivered.

Mr. Chester, his friend, did believe in his guilt.

Such a calamity as that had never occurred to him, and it stunned and deadened, instead of "rousing him to action, as it might have done. He heard Rushton speaking again, hurling more epithets and insults at him, but as yet they glanced aside without penetration.

It was all bullyrag and browbeat, and Rushton was past master of the art. But through it all, at last, something did find an opening.

Rushton was shouting at him:

"Who are you, anyhow, I'd like to know? It ain't nothin' out uh the way that you should be a thief. I guess you inherited it all right. You're just comin' into your own, that's all. You don't amount to nothin'. You ain't got any name that you can call your own, as far as I can find out It's a hundred to one shot, and win at that, that you can't tell where you were born, or who your father an' mother was, an' if they wasn't crooks before you. Oh, I've got your measure. Come, now, give it to us straight. Where was you born?"

Harvard replied in a low tone without taking his eyes from Mr. Chester's bowed head; and the reply was mechanical; more as if in answer to his own thought than in response to the question.

"I don't know," he said; and then: "Mr. Chester, where was I born?"

The banker shook his head negatively.

"Who was your father? Who was your mother? Do you know that?" Rushton shot at him again.

"Can you tell him, Mr. Chester?" Harvard asked, with strange quietude; but again the employer shook his head slowly.

"Well, what d' yer expect from a man of that sort, anyhow, Mr. Chester?" Rushton queried brutally. "It's a s'prise to me that you'd take a guy uh that sort into the bank and give him a lot uh money to handle. You might 'a' known that he'd go the limit if he ever got a show. He don't know who his antecedents was, does he? What was he, anyhow, an' where'd you pick him up?"

The banker replied without raising his eyes:

"He was a foundling. I became interested in him when—"

"Then he didn't have no father an' mother, did he—'r at least you don't know who they was, do you?"

The banker shook his head again.

"Well, then, he ain't got any name, either. Bingham Harvard don't belong to him. It's just an alias. That's all he is—just an alias. Of course he'd rob you, and steal from you, and bite the hand that fed him. It's the way uh that sort. You might 'a' known it all along, Mr. Chester. It's more'n likely that his dad is doin' time right now, in one uh the prisons, an' his mother, too, maybe. Aw, I ain't got no more time to spend talkin' to *him*."

The handcuffs rattled as Rushton suddenly leaped forward toward his victim.

The sleeper awoke. The numbness that had resulted from the accusation was gone. The stunned sensibilities were roused. The fury of outraged manhood was loosed. Harvard was transformed.

"Stop!"

It was only one word, but there was something in the quality of the utterance of it that brought Lieutenant Rodney Rushton to a halt before he had taken the second step forward.

Bingham Harvard's body quivered slightly at the hips. He leaned forward just a trifle. His eyes flamed with concentrated rage at the man who had hurled those insults upon him. Yet, by an effort that was almost superhuman, he managed, partly, to maintain his self-control.

"You rat! You snake! You crawling reptile! Keep your distance while I warn you of the consequences of what you are attempting to do," Harvard said, in suppressed tones, which yet were filled with menace indescribable. I am not guilty of this horrible charge, and you know it. Whatever evidence pointing to my guilt you may have shown to that old man who crouches in his chair and dares not speak what I know is in his heart to say, you, *you*, YOU have manufactured. It is what the men in your business, and of your kind, call a 'frame-up,' and I know that. Don't you dare to interrupt me!

"As for the charge itself, if it were not that you have made this old man, who has been kind to me, and more than a father to me—if it were not that you have made him believe me guilty of that charge, I would meet it, and disprove it. I would give myself up to you, and defy you, if I had *his* confidence and *his* belief in me, to support me.

"But you are breaking his heart as well as mine. You are

spoiling his life, in his old age, even as you are trying to ruin mine, while I am still young in years.

"And you know that it is a frame-up. It could be nothing else. Now, wait."

Bingham Harvard turned once again toward his benefactor, who sat with bowed head and lowered eyes, seemingly heedless of the storm that had arisen; but he was visibly trembling, nevertheless.

"Mr. Chester," he said, "raise your eyes and look at me." Slowly the banker complied. "Do you, in your inmost heart, believe that I am guilty of this thing?"

"I must, Bingham. I cannot help it. I must. I do. God help you, boy!"

Harvard wheeled again upon his tormentor. His eyes were cold and hard and relentless. His muscles were rigid. On his neck they swelled until his collar was near to bursting. He was a dangerous man at that moment, and none knew the fact better than he did.

But he held himself in check for yet another interval.

"Man, do you see what you have done?" he demanded tensely. "Do you know what you are doing? Tell him that you have lied to him. Tell this old man that the charge against me is a false one. Tell him that I am not guilty, and that you know I am not. Confess that you have lied, damnably, or, as surely as you stand there, I will tear you apart with these two hands of mine. As sure as you grin at me, now, I will break your—"

Rushton sprang forward again at that instant. His two aides leaped to his assistance.

But Bingham Harvard was prepared. He abandoned all effort at self-control. He met the attack of Rushton half-way.

He tore the handcuffs from the officer's grasp and hurled them crashing through the plate-glass window. He seized the wrist of Rushton's outstretched right arm and twisted it, turning the man half-way around; then he grasped the officer's elbow with his other hand and brought the forearm down with terrific force across his own bended knee, which he raised to meet it; and there followed a sharply resounding snap, like the rending of a dry stick, and a cry of mingled agony and rage from Rushton.

Then a second snap followed the first one, with scarcely a pause between them, and another and louder cry from Rushton, who staggered or was thrown backward and collapsed in a corner of the room, with his arm broken in two places.

While that was happening the other two men sprang upon Harvard from behind, one hugging him around the neck and body, the other diving to the floor to seize him by the legs.

President Chester started to his feet, dismayed and frightened by what was taking place.

Harvard seized one of the hands that clutched him by the throat with both his own and bent it backward at the wrist quickly and with terrific force, and the crunching grind of the smaller bones as they were fractured by the strain, and the yell of the man whose wrist it was, followed instantly. The hold about Harvard's neck relaxed, and the man fell away from him, moaning with pain.

But Harvard was falling also, for the third man had seized his legs and was lifting and throwing him.

He half turned as he fell, freed from the other encumbrances, and he grasped his last assailant as he went down, pulling the man across him and throwing him forward at the same time; and then, as they both sought to rise, with the advantage with Harvard, the other man made a last desperate clutch at him to seize him by the throat.

Harvard caught the hand in one of his own as it shot forward, and clasped is so that the four fingers were doubled together inside his own grip—and the man sent up a great cry as he sank backward with every finger of that hand broken.

The big library-table had been overturned in the scramble, and its contents had crashed to the floor. Just beyond all that confusion, half crouching in his terror and paralyzed by fear, the banker was standing, wringing his hands together, when Bingham Harvard turned to make his escape from the room.

The banker held up his hands appealingly as Harvard approached him; then he sank backward and collapsed upon a chair beside a door. But the young man who had so defied the power of the law scarcely noticed him at all. One glance only of his blazing eyes rested upon the panic-stricken banker, and one look more he swept around the dismantled room toward the three other men who crouched or groveled upon the floor, now rendered utterly helpless against him—and then Bingham Harvard passed outside of the room and was gone, closing the door after him without a sound, and gliding away into the obscurity and mystery which was to envelop him for a long time to come.

The dismay, the terror, and the broken bones that he left behind him were all the direct consequences of the loosing of that terrible mastering strength which was Bingham Harvard's birthright, which his unknown father and mother had bestowed upon him as an inheritance, and which was coupled with a tempestuous fury and implacable determination whenever it was thoroughly roused.

Outside of the house he paused for an instant to glance backward, for he was his own cool, self-contained self again, and he thoroughly realized the enormity of the thing he had just done.

Innocent of the crime with which he had been charged, he was nevertheless guilty of other things now, and he knew that he must accept the consequences.

He had resisted an officer—three officers. He had maimed all three.

There would be no rest for him now, in the manhunt that would follow, he knew.

With that thought in mind he passed swiftly and silently out of sight. So was born Alias the Night Wind.

CHAPTER IV

THE NIGHT WIND'S WARNING

NOTHING OF ALL this found its way into the newspapers.

More than one ubiquitous reporter scented a "story," but none of them was able to nail it—and a story of that sort has to be verified before it can be printed.

Down at headquarters, Rushton, with his right arm broken in two places, and with a temper that was simply indescribable, excited much whispered comment and many confidential nudges. Banta, with his twisted and fractured wrist, and Coniglio, with his crushed fingers—who were generally known to have been with Rushton that night—nearly took the heads off of any of their brother officers who dared to ask them how they got hurt.

At noon of the day following the episode every available man of the bureau was called into the private office of the "skipper," and behind locked doors and under the seal of secrecy, with a severe penalty if violated, the story of the bank's loss and the belief in Harvard's guilt was related to them.

President Chester of the bank found a recent four-by-five snap-shot photograph of Bingham Harvard, and a supply of duplicates was struck off so that every man of the bureau was provided with one—and there were many yet to spare.

Later, the precinct captains were put wise in about the same manner, and orders went from them to their commands. Within twenty-four hours of the escape of Harvard from Chester's house every uniformed policeman and plain-clothes man in the city was on the lookout for him, and had determined individually to capture him.

But it seemed as if the man had stepped out of President Chester's house upon a waiting aeroplane and flown away to another planet, so literally did he disappear—and it was partly due to that first disappearance of his that the alias, which was presently to become synonymous with profound mystery, was applied to him.

A casual remark has coined many a word, has created a slogan, or named a continent; and so it was that a petulant question impatiently asked by President Chester of the bank when it became known to him that Harvard had actually made his escape in spite of the fact that one other plain-clothes man, and a woman detective from headquarters, were waiting outside the house that night, drew forth the answer that created the sobriquet. The "skipper" called at the bank in person for more direct information concerning the whole affair, and during the conversation that followed Mr. Chester impatiently demanded: "With three of your people inside the house and two more outside at the time, it seems incredible that he could get away. What became of him?" To which the high official replied:

"He blew away like the night wind."

During the week that followed it seemed indeed as if Bingham Harvard had disappeared as mysteriously as a draft of air, and not a sign of him could be picked up anywhere. The ferries, the railway stations, the arteries of the city along which vehicular travel flows, were watched with thoroughness—and in vain; and down at headquarters at the end of the seventh day after his going, Rushton nursing his splintered and splinted arm, confided to his chief this opinion:

"He's got off the earth, skipper. He's tied a ton uh coal to his leg an' gone crab-fishin'. There ain't no other way that he could 'a' kept himself so plumb out a sight from the hull bunch of us. He ain't been near them rooms uh his unless he went right there from Chester's house when he made the get-away—and

that ain't likely. He ain't been seen around any of his former
haunts. Not one uh his acquaintances has put a lamp on him
since that night, an' so the long an' short of it is that he took
the long journey rather than take the long term up the river.
And he done it in some way that his body ain't showed up to
let us know about it."

So, for three more days, that became the generally accepted
opinion among the members of the "force"—until it was rudely
shattered by an experience of a patrolman named Ragowsky.

He was doing his turn around a block in the residential
section of the city, between two and three o'clock in the morning
of the eleventh day after the bone-breaking episode at Chester's
house, when he found an iron grating under one of the stoops
unlocked and partly ajar. So he investigated. He found a servant
of the house engaged in closing it, and he lingered a moment
or two, or three of them, to talk with her. Then, as he turned
away after she had gone inside, a man passed swiftly into sight
and halted directly under the street light that happened to be
located in front of that house.

The man stopped to look at a paper he held in one hand. The
light shone plainly enough upon him. Ragowsky gasped, then
dove a hand into one of his pockets—he was still in the areaway of the house—and brought forth his copy of the snapshot.

One glance at it was sufficient.

Ragowsky was lithe and quick and brave, and he made a dive
for the man under the light, which would have resulted in the
capture of any other than that particular person.

A catlike jump from the top step of the area, and a body-hold
with both arms around his prospective captive by which both
of Harvard's arm were pinned to his sides, was the first act of
the resulting drama.

But Bing Harvard, who could not reach upward because of
the master hold upon him, reached down.

While Ragowsky was endeavoring to hold him and throw
him, he seized the patrolman's right ankle with one hand and

grasped the quadriceps-extensor muscle of the same leg with the other one.

He paid no attention to the effort to throw him, but he pulled that ankle he had seized against the officer's thigh with a sharp and resistless snap. And then they fell to the pavement together, with the uniformed man beneath, still with that leg doubled like a jack-knife under him.

A cry of agony from the policeman followed; and when the Night Wind straightened up, the officer remained where he was, writhing. Then Bing Harvard spoke to him with words of warning and defiance.

"I have not broken any of your bones," he said. "I have dislocated your knee. It is your own fault for taking me unawares. Tell your friends on the force that I'll maim every man who touches me."

Ragowsky, partly raised upon one elbow, suffering and cowed because he felt that he had been in the grasp of a strength that was utterly beyond his conception or description, dared not reply. But later, in telling of the occurrence, he said:

"And then he ducked."

"Where'd he go?" his captain demanded.

"Search me, cap'n. He just blew away. *Himmel!* How strong he is! And there wasn't a sound out of him, only what I've told you he said."

Officer Shuster, of the Thirty-Sixth, met with his experience the following night.

He was crossing diagonally an avenue and a street where two carlines intersect, at three-fifteen in the morning. Two cars traveling at right angles met there at the moment. As Shuster permitted one of them to pass him and stepped behind the other, he came face to face with the elusive one—and recognized him instantly.

He struck out straight from the shoulder with his fist upon that same instant—and his arm was seized and twisted, and he was lifted and thrown over the bent hip of the man he attacked, so that he fell in a sprawling heap upon the tracks, with the arm that would have delivered the blow broken just above the elbow.

He jumped to his feet and blew his whistle. He pounded his stick upon the pavement with his good arm, but the man who had thrown him, and broken him, with some new and improved method of jiu-jitsu, or something better, was gone.

The street and the avenue were practically deserted, save for the two cars already mentioned; yet Shuster swore that the man could not have boarded either one of them, and that he was nowhere to be seen within a second or two of time.

"I met the Night Wind" he told the lieutenant in charge at the station-house. "I started to hand him one, and I got this. He just reached out for it as if he liked it, and took it on the fly, half-way to him; and when I sat up, a second afterward, to look for him, he was gone. And I didn't so much as hear a sound from him—not one."

It was three nights after that when Casey, of the Twenty-Eighth, was taken to St. Vincent's, and headquarters was notified of the fact.

"Three broken ribs and a very slight rupture of the pleura," the night superintendent at the hospital reported over the telephone. "The doctor thinks we'd better keep him here for a few days," *et cetera, et cetera.*

Rushton, whose theory of suicide had been so rudely shattered, went in person to question Officer Casey, who had a slight pleurisy and therefore could not leave the hospital as soon as predicted, and Casey's account of it was no less vague than the experiences of his compatriots had been.

"I had been off duty, and was on me way to report in at the station-house! and I was late at that, and was hurryin' to beat the band. So I was fairly runnin' down the stairs of the Elevated when I sees him comin' up 'em toward me. I didn't *hear* him; I *saw* him, just as he raised his head to look at *me* because he heard me. I knew him that minute; and as he was ten steps 'r so below me I took a flyin' leap for him, rememberin' all that has been said about him, and takin' no chances as I thought And say! I've heard of guys that's lookin' for trouble an' meetin' it half-way, and all that, but I'm the first damn fool that's been known to jump for it. I sure found it. How'd he throw me? Search *me!* I guess he just opened up a valve an' let loose one uh them blasts uh night wind onto me.

"Anyhow, I got mine good an' plenty. And f'r a minute 'r two afterward I didn't know I was hurted—much. I rolled plumb to the bottom of that lowest reach of stairs an' landed on me feet like a cat And I couldn't see him nowheres on the stairs above me. So I says to meself, he's legged it f'r the station platform. An', not realizin' that I was hurted, I chases after him, knowin' that there ain't only that one stairway on that side of the road at that station.

"Well, he wasn't there, an' the ticket-man an' the chopper both swore that there hadn't nobody come up since I went down, an' there wasn't any train pulled in 'r out on either side since the one I got off of, and he had vanished into thin air, to be sure, so he had.

"Then all of a sudden I begun to feel sick an' faint like, an' the next thing I knew I was down here. There's just one thing that I'm dead certain about, an' that is that the Night Wind ain't healthy. Every guy that's laid a hand onto him so far has got a broken bone or so to show for it. There's one thing I'm thinkin'."

"What is it, Casey?"

"They'll have to make some changes and additions to that Sullivan law about the concealed weapons. There ain't anything in it about bottled-up cyclones an' pocket-hurricanes, is there? An' that's what your Night Wind carries around with him. Sure, I ought to have knowed better than to tackle him at all, at all, when he could do *you* up the way he did—you, an' Banta, an' Coniglio—an' you the strongest man on the force."

Lieutenant Rushton returned to headquarters with a thoughtful, yet frowning brow.

"Skipper," he said to his acting chief, as soon as he could get into the private office, "there ain't but one way to get that guy we call the Night Wind. There is one way we can nail him, if we're fly enough about it."

"Well, what is it?" the skipper asked.

"It's Lady Kate."

"Yes," was the reply. "I've been thinking about that, Rushton. She has had a look at him, too, hasn't she?"

"Yes. And heard his voice. She's got his measure, all right. It ain't my place to make a suggestion, but if you'll listen to *me* you'll give her a wide-open assignment on this case. Let her go her own pace, and handle her by wireless until he's pinched."

"Just how do you mean that last, Rushton?"

"Well, nobody but us down here at the bureau knows that she's one of us, and she ain't been here long enough to put the bunch wise even to that much. She's on probation, ain't she?"

"Yes; but she has made good, and we're going to keep her."

"Of course she has, but the bunch don't know that. You an' me, an' two 'r three others of us, know that she's the swell lady, all right, an' she won't have to play no part when she goes out on that lay. She's a good-looker, too—there ain't a better lookin' one in town—an' she's got the wit an' the pluck *and* the ambition to succeed. D'yeh see what I mean?"

"Yes. It's a good idea."

"That night when the Night Wind made his getaway from Chester's, he was a few minutes late in keepin' his appointment because he'd met her on the street, an' she'd played up that she didn't know her way, and wasn't feelin' any too well, to boot; an' so he falls for escortin' her to a car an' helpin' her onto it, an' all that."

"I know about that."

"W r ell, it's a cinch that he'll know her the next time he sees her. Them lamps uh hers have a way of borin' into a guy when she throws 'em at him that he don't forget—an' *he'll* remember 'em all right, take it from me."

"You seem to, anyhow, Rushton," the chief smiled back at him.

"I ain't denyin' it, am I? I'd resign an' quit the force, an' start a mission-house or a church, if she'd ask me to an' marry me for doin' it. But she ain't likely to do either one; an' if you ever tell that I said that I'll resign anyhow, an' go gunnin' for your scalp afterward. I've got sense enough to know that she's just as far away from *me* as if she was back on the upper crust where she belongs, instead of down here among a lot of ginks like us. But that ain't here nor there. The question is, will you put it up to her, an' then let me wise her up to what she's to do when she gets into the game?"

"We'll do that together, lieutenant—and we may as well do it now," was the reply, as the skipper pressed a button beneath the edge of the desk. "I like the idea, and we will have her here now."

Thereafter into the mysterious career of the Night Wind entered Miss Katherine Maxwell—and also many complications not foreseen or considered by any of the hitherto interested parties.

Two hours afterward she took her departure from headquarters, and was not seen there again until—until she returned to the stone building for another and an entirely different purpose.

But it was only a short time after that when she had her first encounter with Alias the Night Wind—an encounter to be remembered by her and by him forever afterward.

CHAPTER V

THE SPECIAL DETAIL

"**LADY KATE,**" **AS** she was referred to at headquarters by the select few of the detective bureau who were wise to her activities, was, in a way, even a more profound mystery than the Night Wind had latterly made of himself.

As a human problem, Lieutenant Rodney Rush-ton had several times undertaken to find the solution of her—as also had some others who were attached to the bureau. But beyond the accepted facts that she called herself Miss Katherine Maxwell; that she was competent, skilful, and apparently fearless; that she possessed remarkable eyes impossible to describe in their varying expressions; that she was undeniably attractive and beautiful, and that she made her home in the second floor front of a house in West Eleventh Street, nothing was known concerning her—with the possible and probable exception of the commissioner of police or the mayor, or both. Nor was the skipper any better informed than the men who served under him.

Her orders from the inspector, commonly referred to as the skipper, were general, although precise and comprehensive. She listened with her eyes half closed while he talked to her; or, if she raised the lids at all, it was to stare through the window while the particulars of the tale, as we now understand it, were related to her.

At the close of that interview, when they both left their chairs and the chief moved to the door to open it for her to pass outside, he paused with his hand upon the knob, and added this:

"You will retain your shield, of course, and will have power to assert whatever authority you may need when the proper time comes; but, aside from Lieutenant Rushton and a very few others who are close in my confidence, it shall be generally understood here that your services have been dispensed with. And in this undertaking you will enjoy an advantage which none of the men possess: the Night Wind will not serve you as he has served them.

"He was a gentleman before he went wrong in this matter, and he will scarcely venture to maim a woman. Here is an order for your expense money. When you need more, send for it. Report to me by telephone when you can; and if there should be anything which you do not care to discuss over the wire, arrange in that manner to meet me outside. And now, good luck to you, Miss Maxwell. If you should win out on this, I think I can promise you the rank and pay of a captain."

These instructions were given immediately after the experience of Officer Compton with the Night Wind, and the interview between Thomas Clancy and President Chester of the bank—a month, approximately, after Rushton, Banta, and Coniglio encountered their Waterloo at the banker's residence.

For a time it seemed as if the Night Wind had indeed disappeared.

Nothing was seen or heard of him for days which lengthened into more than a week, although every man of every precinct in the city carried a picture of him and was constantly on the alert to discover him again.

And in the mean time thousands of the photographs were printed and sent broadcast throughout the length and breadth of the country.

Then, like a bolt of lightning out of a cloudless sky, two incidents happened so nearly simultaneously that the police of two cities were amazed and puzzled, and (none too politely) incredulous concerning them.

Officer Philip Brainard, of the Forty-Third, when he reported at the station-house in the early morning, preparatory to getting his thirty-six hours off, told of an encounter with the Night Wind, at four o'clock that morning, at Park Avenue and One Hundred and Twenty-Eighth Street; and it was a different encounter entirely from those of his brother officers of other precincts.

He had felt himself seized from behind at a moment when he least expected that any person had approached him. His arms had been pulled behind him and held there by one hand, while with the other the Night Wind had jerked his night-stick from its sheath and tossed it into the middle of the street; then, releasing him, the man of mystery helped himself to the officer's gun, broke it, emptied it of its cartridges, and restored it. Then, smiling whimsically into the discomfited policeman's eyes, he said to him:

"Just tell them that you saw me, officer. I had business up this way and thought you might chance a snap-shot at me. Good morning."

While Brainard was engaged in recovering his stick and the cartridges from his gun, the Night Wind had glided away with his swift and noiseless tread, and when the officer chased down to the next corner with his reloaded weapon, intended to try that suggested snap-shot, the Night Wind had disappeared.

"You beat it down to headquarters and tell your story there," was the order that Brainard received; and later, while he was relating it to the acting head of the bureau, a wire from the police department of Boston was delivered. It was:

> Night Wind here. Detective Lamberton met him Summer Street ten-thirty, recognized him, tackled him, and has dislocated right elbow as consequence. Night Wind disappeared, but I have the dragnet out for him. Will get him if possible and put one over on New York.

"Seen in Summer Street, Boston, at ten-thirty last night; seen at Park Avenue and One Hundred and Twenty-Eighth Street, New York, at four this morning," the officer in charge remarked as he reached for a Bullinger and began to turn the leaves. Presently he added: "There isn't a passenger-train that leaves Boston after ten-thirty that could have got him here by four. How'd he do it? Has he got a double, I wonder?"

"It don't sound like no double, him disjointin' that teck's elbow," Brainard replied. "Mebby he's an aviator, cap'n, an' keeps a biplane."

"He's just an animated hell—that's what he is," was the retort. "G'wan home, Brainy, and consider yourself mighty lucky that you've got two sound legs to take you there."

They both forgot, or did not know, that there was a fast mail out of Boston at 11 P.M. which carried no passengers, and which covered the distance to the metropolis in a little less than five hours. The Night Wind might have used that train, notwithstanding the fact that the railroad employees, and particularly the crew of that train, would have said that it was utterly impossible to beat a ride upon it.

The alarm was immediately sent out that the Night Wind had been seen again that morning, and so the entire police force was once more on the alert for him.

During the eight or nine days of the Night Wind's seeming withdrawal from the limelight, Lady Kate had not been idle, although nothing whatever had come of her enforced activities.

She had been abroad every night in the hope of encountering him, and she relied upon the fact that they had met once before, and that he had escorted her to a car on that occasion to make it possible for her to hold him, at least for a moment or two, when the second encounter should take place.

She heard the news concerning the episode in Boston, and the experience of Officer Brainard with the man; and she experienced an inexplicable sense of exaltation, of intuitive foresight—men would call it a hunch—that she would, somewhere and somehow, see and talk with Bingham Harvard during the following night.

Throughout the weeks that had elapsed since the dramatic episode at the home of the banker, the Night Wind had never once been seen by day. He had been encountered always at night, and usually during the wee, small hours of the night.

So it had been Lady Kate's method, since her last interview with the head of the bureau, to sleep by day, and to go abroad in the streets at night; and this going abroad had to be at random, since the object of her search had not been known to frequent any particular section of the city, but had appeared at intervals in widely separated localities.

Nevertheless there was one saving clause in this latter respect, in that thus far he had not been known to visit the slums, or to gravitate toward those localities most frequented by inhabitants of the underworld.

But it would have made no difference to Kate had it been so, for she was well equipped for the profession she had elected to adopt—was fearless, resourceful, and entirely capable of taking care of herself under all conditions.

The night that followed upon the Boston and the Park Avenue incidents became a memorable one to Katherine Maxwell, and to Alias the Night Wind as well.

She left her room in the house in West Eleventh

Street shortly after nine that evening, and went to other quarters that she had secured in one of the West Seventies, about which even her chief knew nothing.

Lady Kate had realized at the very beginning of the game that there was one man who would keep indefatigably upon her trail, by one method or another, if it were possible for him to do so—and that man was Rushton. Hence the small establishment in the Seventies. She did not intend that Rushton, or anybody else, should know of the existence of that retreat.

Arrived there on that particular night, she presently dressed herself exactly as she had been gowned that evening when

Bingham Harvard had so courteously escorted her to a Madison Avenue car. She believed that he would remember her at once, if he should see her so again, and in this, as it proved, she was not mistaken.

Shortly after eleven she went out. At the door a taxi of non-descript character and outwardly mean and common-place appearance awaited her. No one but herself could know that the black man who drove it was her own faithful henchman, and that the cab was as dependable as its driver.

She directed that she be driven slowly east and west through the cross streets of the city for two hours, so that it was after one o'clock when she got down from the cab in Seventy-Second Street, midway between Columbus Avenue and Broadway—within rifle-shot of her starting point.

Why Lady Kate selected just that place to leave the cab she could not have told, save that in a sense she seemed that night to be acting subconsciously, as if she were impelled by an intuition more forceful than reasoning powers. And this young woman was not without her superstitions. She had implicitly believed, since the receipt of the news that the Night Wind was again in evidence, that she was to come upon him that night—that some inexplicable influence over which she had not the power of direction was bringing them together.

She did not address by a word the black man at the steering-wheel, nor did he direct so much as a glance at her when she started down the street toward Broadway. But after a moment he drove on again, turned about, and followed slowly after her, always maintaining a respectful and sufficient distance, so that the girl in the street and the cab that pursued her might not be associated with each other by any chance observer.

Half-way between her starting-point and Broadway, Lady Kate met Rushton. He still carried his arm in a sling, but had refused to be reported on sick leave. He saw and recognized her at a distance, and stopped directly in front of her when they met.

"You're on the job all right, Miss Maxwell," he said to her with extraordinary politeness for him. "Anything doin'?"

"No," she replied, and would have passed on; but he detained her.

"Wait a minute, Lady Kate," he said, somewhat peremptorily. "This is the first time I've had a chance to speak to you since you got this detail from the skipper. We miss you down below."

"Thank you, lieutenant. All the same I don't think it wise for us to be seen together just now. Do you?"

"Did you hear about the Night Wind's bein' in Boston, an' then showin' up here in about five hours' time?" he queried, ignoring her question. She nodded.

"Yes, thank you," she said, and went on past him.

But he turned and pursued her, and overtook her again before she had gone a dozen paces.

"There ain't no need of bein' in such an all-fired hurry," he said. "I want to talk to you a minute, an' besides, I've got some pointers to give you, Lady Kate."

She wheeled squarely upon him then, facing him. She utterly despised the man, and always, in his presence, felt a subtle sense of fear of him, as inexplicable as it was foreign to her character.

"Lieutenant Rushton," she said coldly, "I have received explicit orders from our chief. Part of those orders were, in effect, that I should hold myself entirely aloof from all persons connected with the department while I am on this detail. So, good night, sir."

"But—confound it—I was the one who suggested those very orders to the skipper, an' it goes 'thout say in' that he didn't intend to include me in them directions. I ain't one—"

But she did not remain to hear what he had to say. She turned again and went onward down the street toward Broadway, and Rushton stood scowling at her departing figure, although he made no further attempt to pursue her.

Nevertheless he did not move from the position he had

assumed until after she had turned the corner toward the north—that same corner where Officer Compton had secured his first sight of the elusive Night Wind. Then he wheeled about and went on up the street, turning northward at Columbus Avenue, and hastening his footsteps, muttering to himself as he did so:

"I'll just keep half an eye on you, all the same, Lady Kate."

Katherine Maxwell met and passed Officer Compton, who was again on duty, just around the corner in Amsterdam Avenue, and then she crossed Seventy-Third Street, presently turning into Seventy-Fourth, again toward Columbus Avenue. She had not taken a dozen steps in that direction before her watchful eyes discovered the unmistakable figure of Rushton, who at that moment passed beneath one of the street lights.

For the fraction of an instant, so short as to be unmeasurable in time, she hesitated. Then with abrupt decision she turned in her tracks, intent upon avoiding another meeting with the lieutenant.

Kate had heard no sound of foot-falls behind her. She had no notion that any person was within hailing distance—and yet, when she turned about so suddenly, she came face to face with a man who had approached so swiftly and silently that she very nearly collided with him.

With one glance—with one quick intaking of her breath— with amazement and wonder, and not without consternation, she recognized him, as he, apparently, also had seen and recognized her some moments earlier.

"The Night Wind!" she exclaimed, but without raising her voice.

Then, clattering down the street behind her there smote upon her ears the heavy tread of running feet and the shrill blast of a policeman's whistle, and she knew that Rushton had witnessed the meeting, and had, perhaps, recognized the man who faced her so smilingly, notwithstanding the likelihood that the continued shrilling of that whistle was summoning other officers toward them on the run, and from every conceivable direction.

"Run!" she heard herself cry out impulsively. "Escape if you can, before it is too late."

CHAPTER VI

A SIGNIFICANT STAIN

THE NIGHT WIND seemed in no hurry, although he must have realized the danger that menaced him.

The sharp, clear-noted impact of night-sticks on end against the pavement sounded from front and rear. The shrilling of other whistles mingled with Rushton's blasts. The block, from both ends of it, became suddenly alive with noisily running feet.

Lady Kate, more perturbed and anxious that she would have cared to admit even to herself, stood perfectly motionless and expressionless before the much-hunted man. She did not show the excitement that she felt was consuming her, but she heard the voice of the Night Wind vaguely, nevertheless.

"If they attempt to make trouble for you I will not be far away," he said.

Rushton was within twenty yards of his goal when the Night Wind darted away from Miss Maxwell and started swiftly toward him; and Rushton stopped in his tracks. He recalled his former experience with this man, and he remembered, too, that one of his arms was in a sling.

But the left one was still in commission, and he pulled an automatic from the side-pocket of his coat and sent a staccato of spattering bullets toward the lithe and swiftly moving figure of the man who sprang up the steps of a house that was midway between him and Lady Kate.

Rushton shouted with exultation, too, when the Night Wind plunged forward, head first, through the open half of the vestibule door. Rushton believed that he had "got" his man, although he knew himself to be an indifferent marksman with his left hand.

Renewed courage came to him with the thought. He dashed up the steps of the house into which his prey had disappeared, but only to discover that the door had been closed against him; that the latch had caught, and that he was locked out. He was still profanely and fruitlessly rattling at it when the other policemen who had been summoned to the scene came up.

There was an old-fashioned pull-bell beside the door, and Rushton nearly tore the wires out of the house in yanking upon it ceaselessly, until, after a minute or two—not more—the door fell open before them and the frightened face of a man, clad only in pajamas, peered out at him.

Rushton brushed the man unceremoniously aside, but he called back over his shoulder to one of the officers whom he had recognized by name:

"Watch the door, Dixon, and shoot if you see anything to shoot at. Don't take any chances. Come on, the rest of you!"

Lady Kate was standing exactly where the Night Wind had left her, although she had turned about and was intently observant of all that was taking place.

She saw many things, too, while she watched.

She saw Rushton drag the frightened householder across the threshold after him, and three more officers follow precipitately. She saw the man called Dixon at the top of the steps, with revolver in one hand and night-stick in the other, and she heard the door close and latch again after the hunters had passed through. Then Dixon discovered her and called out:

"Who are you? Come up here while I have a look at you. D'yeh hear? Come up here, you!"

She moved forward without haste and mounted the steps to the uniformed officer's side—and, as it happened, at that side of him which was farthest from the area and the basement entrance, Dixon was thus forced to turn, his back toward the very point he should have watched in order to bend forward and peer into her face.

He was a good-looking chap, and was thoroughly aware of that interesting fact. Vanity, and possibly some past experiences and successes, had partly spoiled what otherwise might have developed into a splendid officer.

He looked into Katherine Maxwell's face and saw that it was beautiful; he looked into her eyes and discovered that they were wonderful. He was young on the "force," but he had been with it long enough to know something about the type of woman that is ordinarily encountered alone in the street at such an hour; and he was instantly conscious of the fact that this beautiful young creature did not belong to that type. She was distinctly misplaced, and Officer Dixon was suspicious.

"Were you with that guy?" he demanded, bending nearer to her, and staring unpleasantly into her eyes

"That was the—never mind who he is—were you with him?"

"I had just spoken to him," she admitted demurely; but she moved backward one step, and leaned against the stone balustrade. Dixon's suspicions were thoroughly aroused, and he thrust his face still closer to hers.

But in that instant Katherine saw something more than the policeman's face—something that shot a thrill of expectancy through her. It was something which Officer Dixon did not and could not see, because his back was toward the area.

Kate was barely conscious of the fact that Dixon, with the hand that had flourished the night-stick, had seized her by one arm, and that he was half shaking her to compel an answer. She was intent upon the discovery she had made in the areaway.

The man who had loomed suddenly and noiselessly into view there glided swiftly toward the three steps that' led to the sidewalk. For an instant he paused there and peered up and down the street—and then he saw the two figures at the top of the steps which led to the vestibule door.

Possibly he misunderstood the scene. Perhaps he did not. At all events he interfered.

Officer Dixon's first warning of another presence near him came at the instant when he would have shaken Lady Kate again, and even more roughly. But it was effective and entirely adequate.

His arm was seized upon and jerked backward, night-stick and all. It was twisted behind him with terrific force, until, with a sharp snap, the ball of that shoulder-joint left its socket. Dixon cried out with the pain of it.

Then the revolver was torn from the grasp of his other hand and hurled into the street; and the man himself was pitched head first down the steps after it.

"You had best go while there is time," Kate heard the voice of the Night Wind say to her, and add, after an imperceptible pause: "Good night."

She saw him go.

It was incredible how swiftly and silently he moved.

Then she bethought herself and went also, but toward the opposite direction, noting only the prone figure of Officer Dixon on the sidewalk as she passed. He had fainted; or at least he was silent and motionless.

The Night Wind had disappeared. Kate had been afforded time to reach the nearest corner and to turn it before Rushton with his three satellites came from the house door with almost the same haste they had used in entering.

On the pavement at the foot of the steps Dixon was begin- ning to stir uneasily, and he uttered a moan of pain at the instant when Rushton appeared and could hear him.

The search inside the house had been fruitless, as we already know, and Rushton was proportionately incensed. He found some relief for his overcharged brute rage in visiting it upon the hapless Dixon. He jerked the man to his feet by seizing him by the dislocated arm. Dixon could not repress a cry of agony, and the condition of the officer who had been left in charge of the door told Rush-ton instantly that the Night Wind had made good his escape by the front of the house, and that he had left his customary trail of maimed anatomy behind him.

"A fine copper you are!" Rushton shouted at Dixon, punctuating his remarks with unprintable epithets. "I'll have you broke for this, Dixon. I don't know what happened, but I do know that if you'd obeyed orders it wouldn't have happened at all. How'd he git you?"

"He came behind me and grabbed me before I knew it."

"Outath' frontdoor?"

"No. From the street."

"An' what the blazes were you doin' that you didn't see him?"

"There was a woman—a girl—down on the sidewalk; his pal, I thought. Anyhow, I guessed she was with him. I thought maybe she'd know something, so I called her up to me. And I was—"

"Aw, shut your trap. I know th' rest of it. She had a pretty face, and you couldn't see anything but her, an' that's how th' Night Wind got your goat. I'm sorry he didn't break your neck, Dixon. Where's the girl?"

"I don't know, sir. I—"

"Beat it, now! Get to your nearest box an' call f'r a relief. I'll 'tend to your case to-morrow. Duck, now, all of you. There won't be anything more doin' this night. You can bet on that."

Rushton strode away by himself, and he muttered, half aloud, but with savage emphasis:

"To think that that guy musta gone to that house yesterday mornin', in broad daylight, after he saw Brainard, to take that room an' pay a week in advance for it!" And Rushton kept on muttering to himself until he was lost in the subway at Seventy-Second Street.

Katherine Maxwell had gone toward Columbus Avenue. A taxi that had been standing before a door at the opposite side of the street some distance away, with the chauffeur apparently sound asleep in his seat, followed slowly after her. It was never very far away from her when she was on the street alone at night, and the slightest signal from her would always bring the black man to her assistance instantly.

She turned north in Columbus Avenue. She was thoughtful, but she had no idea of continuing the search for the Night Wind. She had encountered him this once, and he had remembered her. That was sufficient for the present. Further developments must await another opportunity. Then suddenly, and without warning, she was so startled that she gasped outright in her amazement.

The Night Wind reappeared without sound or announcement of any kind, walking beside her like a shadow—nor did he address her by so much as a word.

For an interval she bore the silence, waiting for him to speak; but when he did not do so, nor show any sign of such an intention, she ventured a remark.

"Is this prudent?" she asked him in a low tone. "Yonder, just ahead of us, is an officer. His relief, the patrolman, cannot be far distant."

"The fact that I have a companion will protect me. I am usually seen alone," he replied coolly, and was again silent.

"Why are you here at all?" she demanded presently. He shrugged his shoulders, but did not turn his eyes toward her as he replied with quiet finality:

"To see that you get to your home without further molestation."

"But if I resent it—if I tell you that you must not do—"

"In that case I will follow after you at a respectful distance. The purpose will be accomplished just the same."

"*Why* do you insist? Is it really to afford me the protection of your presence, or is it a cloak to hide your wish to discover where I live?"

He replied with simple directness and entire truthfulness.

"The principal reason is the one I have already given. In addition, there are two more facts. You made use to-night of the name the police have given me, and you did so the instant you saw me. Also, you tried to warn me of danger. I assure you I have no interest whatever in discovering where you live."

"Nor what sort of a person I may happen to be?" She turned toward' him when she put that question, but he did not respond to her gaze. Instead, he replied quietly:

"No. That does not concern me."

She was silent, and after a time he remarked dryly:

"You have learned to know the city much better since our last meeting."

"I have known this part of it quite thoroughly for a long time," she replied with perfect truth.

"You are dressed exactly as you were then, even to your hat," he went on whimsically. "That is somewhat unusual, isn't it? Also, is not the hour a bit unusual for one like yourself to be abroad and alone? You see," he went on before she could reply, "that evening when we met before proved to be a tragic one for me. Possibly that is why I recognized you at once when I saw you."

"Are you sorry that you did see me to-night—and remember me?" she asked him.

"No." He spoke shortly.

Lady Kate glanced toward him from the corners of her eyes.

"Have you classified me?" she inquired after they had walked onward a short distance.

"Yes."

"How—if I may venture to ask?"

He turned his eyes toward her then, and looked her over from the plume upon her hat to the hem of her gown with calm scrutiny. Then, in the same neutral tone that he had used since the beginning of the conversation, he replied:

"If it were not that you bear the unmistakable evidences of refinement and gentle breeding, and that you speak with the voice and in the tones of one who has been always accustomed to a drawingroom and its environment, I should feel no hesitation in pronouncing you to be a woman detective who has been put upon my trail in the wild hope that your fascination and your beauty might lead me into a trap, sooner or later."

"And—as it is?" she asked, coolly meeting his searching gaze. He shrugged his shoulders and looked straight ahead of him again.

"As it is, I shall keep in mind the fact that you are just a young woman who is at the present moment very much in need of an escort," he replied with conviction.

They had turned toward Amsterdam Avenue again at Seventy-Fifth Street. Lady Kate halted at the corner and faced him.

The impulse was upon her to confess to him exactly what she was and why she was abroad alone at so late an hour. He was not at all the sort of personality she had expected to encounter—and yet, in a way, he was, too.

She had discovered during the last few minutes that she had formed an unconscious estimate of him already—the outgrowth of their first meeting when he had so courteously escorted her to the Madison Avenue car.

She was suddenly aware that she regretted the assignment that she had been so eager to accept—to lead this man into a trap. And all the time she was quite conscious of the fact that she was also glad that she had undertaken the task. Her own assignment would at least prevent another from getting it.

It happened that there was no policeman in sight at the moment. They had come to a stop almost directly beneath a street light. Kate turned to face her companion when they halted, and began in what she meant to be a tone of finality:

"You must leave me here, because—"

She stopped speaking right there. Her eyes widened. Her face blanched ever so little. She took one impulsive step nearer to him and paused with her hand partly extended, for she had seen him thrust his right hand inside of his waistcoat where one button had been loosened, and withdraw it stained. Then he had thrust it back again in haste to conceal it from her.

But she had recognized the significance of that stain.

"You are wounded!" she exclaimed. "One of those bullets—"

"It is nothing—nothing at all," he interrupted her. "I partly satisfied myself of that much before I came out of the house where those policemen searched for me. That was why I was so long in reappearing."

He was facing the street through which they had just passed, and as he ceased speaking he grasped her gently by the arm and led her unresistingly along their back track. "Yonder is a cab which appears to be disengaged," he added without pause. "If you will let me put you into it you need not give the man your home address until after I have gone away."

They approached it even as he ceased speaking, and he signaled to the driver. Unperceived by the Night Wind, Katherine also made a gesture toward the chauffeur. The consequence was that the cab at once came to a stop quite near to them. Nevertheless, the Night Wind had barely ceased speaking when she exclaimed, with genuine protest in her voice:

"But your wound! It needs attention, and you dare not visit a surgeon. Your picture is everywhere. You are a marked—"

The Night Wind was regarding her strangely, and she paused in confusion. With a half smile he abruptly turned from her and approached the black chauffeur of the imitation taxicab. He looked into the black face and eyes for a silent moment. Then he said with slow distinctness:

"This lady wishes to be taken to her home. She will give you the address after I have gone. You will carry out her orders directly and implicitly, or I will find you again, and you will be sorry that you did not. Here is sufficient for your fee, and more. After you have delivered your fare at the proper address, you may drive to the nearest police station and inform the officer at the desk that you have seen the man called Alias the Night Wind."

Without so much as another glance toward Katherine Maxwell, but with a courteous lifting of the soft hat he wore that night, he moved swiftly away from them and disappeared around the corner into Amsterdam Avenue.

Lady Kate bit her lips in real vexation and with honest concern.

She feared—nay, she believed—that the Night Wind's wound was of much more serious character than he had admitted.

She marveled at the man who could so coolly walk beside her in the street with a freshly fired bullet embedded somewhere in his body. Then with sudden determination she sprang into the cab.

"Follow him!" she called out to her black man. "Follow and overtake him!"

CHAPTER VII

A MODERN SAMSON

BINGHAM HARVARD REALIZED that he had need of
the immediate attention of a competent surgeon, although he
was also convinced that the wound he had received was not
serious; else he must have experienced more inconvenience
from it than he had done.

He might have dressed the wound himself, and would doubtless have done so had facilities been procurable. But he had
been driven from the house where he had taken a room the
preceding day, having paid for it a week in advance in the belief
that he could so direct his movements that he might occupy it
that long without discovery. But fate had decreed otherwise.

The small chain of events which had begun with the meeting
between Lady Kate and Rushton, which had continued with
Rushton's determination to spy upon the young woman, and
which had reached its climax in his own encounter with her,
had rendered him again homeless. The one fortunate circumstance of the whole affair was the fact that he had been so near
to that house to which he possessed a key at the moment of
the attack upon him; otherwise he might have been captured
or killed.

That act of his in pitching forward into the vestibule of the
house while Rushton was firing at him was strategy intended
to deceive Rushton. More than likely the bullet would not have
touched him had he not done that.

When he walked so swiftly away from Katherine, leaving

her at the cab, he was thoroughly alive to the fact that the wound must have attention, and that because he was without place and the necessaries to give it that attention he must, perforce, apply to a surgeon.

He recalled one—only because he had frequently noticed the sign on the house beside the door—in an adjoining street. He went there, and it so happened that he turned the corner from the avenue at the instant when the cab with Katherine for its passenger darted into view.

The keen-eyed black man saw him and followed. Those same eyes discovered him as he mounted the steps at the doctor's house, but the cab did not alter its direct course until it had passed the street and was out of sight just beyond the intersection.

Then the black man sprang to the pavement and ran back until he could peer into the street where presently he saw the doctor's door swing ajar. After some sort of parley at the doorway, which might have endured for a minute or less, the Night Wind disappeared into the house. Then the black man returned to his mistress and reported.

Bingham Harvard's gentility of appearance and demeanor was never lacking. The hour was approaching three in the morning, and the doctor responded to the summons at his door in person.

"I have been attacked in the street and have received a bullet-wound. I have no idea that it is serious, but I would like to have you examine it," Harvard announced with that directness of speech which was a characteristic with him.

The doctor was silent for a moment before he replied. He was startled by what he saw, for it happened that he instantly recognized the man on his door-step. But he did not make that fact manifest.

His hesitation quickly passed. He had decided what he would do. One of the capacities he filled was that of police surgeon. As such he had been shown the photograph of the Night Wind.

He knew the identity of his impromptu patient, therefore, the moment he opened the door and had obtained a good look at him.

"Come inside," he said, and led the way through the wide hall toward his office at the rear.

"Where is the wound?" he demanded the moment the door was closed behind him. "You haven't the appearance of a man who has been shot."

By way of reply Harvard removed his coat and waistcoat— not without a certain tightening of the lips as he did so—and laid them upon a chair. It could be seen then that his shirt at the right side was stained with red, although not shockingly so. But it was there, and enough of it to excite concern. The doctor aided him in divesting himself of the two shirts. The bullet, somewhat flattened and misshapen, dropped to the floor.

It had passed through the contents of the inside pocket of Harvard's coat, also through the contents of the upper waistcoat pocket (through letters and papers and a thickly filled leather pocketbook in the one and a small silver card-case in the other), and had thus been flattened and deflected so that it had gouged its way just beneath the skin and against a rib for a distance of five inches. There it had stopped and clung until dislodged by the removal of the shirt.

"You've got one fractured rib, which will give very little inconvenience, and a slight wound which will only trouble you by smarting," the doctor announced, and at once began preparations for dressing it. "There is a chance that the broken rib may have ruptured the pleura. Time will tell that. You will have to keep quiet for a few days, and I should advise that you avoid taking cold."

He prepared a basin with some sort of antiseptic and brought out some absorbent cotton. Then he stopped for a moment, as he was about to begin bathing the wound, and was apparently thoughtful for a time; then he stepped backward a pace and gave the bunch of cotton into the Night Wind's hand.

"Will you bathe it yourself with this antiseptic for a moment?" he asked. He made no excuses for leaving the room. Had he done so Harvard might have been suspicious. As it was, Harvard was not so.

But the doctor, once outside the office with the door closed behind him, hastened to the stairs and ran up them two steps at a time to the second floor. There was a telephone in the doctor's bedroom. From it, by turning down a switch, connection could be cut off from the telephone in the office.

The good doctor, in the belief that he was aiding justice, called up police headquarters, and for a moment he talked rapidly. Then, replacing the receiver, he seized upon a small bottle of liquid from a shelf near him and returned hastily to the office.

The Night Wind was still diligently employed in bathing the wound he had received—and his own judgment had already informed him that it was far from being a serious affair. He knew that he might easily have cared for it himself, and regretted now that he had called upon the doctor at all.

The surgeon made no comment when he reentered the room, but began busily to affix the necessary appliances and dressings where the bullet had plowed its way along the surface which covered the fractured rib. Over that he drew a strip of adhesive-plaster to hold the broken ends of the rib together.

"Now sit tight for a moment before you put on your clothing," he said. "I'll fix you a drop of medicine that I think you ought to take. Then you can dress and go about your affairs. I don't believe that you will suffer any inconvenience to speak of from the wound. Only beware of catching cold."

Harvard nodded and watched him.

The doctor poured a small quantity of liquid into a graduate from the bottle he had brought down-stairs with him, added some water, and passed it to Harvard.

"Take that," he said.

"Why?" Harvard asked him, smelling it.

"It will do you good," the doctor replied, turning away as if utterly indifferent whether the patient swallowed the mixture or not. He was almost too indifferent about it.

"Oh, all right!" Harvard said. And straightway, the doctor's back being toward him, emptied the medicine into a convenient cuspidor and put the graduate upon the table. Then, with expedition, but without the appearance of haste, he began to resume his clothing.

While at college Harvard had taken great interest in the study of chemistry. He possessed a natural aptitude for it, and at one time had seriously considered it as a profession. He had recognized the faint odor of the drug proffered him by the doctor as one of the preparations of Cannabis Indica, called *bhang*. It is a powerful and quick-acting hypnotic when properly administered.

Instantly, when Bingham Harvard detected the significance of that faint and all but imperceptible odor, he became again the Night Wind, for he knew that danger threatened.

His muscles flexed and became tense. His eyes were cold and hard. He drew in several deep inhalations while he resumed his clothing. He knew now, quite as well as if he had followed, why the doctor had left him alone for a few moments. The man had recognized him and knew that he was "wanted."

While he dressed he thought deeply and swiftly. The doctor had no suspicion that the patient had not swallowed the mixture. The Night Wind taxed his brain to remember how soon such a dose as he was supposed to have taken should begin to affect him.

He hurried with his clothing and finished dressing before he permitted himself to sink gently upon one of the chairs.

"I appear to be a trifle faint, doctor. Would you mind opening a window?" he asked; and the doctor complied with the request at once, smiling as he did so and assuring his patient that it would soon pass.

The Night Wind permitted his eyes to close, or nearly to

close, for he kept open a slit between the lids. His long lashes concealed that fact, but he could see the doctor, who at once came nearer to him.

Just then the door-bell rang.

The doctor hesitated for one brief moment. Then he crossed to the entrance from the hall, where he paused and looked back. His patient seemed to be unconscious or indifferent to what was taking place. The doctor opened the door, glanced back once more, passed into the hallway, and closed it after him.

The Night Wind awoke.

He darted to the door and turned the key, leaving it in the lock. He sprang to the open window and peered into the darkness beyond it.

Plainly there was no means of escape in that direction.

A double row of back yards, with high, spiked fences between them, confronted him. An old wistaria vine, the main stem nearly as large as his own biceps, passed over his head and had been trained and supported against the building just beneath the second story. He believed that he could reach it from the rail of the iron balcony outside the window.

But the room above him, even if the window of it were open, was probably occupied, and he hesitated to take that way out of his present difficulty—if indeed it offered a way out.

He turned back and crossed swiftly to the folding-doors which communicated between the office and the reception-room for patients. There was a hook-catch between them, and he dropped it into place just at the moment when the knob of the other door was turned and the person outside of it, whoever he might be, discovered that it had been locked against him.

There was no choice left to the Night Wind.

He sprang to the open window and through it, thence to the top of the balcony-rail.

His powerful arms lifted him easily when he seized the stem of the wistaria. He forgot that he had a broken rib and a bullet-wound. He could hear a grating sound at the office door, and detected the shooting back of the bolt of the lock just as he drew himself upward out of sight from the open window. He remembered even in his extremity that there are such things as burglars' forceps with which the post of a key may be seized and turned from the opposite side of a door. He had been none too quick in going.

The window of the second story near the vine was partly raised. The Night Wind pushed it up as far as it would go and swung himself into the room. A dim light reflected from the world outside assured him that the bed was occupied, but he passed it silently as a shadow and in another moment stood in the hallway of the second story, with the doorway through which he had passed closed behind him. Nor had the occupant of the bed been disturbed.

Harvard bent over the balustrade and listened.

Many voices from below assured him that several officers had been sent out to effect his capture. It did not matter to him what they were saying. Possibly there were more men outside of the house. He did not know.

Nevertheless he realized that his only means of escape was to fight his way through them and past them. To accomplish this he must first gain the first floor—or the basement, if that were possible.

He started down the stairs.

The incredible swiftness of the Night Wind was always his best asset. He never carried a weapon of any sort. That wonderful, God-given strength of muscle which was his always served him far better than any mechanical device could have done.

When he was three steps from the bottom of the stairs one of the two officers stationed just inside the door discovered him. The man uttered a cry of warning and reached for his gun; his companion did the same.

The Night Wind, even as the cry rang out, sprang toward them from his vantage-point of that slight elevation.

With the outer edge of his right hand he struck the foremost of the two men squarely across the bridge of the nose, and the fellow went down as if he had been shot. It is a terrible blow when properly delivered and silences effectually where the clenched fist would only stun. It is one of the popular jiu-jitsu blows.

The second officer fired his revolver just as his companion collapsed beneath the terrific blow; but the bullet went wild, as policemen's bullets are likely to do. The Night Wind seized the wrist of the extended hand that held the gun, twisted it, turned his own body half around, and pulled the arm down across his shoulder.

He bent suddenly forward. The legs of the officer he had seized upon described the arc of a half circle above their heads. They crashed into the chandelier, demolished it, and extinguished the lights. One foot smashed against the post of the balustrade. Ten weeks elapsed before that officer pounded pavements again.

The shout, the pistol-shot, the crashing of the chandelier, the cry of the cop whose ankle was broken, drew every man of the attacking party toward that spot.

They seemed to come from every direction—from the office, from the reception-room, from the parlor. One might have supposed that the reserves had been called out to capture this one man.

And yet there were not many. They had anticipated an easy capture, because the doctor, over the telephone, had promised to have their man well drugged and insensible by the time of their arrival.

There was no pause in the Night Wind's onward progress. Never had he needed his great strength so much as then; never had he used it to such purpose.

With the two men disposed of who had opposed his escape at the door, the way outside seemed momentarily cleared. He seized the knob and tore open the door, but somebody had put the chain-bolt in place, and for one brief instant it caught and held.

But even that—a small brass chain, in reality—was not proof against the unnatural strength of this remarkable man, born of unknown parents. The chain snapped in the middle with the Night Wind's second effort, which followed instantly upon the first one. He threw the door open and dashed outside.

His enemies were behind him, some of them disqualified for further pursuit; but he knew well that there were others, two or three, perhaps, who would be hot upon his trail without delay.

A cab was passing through the street slowly—barely moving, it seemed to the Night Wind in his haste.

He sprang down the steps toward it. He darted into the middle of the street after it. He vaulted to the seat beside the chauffeur—and would have seized the man and thrown him out, and so have made use of the cab to help his escape, but, as if the man realized his danger, he instantly speeded up.

The Night Wind held his hands and all his muscles ready for action; but there seemed to be no need of it.

In a moment they were at the corner. In an instant more they had turned it and were out of sight from the street through which they had just passed.

"Turn here, to the right," the Night Wind ordered when they had gone one block toward the north; and when they were nearing Central Park West he added, "Turn out here. If you see a policeman, go slowly; avoid him. You will be sorry if you do not."

Somewhere in the middle of the Sixties he told the man to stop. Then he sprang to the ground and turned to press a fee into the hand of the man who had saved him.

The door of the cab was thrown open at the same instant.

The face of a woman looked out at him.

Once again that night the Night Wind and Katherine Maxwell faced each other.

CHAPTER VIII

ANOTHER NIGHT
WIND MYSTERY

BINGHAM HARVARD RECALLED then what it was that had seemed so familiar to him in the manner and general bearing of the chauffeur who had obeyed him so implicitly during the rapid ride away from the front of the doctor's house.

Not once had the Night Wind turned his head to look at the face of the man who drove the car; now involuntarily he did so, and he saw that it was black.

It was all plain now—or, at least, he thought it was so.

He turned quickly toward the young woman again.

"You told this man to follow me when I left you," he said quickly. "Why did you do that, please?"

"Naturally I was alarmed about you," she replied without hesitation. "You were wounded. You did not tell me of your intention to seek a doctor, nor did I know that you were not seriously injured. Common humanity—"

"Thank you," he interrupted her and glanced quickly in both directions along the wide avenue. "More than all, I thank you for the service you have permitted this man to render me. I do not quite understand, and there is no time for explanations now."

"No," she said.

"I feel that I should apologize to you, however, because for a moment during our former meeting to-night I associated you with the powers that are hunting me. I am aware of the mistake now. You would scarcely have done what you have done if that

64

were the case. You have befriended me twice in ways that I shall not soon forget. I thank you. Good-by."

"Please wait a moment," she said. "I wish—"

"No," he interrupted her a second time. "Pardon me. Whoever you may be, you can ill afford to risk the discovery of having aided me. I would be a cad to permit it. Good night."

He swiftly crossed the space that separated them from the park wall, vaulted it, and disappeared.

Katherine watched him go, saw him leap the barrier, and pass out of sight beyond it.

Even then, for a space, she sat silently regarding the point where the Night Wind had disappeared. But presently, with something very much like a sigh, she closed the door of the car, seized the signal-cord, and pressed the plunger at the end of it in a way that indicated "Home."

Inside the park, concealed by the shrubbery that surrounded him, Bingham Harvard was suddenly conscious of the terrific strain he had been under since Rushton's attack upon him, and the slight, though somewhat telling, wound he had received as a consequence. The broken rib ached. The unimportant flesh-wound smarted. Every muscle of his body seemed oddly to protest against the calls he had made upon them.

He was tired. Already the gray approach of dawn was chasing away the shadows of night which were so necessary to his liberty. And he had no place to lay his head.

That room in the Seventies which he had taken and where he had hoped to remain for a few days at least, was no longer a haven for him. He must seek elsewhere for a resting place, and already the obscurity of night, with its deeper shadows to conceal him, was gone. He smiled grimly at the predicament he was in, touched his wounded side tentatively with hesitating fingers, coughed slightly in the hope to reassure himself that the pleura had not been injured—and became instantly conscious of a sharp twinge of pain which told him that it had been. The fact was not to be denied.

He started away across the park, heedless of paths and traveled ways. He came out at Seventy-Second Street, crossed Fifth Avenue, and presently boarded a northbound Madison Avenue car. He rode in the vestibule occupied by the motorman, and got down again at One Hundred and Twenty-Fourth Street.

He walked onward slowly to One Hundred and Twenty-Fifth Street and jumped upon a westbound crosstown car. But in doing so he passed a policeman, who peered curiously at him, and then turned upon his heel.

The Night Wind was not deceived. He knew that the officer had recognized him, or at least believed that he had done so.

Looking backward from the moving car, Harvard was convinced of it. He saw the policeman climb into the front vestibule of an Amsterdam Avenue car that followed closely behind the cross-town, and he knew that no uniformed officer on duty would dare to abandon his post save on a matter of grave importance, and in the utmost extremity.

So, again he had been recognized.

For the third time within a few hours he was to be hunted like an animal—for the Night Wind also knew, by implication but none the less certainly, that the policeman who had boarded that car that was following after him had managed somehow to pass the word along of the discovery he had made before he did so.

Bingham realized that telephones would be working, that word would be sent ahead of him, and that the car upon which he was a passenger was likely to be intercepted.

And now it was broad daylight. Darkness, which had so often stood his friend at other times, had disappeared.

The hour was early, nevertheless. Comparatively few people were abroad in the streets. The car he had taken was not signaled as often as the Fort George car that followed, and the consequence was that it gradually drew ahead, so that when it came to a stop at the near side of Eighth Avenue, the pursuing car with the policeman aboard of it was just crossing Seventh Avenue, seven hundred feet in the rear.

Ahead of the Night Wind, a couple of blocks distant, was the 36th Precinct station house in West One Hundred and Twenty-Fifth Street. That would be the place to which warning messages would have been sent by telephone. He knew that it must be avoided—or that the men who would dash out of it in search of him must be outwitted.

Quick to realize the difficulties he must encounter, as quick to meet and to overcome them, Bingham sprang from the car and went swiftly down Eighth Avenue as far as One Hundred and Twenty-Third Street, where he turned the corner to the right, his intention being to seek the cover afforded by Morningside Park in order to avoid his pursuers.

But at St. Nicholas Avenue, which runs diagonally across the other streets and avenues, fortune favored him. A One Hundred and Tenth Street car, westward bound, was just passing, and he sprang aboard of it without an instant of hesitation.

It happened that the car was well filled with Italian laborers bound for the One Hundred and Thirtieth Street ferry, and Edgewater, and the fugitive easily lost himself among them. When the car crossed One Hundred and Twenty-Fifth Street within sight of the police station, Bingham could see some of the signs of activity around it, doubtless induced by the telephone messages that he had surmised.

He saw more than that. The crosstown car in which he had been a passenger a few minutes before had been held up at the junction of One Hundred and Twenty-Fifth Street and Manhattan Streets and had only just been permitted to proceed on its way. Apparently it did not occur to the officers of the law to search the One Hundred and Tenth Street car. Perhaps it did not even remotely suggest itself to any of them that the Night Wind might have managed to board it. At all events, it passed on, unheeded, and so arrived at the Fort Lee ferry.

Harvard anticipated more difficulties there; but he could think of no better way for him to follow than to risk the ferry, and so escape from the immediate environment of the city while daylight lasted.

He got down from the car in the midst of the swarm of Italians, hunched his wide shoulders, pulled his hat down over his eyes, carried his coat over his arm as many of those around him did, covered his features as much as possible with his handkerchief while pretending furiously to blow his nose, and thus passed upon the ferryboat unseen—as he supposed.

But the handkerchief he pretended to use so vigorously was much too white for the company he was in, and there were sharp eyes watching that saw it, wondered at it, and acted upon the suggestion it conveyed.

Fortunately the car had been a trifle late. The big gates were already closing when Harvard dashed into the ferry house. He was among three or four of the last ones to pass the waiting-room door which slammed shut close behind them.

The ratchets of the mooring wheels were rattling, the hooks had been cast from the steel eyes that held them, the long blast of the ferryboat's whistle had begun to sound, and the propellers had actually begun to turn, pulling the boat inch by inch away from the bridge in the slip, when one of the big gates past which teams and vehicles go aboard of the ferry was swung open, and a half dozen policemen in uniform dashed through.

Even then they might not have succeeded in gaining the boat had not a tug, with a laden barge lashed abreast of it, been passing the slip at that moment.

That fact compelled the momentary stoppage of the ferryboat before it had fairly started—and so the officers who rushed down the bridge toward the craft were able to leap aboard of it.

Harvard had lingered where he could watch the approaches to the boat, and he saw all this—and he was forced to confess to himself that he was no longer in condition to contend against those men. Moreover, they were in uniform, and had the power to summon to their aid every citizen who happened to be on the boat.

He had been wounded; he had undergone superhuman exertion since receiving the wound; his great strength and phenomenal endurance were spent; he had been taxed even beyond his marvelous resources.

Nevertheless he darted out of sight among the passengers the moment he saw the approach of the officers. He started forward among the teams in the middle gangways, dodging in and out and constantly looking backward to discover if he had been observed, and presently, seizing upon an opportunity which offered itself, he pulled open the door which gives upon the stairway to the hurricane deck, for the use of the pilots, and passed out of sight.

But he was well aware that it could not be for long if he remained aboard.

He was known to be on that boat, else the policemen would not have followed him there. Before it could arrive at the slip at the opposite side of the river they would have searched everywhere for him, even to the hurricane deck and the pilot houses as well, and would have enlisted every man there in their service.

He decided, even while he mounted that narrow stairway, what he would do. He knew it to be a desperate chance to take, but there was no other way—so he lost not a second of his valuable time in taking it.

From the hood which covered the stairway at the deck he ran aft again, keeping it as a shield between himself and the occupied pilot house; and just abaft of amidships on the port side, he dove headfirst from that height into the foaming water of the Hudson River.

Bingham Harvard could swim almost as well as he could fight.

He chose the up-river side of the boat because the tide happened to be flowing swiftly in that direction, and also because the tug with the barge lashed beside it, which had momentarily delayed the ferryboat in leaving the slip, was still perilously close.

He dove deep, and swam still deeper, taking the direction of the tide for his guide and exerting every ounce of remaining strength he possessed to make speed.

He knew by the foaming of the water that he was directly astern of the tug, and he believed that he was gaining upon it; and then the great good fortune which at times seemed to try to balance the account with his ill-fortunes worked once more in his behalf. He discovered the dangling end of a heaving-line trailing through the water just in front of him.

With a last superhuman effort, for he was nearly spent by now, he succeeded in grasping it—and there for a space of time he hung, forcing his body to remain beneath the surface out of sight, but, with it all, mercifully resting, and catching an occasional breath of air to sustain him.

Nothing reminded him of the doctor's warning concerning exposure and catching cold.

He was most concerned, just then, about making good his escape.

DOWN at police headquarters at ten o'clock that morning the skipper gazed across the top of his desk quizzically at Lieutenant Rodney Rushton, smiling grimly, and with something of the contempt he felt gleaming in the expression of his eyes.

"The Night Wind established a record last night, Rushton," he said. "He made a complete getaway three separate and distinct times. Eh? What?" That Eh? What? from the skipper was equivalent to a whole paragraph of scorn from most men, and Rushton winced under the sting of it.

"Not from me, he didn't," he retorted.

"Oh, well, it amounts to the same thing. He gave you the happy ta-ta once all right, and he fought his way out of the doctor's house—and he left the usual collection of broken bones behind him, too. If he keeps on at this rate, Rushton, he'll have the whole force laid by the heels and in the hospitals before he gets through." Then the skipper's entire manner changed as he added, severely: "Something's got to be done to put a stop to it."

"It looks to me as if he had put a stop to it himself, skipper," Rushton replied.

"Oh! Does it? How so?"

"That ferryboat business."

"Well, what of it?"

"He drowned himself; that's all," was the sullen response.

"Are you refreshing yourself with some new kind of humor, Rushton?" the skipper inquired, indulgently. "Of course that last remark of yours is some sort of a joke, and I am not quite keen enough to see it. What's the point?"

"The *point?* Wasn't he seen to go onto that ferryboat just before it left the slip? Didn't those six cops chase him onto it? Didn't they hunt everywhere, from the stoke-hole to the pilot houses, for the Night Wind? Didn't they compel the pilot to keep the boat in mid-stream until they completed the search?

"Didn't they find two men who swore that they both saw a man dive into the water from the hurricane deck soon after the boat left the New York slip; and didn't both of those men swear on their solemn oaths that the man never came to the surface again? *And* didn't those six cops watch every man that left that boat, at either side of the river, for three hours afterward? And so, ain't it logical to say that the fellow who dived from the top of it was the Night Wind?"

"The one word, 'yes' will suffice to answer all of your questions, lieutenant. But all the same I don't see how it establishes your point," the skipper replied quietly.

"The Night Wind ain't no fish, is he?"

"I find it difficult to determine just what he is, Rushton."

"Well, if he didn't come to the surface—"

"You have only the words of those two men for that."

"Do you think it's likely that they lied about it, skipper?"

"No; but I regard it as quite logical that the man might have come to the surface without having been seen by either of them. Argument as to that amounts to nothing. The facts are these: That the Night Wind succeeding in getting away from you once, and that was done when you thought you had him well trapped inside of the house where he had taken a room, when you had four men with you to help you, and after he had been wounded—he did not know how badly.

"And he left a dislocated shoulder for Dixon behind him. Later he made his getaway from the house of the doctor after smashing a wrist for one man and breaking a collar bone for another. Still later he eluded those six cops from the Thirty-Sixth, besides a whole ferryboat full of passengers. I tell you, Rushton, this sort of thing has got to be stopped."

"Well, *you* stop it!" snapped Rushton savagely.

"Be careful, lieutenant. Don't be impudent."

"I ain't. I didn't mean to be so. I'm just plain mad clear through. And, cuttin' out the argument, I think that last getaway of his'n spelled down an' out f'r him. You'll find that he won't show up agin—goin' into the water like that, an' him wounded to boot. Bet you a hat he's croaked."

"You're on. How's that arm of yours, Rushton?"

The lieutenant ground his teeth together savagely by way of reply. The skipper smiled grimly.

"It would get well qucker if you'd take a rest," he suggested.

"I won't do that," Rushton replied. "He's got to break my neck in order to lay *me* up. That's what!"

"The one thing that I do not understand concerning the whole affair last night, Rushton," the skipper said presently, "is that taxicab incident, when the Night Wind got away from the bunch at the doctor's house. It was altogether too opportune to have been entirely due to accident."

Rushton snorted without replying.

"If he had jumped into the front seat beside the driver and

chucked him into the street and run the taxi himself, I could see through it. But, as nearly as I can make sense out of the reports, it looks as if the chauffeur speeded up the car the moment the Night Wind got there. What's the answer to that?"

"Give it up, skipper."

"Has he got somebody working with him?"

"I give that up, too; only, I don't think so."

"Well, it's up to you to find that cab and to bring the driver of it here to me. And you're not the only one I've sent out to find it, either. That's all."

Rushton saluted and went out.

The chief of the detective bureau, left alone, called up the house in West Eleventh Street which he knew to be the address of Lady Kate. He was informed that Miss Maxwell was not there, and had not been in the house since shortly after nine o'clock the preceding evening. He left a message which she would understand as an order for her to call him up as soon as she came in.

But he received no call from her that day nor the next one.

At noon of the third day thereafter he sought the West Eleventh Street address in person, and found that Miss Maxwell had not yet returned. He knew nothing about that other address of hers in the Seventies. Nobody knew anything about it save herself and the black man.

In the middle of the afternoon of the fourth day she telephoned to him—from the Eleventh Street house—and he ordered her to remain where she was until he arrived there. He wished to talk with her at once.

In the mean time not a word or a sign had been heard, or seen, or reported, concerning the Night Wind.

That mysterious character had indeed disappeared. Many men on the force, the skipper included, began gradually to adopt Lieutenant Rodney Rushton's view that the Night Wind had "cashed in" when he went over the side of the ferryboat into the rushing waters of the Hudson.

"You received my message, didn't you, that I telephoned here three days ago?" the official demanded as soon as he entered the presence of Lady Kate.

"I received it an hour ago—yes, sir," she replied quietly. "I called you at once."

"Then you have not been here?"

"No."

"Where "have you been, Miss Maxwell?"

"I have been attending to my duty—as I have seen and understood it," was the calm reply.

"Lieutenant Rushton reports that you have apparently succeeded in making the acquaintance of the Night Wind. You were talking with him that night of his last—I was going to say appearance, but 'cyclone' would be a more apt word to apply to it and to him. How did that happen, Miss Maxwell?"

"He approached me from behind. He had recognized me from that other meeting the evening of the attempted arrest at Mr. Chester's house."

"Officer Dixon says—he does not know who and what you are, of course—that *he* had called you to the top of the steps and was talking to you when the Night Wind attacked him from behind; and he expresses the opinion that you went away with the man after Dixon was thrown to the bottom of the steps and rendered senseless. How about that?"

"Officer Dixon, if that is his name, evidently supposed me to be an acquaintance—perhaps even a friend—of the Night Wind. He called me to the top of the steps, and, in his eagerness and zealousness, grasped my arm. He shook me rather roughly, and was still doing it when the Night Wind reappeared. I assume that he thought he was defending me when he attacked Dixon. Then, having thrown Dixon down the steps, he ordered me, gruffly, to 'beat it,' as Mr. Rushton would express it. I went one way, the Night Wind went the other. One does not stop to argue with the Night Wind when he says things. I have discovered that much."

"Is that *all* that you have discovered?"

"Practically."

"You are still on the job?"

"Assuredly. And I will report whenever there is anything definite *to* report. My understanding of the orders I received was that I was to have a free hand, inspector. If that is not the case I would much prefer to return to my regular duties," she replied concisely.

"It *is* the case. Go ahead in your own way, Miss Maxwell. You're all right. Only don't leave me guessing too long at a time," the inspector said, smilingly. Then he went away. In the mean time the Night Wind was having a startling time.

CHAPTER IX

THE HOUSE
OF THE SEVENTIES

BINGHAM HARVARD, ALIAS the Night Wind, opened his eyes and stared.

There was nothing familiar in any object that his gaze encountered. The room was strange; everything in it was strange.

He became conscious, too, of an old lassitude that was upon him; an unaccountable weakness; and, more remarkable than all else, he felt no desire to move a muscle.

There was no ambitious effort latent in his mind, to be put into effect on the moment of his awakening, as had been the case with him of late.

Sunlight streamed in at the open window. Beyond it he could see the walls and windows of other houses across the street—or avenue; which was it? he wondered.

At first he was not greatly concerned about the strangeness of things around him—and that was odd, too. But his mind, newly active, was working slowly.

He was in bed. He knew that. A sheet and an immaculate spread covered him. One of his arms rested upon it; the other was beneath it. He raised that arm and hand before his eyes and was amazed by the effort that was required to do so.

The sight of his right hand and forearm astonished him still more. "Surely," he thought, "they are not mine;" and yet he knew that they were his own.

He withdrew the other arm, with considerable effort, from beneath the bedclothes, and examined it. It was undoubtedly the mate to the other one. Startling things had happened to him during the past weeks, but this one was the most startling of all.

"I wonder what has happened?" he asked himself aloud, and met with still another surprise. Was that his voice that had spoken—a weak, small voice not at all familiar to his ears? "Oh, well, I'll get up, and find out about it," he added, and made the effort to do so; but he sank back upon the pillow, helpless, weak, incapable of further effort.

For the first time in his life, Bingham Harvard was frightened.

He had never been helpless like that before. He could not remember when his muscles had refused to respond to his will until then.

He stared about him again, and then through the windows a second time, for, with a rush of comprehension, he remembered that he was a fugitive from justice, a hunted outcast, a man outside the law.

But surely the room he occupied formed no part of a prison. There were no bars at the window, and no prison-house ever held a room like that one, spotlessly clean, with pictures hanging against the walls, and freshly cut flowers in a vase on the table where he could see them.

A hospital, then? No. He decided against that view for the same reasons. And, besides, he could detect nothing in the atmosphere of the room that suggested hospital odors.

The table that held the vase of flowers contained also a bell which he discovered that he could reach with that same right hand which had so amazed him with the first sight of it.

Hesitatingly, tentatively, he reached out, hesitated again another moment, then, with decision and some force, touched the plunger of the table-bell.

He could not see the door to the room, as he was lying, but he heard the click of the knob and knew that it had swung open, realized that some one had entered, and had softly closed the door.

He remained perfectly quiet and motionless, listening expectantly, but no one came into view; there was no sound of further advance across the rug which covered the floor. Evidently the person who had entered the room was waiting to discover if the stroke of the bell had been an accident, or if it had been done with intelligence and purpose.

"Well, *well, well!*" he exclaimed petulantly, and was again surprised by the sound of a voice which he could barely recognize as his own.

Something resembling a gasp of mingled pleasure and dread replied to him. The delicate swish of silken skirts fell upon his ears. The figure of a woman glided almost noiselessly to the bedside. He raised his eyes and met hers, and then stared on and on at her in speechless amazement.

She was the woman of the taxicab!

He recognized her instantly. Incredulity became certainty. Astonishment held him in its grip, utterly silent. He asked himself what sort of necromancy was this, which conjured up before his eyes the face and form of the only person who had befriended him since his unfortunate outlawry?

He knew it to be true that she was there beside him, looking down upon him with a kindly smile in her eyes and upon her lips—and yet he doubted the truth of it, too.

"You are better," she said. "I am glad." And she reached out and laid one soft palm gently upon his forehead.

"What has happened?" he managed to ask her. She replied, still smiling:

"You have been quite ill, Mr. Harvard. But you are better now."

"How long? How long a time have I been here?" he demanded, weakly.

"Five days. No more. Not quite that long, in fact. The sixth day will not begin until to-morrow morning."

"And you—*you* have taken care of me?"

"Partly. Not entirely. I have had assistance," she replied; and then, seeing the sudden wave of alarm in the expression of his eyes, she added hastily: "But you need feel no concern about that. The person who has assisted me is entirely trustworthy. He is the same one who drove the cab for us when you escaped that night. Do you remember?"

He nodded and would have spoken again in further questions, but the soft hand that rested upon his forehead was transferred quickly and the tips of her fingers closed his lips.

"You must not talk—now," she said, with quiet decision. "I will tell you sufficient to still your curiosity, and you must be satisfied with that until you are better and stronger, and all danger of a relapse has passed."

"Has there been—a doctor?" he managed to say, notwithstanding the delicate finger-tips that pressed against his lips.

"No," she assured him. "And you *must* not talk. Talking will make you cough, and one fit of violent coughing might throw you into a worse condition than you have been in. Do you remember the bullet wound? Don't answer me; nod your head, or turn it from side to side when I ask a question. Well, that broken rib ruptured the pleura very slightly, I suppose. It could not have been more than slight, else you would have been much worse off than you have been. Perhaps it might not have inconvenienced you at all, but for the strenuous times you encountered after you received the wound. And then, finally, you must have been a long time in the water. It was cold, too. It put the finishing touches upon what the violent exercise had begun."

He nodded vigorously.

Temporarily he had forgotten the dive from the hurricane deck of the ferryboat, but now he recalled it vividly enough.

He remembered that he had clung to the end of the rope he had grasped, for a long time, keeping himself immersed beneath the water as much as possible to avoid discovery. He remembered that at last, when he decided that it would be safe to do so, he had pulled himself hand over hand closer to the barge that was lashed to the tug, and had finally succeeded in establishing himself upon the top of the rudder of the barge which had been only a few inches beneath the surface, and that he had clung there desperately until the craft was being docked.

He had slipped into the water again after that, and had swam, unseen, to one of the numerous small craft moored near by. He had climbed into that, and rested for a time, after which he had made his way to the shore, to discover that he was on the bank of the Hudson, not far above One Hundred and Fifty-Fifth Street.

He remembered that he had crawled beneath the upturned derelict of an old cat-boat, to hide himself away, and to rest and sleep, if he could do so, until darkness should come again.

Somebody had made use of that retreat before him. There was an old sail and some burlap bagging which he utilized for bed and covering, and some old newspapers which he used for a pillow. All save one of them, which attracted him, and which he tried to examine because it happened, in glancing at .it, that his glance first found the column which was headed "Furnished Rooms to Let."

An isolated furnished room was what he most needed just then.

Now, he vaguely recalled that he had marked a circle around one of the advertisements, with a blue pencil that he carried in his pocket, intending to seek that address when night should come again.

Then, the awful chill!

He would never forget that, and the terror and helplessness of it.

There was a confused recollection in his mind of staggering from his hiding place, of climbing a steep hill, of the roar and confusion of the subway—and that was all.

But he did not tell his new friend of any of these things that

he now recalled. He did not speak, because she had commanded him not to do so.

"Did you know of this address?" she asked him when he
again raised his eyes for further information. He shook his head
negatively. "Do you know where you are now?" Again a negative.

"It was long after dark when Julius found you," she went on,
resting her soft palm upon his head again to quiet him. "You
were seated upon the steps of this house. Julius is the negro
who serves me; who has helped me to care for you. You were
shaking with a terrible chill when he discovered you. You were
delirious, and had no idea who you were, or where you were.
But Julius recognized you. He had brought the cab to the door
by my order. He summoned me from the house and we brought
you inside—to this room. Shall I tell you more, now?"

He nodded.

"Don't you think you can wait in patience until another time?"

He shook his head in protest. She gave him a sip of water
and went on:

"There was an old newspaper clutched in your right hand
when we brought you to this room, which even in your delirium you seemed reluctant to part with. While Julius undressed
you and put you to bed I carried it into the adjoining room and
examined it, wondering why you clung to it so tenaciously. The
paper was more than a week old. There was a blue-pencil mark
around one of the advertisements. Inside of the blue circle was
the address of this house. Perhaps that is what directed your
steps here, subconsciously. You were seeking a room, half realizing that you were ill, and very much in need of one. That
week-old newspaper contained an advertisement from this
house. The location suited you. That is the explanation. It has
puzzled me greatly. It was merely a coincidence that I have the
top floor."

The explanation seemed quite simple now.

"In your delirium you have told me much that happened to
you after we parted that early morning when you sprang over

the park wall and disappeared. In other ways I know more about the circumstances," she concluded.

She was silent a moment, then she added:

"There is just a little more to tell you, after which you must rest, and try to sleep, until I can come to you again. I tell you this, so you will understand, and in order that you may not be troubled by misgivings and apprehensions while you rest here, and get well again. It is this:

"I have always been rather an ambitious young person. Once upon a time I believed that the career of a trained nurse filled my desire for usefulness, so I studied and graduated as one. Because of that fact I have felt that I was equal to the emergency which confronted you. "To summon a doctor to attend you was out of the question, save as a last extremity. So I took the chance. You have nothing to fear while you are here. Nobody suspects who you really are. Nobody will suspect. Now, get well again as quickly as possible; and, to do that, avoid, if you can, every inclination to cough, force yourself not to talk or ask questions, and compel yourself to patience until you are stronger."

"I must ask one question," Harvard said quickly—"just one; then I will be content. I must know who you are, and why—"

She closed his lips again with the tips of her fingers.

"The 'who' is sufficient for the present," she said. "Never mind the 'why.' You may, when you are able to talk, address me as Katherine. Let that suffice. I know your name, but I prefer to think of you as the Night Wind. I like it."

She moved quickly away from him and he heard the door close behind her before he realized that she was going.

Left to himself he fell to studying the pictures on the walls, and the other decorations of the room he occupied so strangely, nor was he long in determining that it was the parlor, or living-room, of a suite. Undoubtedly the place was the home of this remarkable young person who had befriended him. The bed, he decided, was one of the davenport creations.

Then the door opened again, softly, and he thought that she was returning. But the face that appeared beside him was intensely black, though well featured and kindly in its expression.

The jet-black hair on the man's head was wavy instead of kinky, and his skin was entirely without that shininess which is the usual quality of a negro's complexion.

"I am Julius, sir," he said. "If you should want anything, touch the bell. I will be in the next room."

He went away, and Bingham Harvard, alias the Night Wind, being again alone, slept.

Chance alone—possibly fate had a hand in it—had placed him where he was. In that old newspaper he had discovered the address of a room to let in the locality he desired. Being ill, he required one. In his delirium he had wandered there, unrecognized.

Fate decreed that it should be that unknown address of Lady Kate in the Seventies.

CHAPTER X

THE ALARM

"**WELL, MY LADY,** good evening to you."

Katherine Maxwell turned swiftly and Rushton confronted her. She had recognized his voice with the first of his uttered words.

He was undeniably pleased by the encounter. She was the reverse, although she managed not to betray the fact. His expression, which was meant to be an engaging smile of welcome, was to her merely a leer. She noticed that the sling which supported his arm had been loosened and lengthened, and that the splints had been removed. These facts suggested that he would be, very soon again, as active and as competent as ever. Unconsciously she resented that quite as deeply as she did his nearness.

By many persons, Lieutenant Rushton would have been adjudged a handsome man. He was himself one of the many. He was entirely convinced of it, and it never occurred to him as possible that anybody should hold a different view.

He was big and burly and brutish. His eyes were too widely apart, indicating cruelty. But his features were regular, his face was intelligent, he carried himself well, dressed immaculately, groomed his black mustache carefully, was alert, quick, and as graceful as so ponderous an individual could be.

"It is two weeks—more than that, nearly three—since I have seen you," he said to her. "I have missed you. Where have you been keeping yourself, Lady Kate?"

"On the job," she replied, speaking rather shortly.

"Yes? There isn't much need of that now, is there? The Night Wind hasn't blown through a city street since that eventful night."

"I haven't been called off it. Have you?" she retorted, ignoring the last part of his remark.

"No," he answered. "None of us have. The 'skipper' is still of the opinion that he will show up again somewhere before long. But nobody has seen anything of the guy since that night—unless you have."

She was silent.

"Have you?"

"Would you believe me if I should tell you that I *have* seen the Night Wind since then—seen him and talked with him?" she responded, smiling upon the lieutenant for the first time.

To use an expression which was frequently voiced by himself, that smile of hers got his "goat." He fell for it without in the least realizing that he did fall, and that he walked, open-eyed, into the trap she had set for him. He grinned broadly, then closed one eye in a prolonged wink.

"I'm on," he said. "I get you. You like the job, eh? You'd like it to last as long as possible. But, on the level, have you seen him?"

"You haven't replied to the previous question yet, lieutenant."

"Well, considering the matter from the standpoint of your superior officer, I think that I should take such a statement as that with a considerable grain of salt, Miss Maxwell."

"Thank you," she replied, and bowed mockingly. "After that statement I need not answer your question. But I agree with the skipper in that I confidently believe that the Night Wind will be seen—and felt—again."

Rushton regarded her narrowly for a moment, then abruptly altered the trend of the subject.

"You were talking with him that night when I chased down the street after him," he said. "What did he say to you?"

Again she radiated a smile for his benefit.

"He recalled our former meeting—the evening when your arm was broken." Katherine let her eyes fall toward the crippled arm for an instant. Rushton scowled.

She continued: "One of the things that he said to me that night was that I seemed to be better acquainted with the city streets than I was on the former occasion."

"He was on to you, was he?"

"I don't think he suspects that I belong to the police—now, if that is what you mean, lieutenant."

She was smiling upon him for the third time; but Rushton took note of her use of that word "now," and called her attention to it.

"What did you mean by that?" he demanded. She tossed her head, and replied:

"I could not afford to have him suspect that I was a female police officer, so I took instant means of dispelling that idea. I warned him of your approach and told him to beat it."

"Well, now, what d'ye think of that? Say, you're gettin' wise to our parleyvoo, ain't you? But what the dickens did you do that for—tellin' him to duck when I was headin' for him?"

Katherine smiled frankly at him this time, but it was a frankness which he did not in the least comprehend.

"I scarcely wanted to see you killed, Lieutenant Rushton," she said—"you, with one of your arms in a sling, and useless. And I could not know that there were several others coming to your assistance—could I? Besides, I knew that my warning, in addition to sparing you, would put me right with him. See?"

She bent nearer to him and he did not draw back. Then she laughed aloud and started away, but he put out a detaining hand. She stopped again, before he could touch her.

"Between you 'n' me, Lady Kate," he said, "that guy is dead—deader'n a herrin'. You take it from me. But let's cut him out of it. Where are you goin'? It's early yet. Only a little past nine. Had your dinner yet?"

"Oh, it is only a little more than an hour since I ate heartily—

thank you, all the same, Lieutenant Rushton. Besides, I am on duty, you know. So are you, for that matter, I suppose. Good night."

She was gone before he could detain her.

They had met directly in front of the Hotel Manhattan, in Forty-second Street. Katherine crossed the avenue, when she parted with the lieutenant, and went into the subway; but she crossed over by the underground platform and mounted the stairs at the opposite side of Forty-second Street, for something told her that Rushton intended to keep trace of her.

Indeed, that was his intention, although not directly so.

He had another method, quite as available, and much more logical in practice with such a woman as Katherine Maxwell, than to attempt to follow her in person. The truth was that he had discovered her some moments before he spoke to her, and that he was not alone when he made the discovery of her nearness. There was with him, at the time, a new man lately promoted to the bureau, and therefore unknown to Lady Kate. Before Rushton spoke to her, he said to his side partner:

"I'll give you a tryout on a stunt that won't be easy, Merton. I'm going to speak to a lady in a minute. When I leave her, whether it's now or an hour from now, you take her trail. She ain't livin' where I thought she was and where the skipper thinks she is—not so's you could notice it. She's got a 'go-bye bye' some'er's else, and I wanta know where. Y'understand?"

"Yes, sir."

"Well, you trail her to it. She's one of us, all right, but she ain't on to you. I'll hang out near the telephone inside the Manhattan, an' when you've nailed her sleep-house, call me up an' have me paged. I'll be here, all right, or I'll have some other guy here representin' me."

"Very good, sir."

"An' say! if you fall down on this, it's yours f'r poundin' pavements again. If you happen to win out mebby I'll take you on with me, in place of Co-niglio. We'll see about that."

Thus it happened that when Katherine ascended the stairway at the opposite side of Forty-second Street and peered across that thoroughfare, she discovered that the lieutenant was still standing where she had parted with him.

Katherine was not entirely reassured. The lieutenant was playing the indifferent much too well. She was perfectly aware of the "side-partner" business, and she knew that Rushton was not in the habit of traveling alone, particularly since he had carried his arm in a sling. She had discovered, that same day, that Rushton had been quite frequently to the house in West Eleventh street, inquiring for her, and must therefore suspect that she had another address. He would try to discover it, too.

The fact that she had not seen anyone with him did not convince her of his solitude, so she remained beneath the hood of the subway stairs at the south side of the street, watching him, until at last he turned about and entered the hotel—and later, that same night, she learned a lesson in caution which she did not soon forget.

She turned back into the subway, after the lieutenant entered the hotel, and boarded an express for Seventy-second Street. At that hour the cars were not crowded, and she could inspect the appearance of each passenger with little difficulty. She came to the decision before she left the train that her fears had been groundless and her caution unnecessary.

Nevertheless she was watchful when she mounted the stairs to the street level. But nothing attracted her attention. It did not occur to her that the man who walked beside her up the stairs, almost brushing elbows, was trailing her, and that he preferred propinquity, rather than distance, in the shadow game. Merton, the new man, was a born "shadow."

Nevertheless she resorted to her usual tactics of caution in approaching the house where she lived, and which she called her real home, and where the Night Wind was at that moment impatiently awaiting her return. For it had been agreed upon between them before her departure that he was to go away that night, and he was anxious to be gone.

He had been there long enough. He was well and strong again. It was necessary that he should go at once. She entered at last, unobserved, as she supposed.

Ten minutes later a much-bebuttoned boy gyrated among the guests and patrons of the Hotel Manhattan, singsonging:

"Mis-ter-Rush-tun! Mis-ter-Rush-tun!"

Three or four minutes after that incident Lieutenant Rushton hastened from the hotel into the subway.

In the meantime the Night Wind and Katherine Maxwell, unmindful of the danger that threatened, were rather earnestly holding their last interview and conference before the parting of their ways—a parting which the man was determined should be final, and which the woman was equally determined should not be.

The process of recovery from Harvard's recent illness had rendered them oddly intimate, without intimacy. He had decided that for her welfare it must end—at once, and for all time.

The cab presided over by Black Julius stood at the curb several doors below that house, and Julius himself was waiting in the adjoining room of Katherine's suite when the doorbell rang out its warning.

Katherine raised a pair of startled eyes to Bingham Harvard's. Intuitively she sensed the danger that threatened. She "felt" that the person who rang that bell was Rushton, and she was certain that he would not have come alone.

CHAPTER XI

LADY KATE'S BLUFF

"**THAT TERRIBLE MAN** has had me shadowed, despite my caution!" Katherine exclaimed. "Oh, why was I so blind to what he might do? It is Lieutenant Rushton," she added. "I am sure of it."

Harvard had taken several steps away from her, nearer to the door through which any person entering the room must pass.

He had by no means regained all of his great strength, but nevertheless he knew himself to be, even at that moment, more than a match for any ordinary man.

Also, the prospect of battle fanned the fires that burned within him. His nostrils dilated. That ringing of the doorbell had been to him like the boot-and-saddle call of the bugle to a cavalry horse.

Moreover, the entire circumstance filled him with strange misgivings.

They had been talking together for some time when the summons at the bell occurred, and she had made no mention of having seen Rodney Rushton while she was out. Now she admitted in the first few words she uttered that she *had* seen him.

The suspicions which at one time had possessed him concerning her were again suggested to his mind. He did not admit to himself that they really amounted to suspicions, and yet—

He regarded her silently, from his position near the door,

and he saw her shiver, as if she were half-conscious of the hateful thing that was in his mind.

Then the bell rang a second time, more loudly, more imperatively, than before.

Black Julius tapped upon the connecting door between the rooms, then opened it slightly and inquired:

"Shall I answer it, Miss Kitty?"

"No," she answered promptly. "Whatever happens, you must not be seen. Keep out of sight, Julius, and get to your car at the first opportunity. Then hold it in readiness to serve Mr. Harvard. He may need you."

Julius disappeared. Katherine turned again to her companion. She voiced the unpleasant thought that had occurred to her.

"You suspect me," she said. "You think that while I was out I betrayed you."

"No," he replied to her, with decision. "I do not think that."

She smiled at him sadly.

"You are trying not to think so—you won't admit that you do think so, even to yourself. But in the back of your mind there is the thought. It is not true. I *must* say that much."

"I believe you," he said.

The doorbell rang out a third peal; this time a prolonged one.

"You must answer it," he told her. "There is no other way. If Rushton is there, let him enter. I will not hurt him—badly—now. He is a cripple. But when he gets back the use of his arm, when he is entirely himself again, then—" He paused in his speech.

"You are in no condition to contend against him now," she said, ignoring the implied threat. "You are not strong enough. You must get outside, somehow, before I admit him. Besides, he would not come alone. There is the fire-escape at the rear, and—"

She came to an abrupt stop, startled, for there had come a

loud and determined rapping against the door that opened upon the hallway.

"He has rung another bell than yours, and somebody else has worked the latch on the lower door for him," Harvard said quietly and in a low tone.

"Go in there and wait," she said, indicating the door through which Julius had spoken to them. "Or escape, if there is an opportunity. I will find a way to detain Rushton and whoever may be with him."

Harvard inclined his head an instant and obeyed her silently.

He closed the door after him but did not fasten it, as he might have done. He paused near it to listen, and he heard Katherine throw open the door into the hall.

"Well?" he heard her say, and he barely recognized the voice in which she uttered that one word, so cold and repellent was it. Harvard could imagine her standing before the opening, barring entrance to the room with her own slight figure.

Lieutenant Rushton's coarse chuckle replied to her.

"Nice little nest you've got here, Lady Kate, ain't it?" the officer inquired, with another chuckle louder than the first one, and with an easy familiarity of manner which made Harvard's fingers twitch. Also, the circumstance had another effect upon him. It assured him that Katherine Maxwell *was* personally known to the powers that ruled down at police headquarters. All his former suspicions swept over him again.

In the other room Katherine faced the lieutenant precisely as Harvard had imagined the scene. She stood in the doorway, close to the threshold, barring his entrance to the room; and he, without attempting to pass her, grinned broadly. He felt entirely at ease, and decidedly the victor. He had that cock-sure attitude of the confirmed egoist.

"What do you want, Lieutenant Rushton?" Katherine demanded, ignoring his questioning remark.

"Well, f'r one thing, I wanta come in," he drawled, still grinning. "F'r another, as the personal representative of the skipper, I wanta know what you're doin', livin' in this nice little nest, when all the time you're supposed to be residin' in that West Eleventh Street place. 'Tain't accordin' to Hoyle, Miss Maxwell, an' seein' as I'm the first one to get onto it, it's my duty to make some inquiries."

Without warning as to his intentions he thrust her aside as he ceased speaking, and brushed past her into the room. Then he turned about and stood facing her under the chandelier.

He was still grinning—smiling, he would have called it—but there gleamed in his eyes an expression of dogged insistence upon the position he had taken, which she was wise enough to know it would not be well to combat. She gestured toward a chair.

"Since you have forced your way inside—pray be seated," she said, with mock politeness. "You are not welcome. You have not advanced yourself in my esteem by this act, if you happen to care for it, which I suppose you do not."

"Livin' here alone?" he drawled, accepting the chair and examining the interior of the room with that perceptive intentness which was one of the qualities of his calling.

The question was harmless enough, of itself. But his manner in putting it, and the wider grin with which he uttered it, amounted to a studied insult. She made no reply to it, but continued to stand at the opposite side of the room, waiting.

In fact she was paying little attention to him. Her ears were straining to catch any sound that might come from the adjoining room. None came, however. Her eyes sought Rushton's face again.

He started to his feet at that instant, and crossed the room with quick strides. From a taboret beside a Morris chair he picked up a copper receptacle that had been fashioned to imitate a shell, and regarded it quizzically.

"Do you smoke cigars?" he asked, without turning his head.

She made no reply.

"These are cigar ashes, ain't they?" he asked again.

"Possibly."

"Who left 'em here?"

"A person of my acquaintance." She knew that Harvard, who did not smoke, frequently provided Black Julius with cigars, in order to keep the faithful servant with him for company, when otherwise he might be lonely.

"When?"

"During the early part of the evening, I suppose."

"You suppose! Don't you know when it was?"

"Not definitely."

"Where is he now?"

"I haven't an idea," she replied truthfully. Indeed, she hoped that Julius had made his escape from the house ere then, and that he had the car in readiness for Harvard. She had begun to believe that Rushton had come to her house alone, after all.

"Is he here *now?*" Rushton wheeled upon her, half-savagely. Something akin to jealous rage had been roused within him. "If he is, you'd better produce him, Lady Kate. I ain't in no mood for foolin'. See? An' this thing needs explainin'. Y'understand what I mean?"

"Lieutenant Rushton," she retorted icily, "my private affairs do not and cannot concern you. I am responsible to the inspector and the commissioner; not to you."

"Say, does the skipper know about this here dommycile of yours? Tell me that."

"Instead of replying, I will refer you to him."

He peered sharply at her. He was wondering how far he dared go forward with the attitude he had assumed. But Rushton was not easily bluffed, and he was himself the greatest of bluffers—whenever he thought there was a bare possibility that the other party might "lay down."

"Anyhow," he said, "I'll have a look at the other rooms of this here flat. It is a flat, ain't it? One of the 'made-over-from-old-residences' sort."

Rushton went quickly toward the door past which Harvard had gone when he left the room. Katherine did not move. She knew that it would be quite useless to attempt to intercept the man, and she saw that he was determined. She could only pray, silently, that Harvard had gone; that the adjoining room would be tenantless when Rodney Rushton entered it.

It was.

Harvard had listened but a moment to the conversation in the front room.

He had gathered sufficient to convince him that Katherine was entirely capable of taking care of herself, so far as Rushton was concerned, and he realized fully that it would be far worse for her in every way if he should be discovered in her apartment, and recognized. So he let himself into the hallway and closed the door softly behind him. What happened to him thereafter we will know presently.

The room which Rushton entered from the parlor contained a dining-table, some chairs, and a sideboard. Beyond it was a narrow private hallway, and, opening from that, a small kitchen, and two more rooms.

At the rear, occupying the entire width of the house, and lighted by three windows, one being at the side where it overlooked the roof of the adjoining house, was the largest room of all.

A glance into it would have assured any person that it was devoted to the personal and private uses of Katherine Maxwell herself.

Rushton inspected all of them. A mere glance into all but one of the smaller rooms satisfied him, but in that one he lingered. Presently he returned to the living-room, where Katherine awaited him. Apparently she had not altered her position since he left her.

"Who occupies that little room back of the kitchen?" he

demanded. "It's a man. I know that much. Who is he, and where is he now? I guess it'll make it easier f'r you all around, if you give me the answer, Lady Kate."

"You may ask that question of the inspector, also, Lieutenant Rushton, after I have reported your present conduct to him," she bluffed; and this time the bluff worked. Perceiving that it did, she gave the screw another turn. "You may find that you have exceeded your powers somewhat tonight."

"Aw, come now," Rushton replied, advancing nearer to her, and assuming what he considered to be a particularly ingratiating manner. "You don't wanta git me in bad with the skipper, do you? You can't blame *me* f'r wots happened. On the level now, Miss Maxwell, who's the guy that occupies that little room? You can't blame me f'r wantin' to know, can you, with me thinkin' a lot about you all the time, as I do, an' all the time watchin' out to see that you don't fall up ag'inst any of the raw edges that's layin' around with teeth on 'em, just waitin' f'r your sort?"

"He is a servant who has been in my family since I was a little girl," she replied, quite willing that the scene should take the turn it had. "He looks out for me, and watches over me. And sometimes, when I am gone away, I shouldn't wonder if he sits in this room and smokes. That isn't the first time I have seen cigar ashes here."

"Oh, that's all right. I am kinda onto things now. I hope you'll just overlook my comin' here to-night, an' actin' the way I have. I s'pose this is your real home, ain't it, an' the other place down in West 'Leventh is only a hang-out? Eh?"

"Yes. And I will forgive you, if you will go now, at once—and will promise me never, never to come here again. I do not permit anybody to come here to see me."

"All right, lady. You're on. Just shake hands to prove to me that it's all right, won't you? Thanks. An' I know now that you won't say nothin' to the skipper—an' you can bet your sweet life I won't."

Rushton lingered in the doorway a moment, looking back

at Katherine, and she shot a smile at him. He murmured another good night, meant to be a tender one, and closed the door softly. Then she stood listening for his footfalls on the stairs, for there was no elevator—and in a moment more she heard his heavy tread returning, hastily and peremptorily, too, she thought.

He rapped noisily against the door.

She threw it open, wondering, dreading, fearing she knew not what. Rushton was there, a black scowl on his face.

"Say! What does this mean?" he demanded

"What does what mean?" she answered.

"I goes down to the bottom of this last flight of stairs, an' there I finds Dan Merton, th' guy that trailed you here to-night by my orders. When I comes in along with him a little while ago, I tells him to wait down there for me, while I makes my call on you. Then I goes out, after I've made the call an' every-thing's salubrious between you 'n' me, an' down there at the foot uh them stairs I finds *him* laying all in a heap, breathin' like a chicken with the pip, an' a bump on th' side of his head as big as a goose egg. What does it mean, that's what I wanta know?"

Katherine was relieved; so greatly relieved, indeed, that she feared she might show it.

She went hastily past the police officer and down the stairs. Rushton followed after her.

Merton was in much the condition that Rushton had de-scribed, but the shaking that his superior had given him at the moment of discovery had partly revived the man.

He was trying to get upon his feet when Katherine got to him. Rushton aided her in helping him, and together they assisted him up the stairs and into her front room. Katherine brought him some brandy, and together they waited for him to pull himself together.

"Who rocked you to sleep, Danny?" Rushton demanded, presently.

"Search *me*, lieutenant. I was sitting on the steps at the bottom of the stairs, where you left me, when it happened.

Maybe I dozed off a little; I don't know. I haven't had any sleep for forty-eight hours, but I figured that nobody could get by me, even if somebody did succeed in getting past you, which wasn't likely. Now, was it, sir?"

"Well, nobody did, anyhow. What's the answer?"

"Search *me!* I thought I heard somebody coming down the stairs behind me. Maybe I thought it was you. Anyhow, I half turned. I guess I got the clip side of the head then—with a night-stick, wasn't it?"

Rushton turned his eyes upon Katherine.

"What time did that servant of yours go out?" he asked.

"Oh, it was early. Before I went out myself," she replied. (It was the truth, too. She did not regard it as necessary to tell the lieutenant that Julius had returned from that errand, and was inside the apartment when Rushton rang the bell.)

"Look here, Lady Kate, are you willin' to give me your solemn word that you don't know who it was that hit Merton?"

"Surely. How should I know more about it than you do, lieutenant?"

"I guess you're right about that. Now, if he'd 'a' had a few fingers broken, 'r an arm, 'r leg, 'r his bloomin' head, I'd 'a' felt like sayin' that the Night Wind was blowin' himself agin. But *he* ain't never yet been known to *hit* anybody—and he wouldn't likely be roamin' around here, unless he was searchin' for you the same as I was. Say! You! Dan Merton!"

"Yes, sir?"

"You an' me are goin' to forget what's happened here to-night. See? We ain't neither one of us seen hide nor hair of Lady Kate, only down there in front of th' Manhattan. Get that?"

"Yes, sir."

"An' *you're* going to forgit all about this address, an' everything relatin' to it. An' if I hear a peep about it that could have come from you, I'll break you. Get me?"

"I do, sir."

"Good night, Miss Maxwell."

"Good night, lieutenant," she replied.

This time she waited at the top of the stairs until she heard the street door close behind the two men.

Oddly enough, Katherine felt quite weak and shaken after the ordeal was over. Stranger still, it was of the Night Wind she was thinking; not of herself.

CHAPTER XII

ESTABLISHING AN ALIBI

WHEN THE NIGHT WIND closed the dining-room door so softly behind himself he had already determined upon a course of action, if only he should be fortunate enough to make good his escape from the house. The two had become rather good friends during the interval of Harvard's convalescence. He had found the negro to be unusually intelligent and efficient.

Only a very few moments had elapsed since the going of Julius. It was not likely that the black would be very far away.

At the top of the stairs, Harvard looked down ahead of him, and discovered Julius at the foot of them, beckoning; and, directly beneath Julius, on the floor, was the huddled heap of another man.

Harvard hurried down the stairs.

Making no sound, the black led the way to the street, where, after a hasty glance to the right and left, they hurried to the waiting imitation-taxi. As soon as the Night Wind was hidden away inside of it, Julius thrust his face in at the window, and explained.

"I got down two flights of stairs before the two men entered at the lower door," he said. "There's a little cubby-hole closet on each of the floors, and I stepped into the one that was nearest to me, until after they had passed. Then I came out, and I heard Lieutenant Rushton tell the other man to stay at the bottom of the last flight, and keep watch. Well, sir, I got to him before long. He just went off to sleep. He left his gun lying on the step, at one side of him, and his heavy billy at the other side. I picked up the billy, and tapped him with it, because I knew that it wouldn't do to make any noise. I don't think I hurt him much. Just stunned him. Then I waited for you. Now, sir, where shall I take you?"

"Around the corner, out of sight of that house, first, Julius. Then stop for orders."

When they came to a stop, and Julius again appeared at the door, Harvard's face was all aglow, and his eyes were shining with the full appreciation of having perfected a plan which had only dimly occurred to him before.

In every sense of the word he was again the Night Wind. Strength had flown back into his muscles, and courage into his heart, and he knew himself to be equal to anything that might now happen.

"Julius?" he asked, "how fast can you go?"

"I could speed her up to seventy miles, if I should try," was the reply. "You see, sir, we've the chassis and the engine of a racer. Miss Kitty had this body, and that fake taximeter put on just to fool people. There isn't anything that can pass me on the road, or catch me, either, if that is what you mean, sir."

"It isn't exactly what I mean," said Bingham Harvard, "but I'll get to that in a moment. How about your license number?"

"What do you mean by that question, sir?"

"If we speed up too high, and some officer catches a glimpse of your number, you would be hauled to court for it. I don't want that to happen."

"I've got half a dozen fake license numbers stowed away under the seat, sir. I can adjust one of them in a jiffy, right now."

"Do so before we start. Now, listen to what I have to say."

"Yes, sir."

"I have no means of knowing what is happening, or what may happen, back there, to-night."

"No, sir. But I would like to say this much. Miss Kitty is safe enough. Those men won't dare to harm her, even if they wanted to—and they don't want to."

"All the same, that scoundrel, Rushton, is shrewd enough, in his way. He proved that, by having her trailed to-night, when she did not suspect such a thing."

"Yes, sir."

"Do you remember, Julius, that I permitted you to smoke a cigar, when you were in the sitting-room with me to-night, while your mistress was absent?"

"Yes, sir. I do. Yes, sir."

"The ashes of that cigar are still there, on that copper shell, where you left them. Rushton will see them. He will know that a man has been there. It is not unlikely that he will suspect that I may have been that man.

"He doesn't know that I don't smoke. He does know that Miss Katherine and I are known to each other. At least, he knows that we have met, and spoken, and have a sort of acquaintance. It will never do, Julius, for him, or any other person, to suspect that *I* have been in that house."

"No, sir. You are right about that," Julius replied.

"And so, I must find a way to avoid the possibility of such a suspicion."

"Yes, sir."

"I must establish a perfect alibi, Julius."

"Yes, sir." Julius's eyes were opening wider and wider.

"And you shall help me to do that—with this car. I will do the rest—with these."

He reached out both his arms and grasped the negro by the biceps, and Julius winced beneath the pressure of his fingers. "It is against my principles to attack the men who hunt me, unless they first attack me," he went on, without pause. "But I feel that I must make an exception to that rule, to-night—for Miss Katherine's sake."

"Wait a moment, sir," said Julius, interrupting him. "Look there."

He jerked one thumb over his shoulder in the direction indicated. Up the street, still a hundred feet or more distant, the Night Wind could see two policemen who were slowly coming toward him. They were engaged in earnest conversation together, and apparently had not noticed the cab; or, if they had done so, had paid no attention to it.

One of them was probably a roundsman; the other, the patrolman of that beat.

"I must be quick with what I have to say, Julius," the Night Wind said hastily. "Stand ready to jump to your place, and to hike out of this. The Night Wind will blow strong to-night, my black friend."

"Yes, sir."

"Listen, now. Heed everything I tell you. Try to obey my orders to the letter."

Then the Night Wind talked rapidly, and with emphasis, to the black chauffeur. He gave specific direction concerning what would be required of him. He permitted no detail to escape him, and he saw to it that the black man understood thoroughly each one, as he explained it.

All the while he kept his eyes directed toward the approaching officers, and there was a strange and eager light in them, as he outlined his plans for the night to the man who listened and grasped every detail.

Even the eyes of Julius sparkled with excitement, and he showed his white teeth in answering smiles of approval.

"That is all," the Night Wind said at last. "Now, go!"

The black sprang into his place.

The two policemen were not thirty feet away when the car started. They raised their heads and looked toward it, but they saw only its red tail-light as it flashed around the nearest corner and was gone.

"Send Lieutenant Rushton in to me the moment he arrives," the inspector ordered.

"He just this moment came in, sir," replied his secretary.

"Tell him I want him."

"Good morning, skipper," Rushton said, a moment later, saluting his superior officer.

The inspector nodded curtly. He was fingering nervously a little pile of slips of paper on the desk in front of him. He said grimly:

"I assume that you have heard part of the news of the morning, lieutenant; sufficient to know that you lose the bet you made with me. Eh?"

"I have heard nothing this morning, chief. I just this moment came in," was the reply.

"Well, the Night Wind—you thought he was drowned, re-member—has furnished proof that he is very much alive. That's what!" Then the inspector started from his chair and began to pace the floor. "How many Night Winds are there, anyhow, I'd like to know. How many? How many?" he demanded impa-tiently.

"I never heard of but one," Rushton rejoined mildly. "I'm willin' to admit that I'm hopin' there'll never be another like him."

"Will you tell me how in blazes he can be in two places at the same time, when those two places happen to be apart? Can you tell me that, Rushton?"

"I can't, sir."

The inspector returned to his desk and slammed one hand forcibly down upon the small bundle of papers he had left there. He bent over the desk toward Rushton, glowering at him.

"Listen," he said, "and don't interrupt me."

"Yes, sir." Rushton was somewhat alarmed by the attitude of the chief. For one fleeting moment he wondered if Katherine Maxwell had broken her word to him, and had reported the happenings of the preceding evening. But he dismissed that idea from his mind instantly.

The inspector picked up the small bundle of papers. He read from them, one by one, laying each one face down upon the desk before him as he finished with it.

"12.44 A.M.—these things refer to last night, Rushton— 12.44 Two Hundred and Fifteenth Street and Broadway. Officer Thomas Whalen patroling his post. Met the Night Wind. Tackled him. Whalen now laid up with two sprained wrists. No bones broken. Detailed report attached. That's the substance of one of these slips, Rushton. I'm reading just the bare facts to you."

"I understand, inspector."

"12.58—that's fourteen minutes later—Aqueduct Avenue and Fordham Road. That is three or four miles away from the other place by the route that would have to be traveled."

"Yes."

"Well, the Night Wind loomed up suddenly, directly in front of Officer Cregan. He took Cregan's gun and nightstick and billy and whistle away from him, and then stood in front of him, guying him, and laughing at him, until he got Cregan so hot around the collar that the plucky chap sailed into the fellow. Result: Cregan was chucked over the Night Wind's head into the ditch, and has got a broken collar-bone to show for it. Get that?"

Rushton nodded.

"Willis Avenue and One Hundred and Thirty-Eighth Street, i.io A.M. Got the distance down in your mind? And the time?"

"Yes."

"Officer Birch on peg. Busy corner. Night Wind appeared as if he had dropped down out of the clouds beside Birch. Birch made a grab for him. Result: Night Wind grabbed him by both hands, crushed the fingers together in his terrible grip. Broke two small bones; one in each hand."

"Say, inspector, how many more uh them things are there?" Rushton asked.

"Plenty. You listen till I'm through."

"Go ahead."

"1.40 A.M. Listen to this one. It'll give you a chill, Rushton. Thirty minutes later than the last one. Away out in Queens. Twelve miles and more away by the nearest route—unless he used a flying-machine. Officer Rudolph Schmidt took a fall out of the Night Wind. He's got a dislocated shoulder, same as Dixon, who was with you the other night.

"2.40 A.M.—one hour later—Fort Hamilton section. Ninety-First Street and Fifth Avenue. Between fifteen and twenty miles away. Roundsman Green stepped into the middle of the street at the intersection to talk with Officer Mercke. Neither of them noticed anybody near them at the moment. Somebody said in their ears, 'Good morning, gentlemen.' They turned. It was the Night Wind. Both men recognized him. There were two of them. They took a chance. Green has a broken leg, below the right knee. Mercke has a sprained ankle that is as bad, or worse, than a fracture. The Night Wind didn't get anything—but satisfaction.

"Wait a minute. You can talk presently. Coney Island. Surf Avenue near the entrance to Sea Gate. Time 3.10—thirty minutes later. Officer Maddox of that precinct saw the Night Wind approaching him; discovered him while yet the fellow was several yards away. Reached for his gun. Night Wind jumped at him, knocked the gun aside, or down, rather. It went off. The bullet smashed the great toe of the cop's left foot. Night Wind kicked the gun into the gutter, and disappeared before Maddox could follow him or summon assistance. Got all that, Rushton?"

"Aw, what's the use readin' all that truck to me? I guess I know that it's the work of the Night Wind, all right," was Rushton's reply.

"Hold on a minute. I'm not through yet. Brooklyn. Flatbush

Avenue and St. John's Place. Six miles away. Time, 3.25. Fifteen minutes later. What do you think of that?"

"What happened there, inspector?"

"He got three of them all at once."

"Three?"

"Conover and Denton, in plain clothes, were talking to Officer Morris, on post. The Night Wind stopped directly in front of them, under a street light, and asked the time. They knew him at the drop of the hat. Three to one was good odds, and they took the bet—and lost. He smashed two of their heads together and chucked the other one over his head. Result: Conover's got a broken nose; Morris has a beautiful black eye where Conover's nose hit it when their heads came together. Denton has a broken arm where he fell on it himself when the Night Wind tripped and threw him.

"Hold on another minute, Rushton. That isn't quite all. Police headquarters over in Hoboken telephoned to this office a little while ago that the Night Wind appeared there shortly after four o'clock this morning. You don't need the details. Two cops who tackled him are laid up for repairs. Could one man do it?" the inspector asked.

"One man must 'a' done it, chief. There ain't any other man that I ever heard of that could 'a' done it—and I'm blowed if I'd 'a' believed that *he* could."

"And you, Rushton, were prepared to take your oath that the Night Wind was a dead one," the inspector sneered at his companion.

"I ain't no oracle, chief."

"So I perceive. Now, take this tip from me. The whole bureau turns loose to-day to get that fellow, alive or dead. All other business has got to take a back seat from now on, until we do get him. Orders are going out to shoot him on sight, and to do the explaining about it afterward.

"And if the men of this bureau can't nail him within the next week, some of you are going back to pounding grass instead of pavements, out among the goats. You can get out, now. I'll have a special order issued from the commissioner's office in about fifteen minutes."

"I'd like to ask you one question before I go, inspector," Rushton grumbled.

"Well, what is it?"

"Couldn't he have done it all with a big racing car?"

"Maybe. I thought of that. But there wasn't any big racing car reported as speeding last night. There were a few taxicab spurts in different parts of the city—but the taxi hasn't been made yet that could have followed and kept up with the Night Wind last night."

CHAPTER XIII

THE NIGHT WIND WAITS

BUT THEY DID not get the Night Wind within the next seven days. In fact, "the finest police force in the world" did not secure so much as a look at him. He was not shot on sight, for the very good reason that there was no "sight" obtained.

Word was received concerning him, however, very shortly, and somewhat astoundingly—because it came to the detective bureau across the space of a thousand miles. In a word it came from Chicago.

The second morning after the talk between the inspector and the lieutenant, the head of the detective bureau received a wire from the windy city, which read:

Your man is here. He laid up two of our men right in front of headquarters at three this morning. Drag net out for him.

At midnight, sixteen hours after the receipt of the Chicago message, the following telegram came from St. Louis:

One of our men attempted to hold up supposed Night Wind in third precinct two hours ago. Night Wind got away. Officer had his right arm broken.

From Cleveland the succeeding morning, this:

Man recognized as Night Wind by pictures seen Euclid Avenue early to-day. No casualties.

Buffalo sent the following message twenty-four hours later:

Night Wind seen here, Genesee Street, three this morning. Officer tackled him and got hugged at expense of two ribs.

"He is evidently working back again, toward home," the

commissioner of police remarked after the inspector had finished reading the telegrams to him. "Can't you figure out a way to get him, George? We cannot afford to let one man paralyze the entire police force of the city. Something has got to be done."

"Possibly," the inspector replied quietly, but with malice concealed behind the soft tones of his voice, "you can think out a way yourself, commissioner. You are big and young and lusty—and brave."

"I am here to suggest, to direct; not to perform," the commissioner retorted, flushing slightly—and returned to his own private office.

The inspector sat alone for a long time after the commissioner left him. He scarcely moved in his chair. Summonses at his door he did not heed. Papers upon his desk remained there, unnoticed. He was thinking.

He had been long on the force, although, as yet, apparently young in years, as compared with many of his colleagues. He knew the police business from the ground up. He knew men, too, and more particularly the men that formed the personnel of the "finest."

After an hour he closed the lid of his desk with a bang, and summoned his secretary. Then he went out and sought the office of the commissioner.

"I think I'll do a little scouting myself, commissioner, if you'll assign somebody to hold down my desk while I'm gone," he said tentatively. "And if I might make a suggestion, it wouldn't be a bad idea to give Lieutenant Rushton the job for a day or so. His arm will be in working order again by that time, and I'd just as soon he was kept quiet while I'm out. I'll report sick, if you're agreeable."

The inspector sought a telephone booth in a drug store half an hour later and called up President Chester of the bank where Bingham Harvard had been employed. The result of that telephone call was an appointment for the inspector and the banker to meet at the home of the latter that same evening.

President Chester called up Thomas Clancy, Bingham Harvard's college friend, before he left the bank to return to his home that afternoon. This was at the request of the inspector, who wished to talk with both men, and together.

At nine o'clock that evening the three men met in the banker's library, behind closed doors, and protected by specific orders that Mr. Chester was "not at home" to any person for the balance of the evening.

The appointment had been made for eight-thirty. The inspector was purposely half an hour late. He especially desired that the banker, and the broker who had been a close personal friend of Bingham Harvard's, should have ample opportunity to compare notes before he butted in upon them.

"Gentlemen," the inspector said as soon as the conference began, "I am, just at this moment, in the character of representing the entire police force of the city of New York. I have given myself this assignment. In your talk with me I wish you to try to consider me as the composite representative of the department, for I intend to pass along to whomsoever it will best assist all the information I may get from you. Now, to begin, you have both known Bingham Harvard a long time, and both of you have been fond of him. Is that correct?"

"I am fond of him now," Clancy replied bluntly.

"And I, also—aside from this deplorable affair," the banker admitted.

"You both believe him to be guilty of that affair at the bank?"

"No. Both of us *do not*. I don't," Clancy replied. The banker made no response.

"*Why* don't you?" the inspector asked, turning toward Clancy.

"Because I don't believe it was in him to do that thing. Do you want my honest opinion, inspector?"

"That is precisely what I came here to get, Mr. Clancy."

"Well, then, it is this. Chester was bluffed into thinking that Bing Harvard took that money. Your man Friday—I don't know his name, and don't care a hang what it is—who was sent to the bank to investigate just had to have a 'goat.' He probably found a blind lead, an absence of clues, and he had to get something on somebody in order to keep up his own reputation. Now, if you care to bunch all of that together, inspector, it means that I consider the whole case against Bing Harvard to have been a deliberate frame-up."

"That is rather a serious accusation, Mr. Clancy, without evidence to sustain it."

"All right. Take it that way. This is a private conference. You asked for my opinion, and you've got it. You couldn't make me believe in a thousand years that Bing Harvard ever stole a cent in his life."

"He certainly has outlawed himself a sufficient number of times since then," the inspector replied, smiling at Clancy's enthusiasm. "He has resisted arrest. He has assaulted officers in uniform. He has maimed them, broken their bones, and laid a good many of them up for repairs."

"Well, who wouldn't do the same things in his place? Wouldn't you do it, inspector, if you had his strength and *could* do it, if you had been wrongfully accused of such a crime, as he was?"

"Possibly."

"I have yet to hear that he has assaulted any officer who did not first attack him. When one of your men lays a hand on him, it gets broken. When one of them lifts a leg at him, it gets smashed. When one of them pulls a gun on him, it is taken from the man and chucked into the gutter, and the owner is speedily sent spinning after it."

"Did you know, while you were at college with him, Mr. Clancy, that he possessed such remarkable muscular strength?"

"Oh, yes. Why not? We all knew it. He himself was more or less ashamed of it—and he was always deathly afraid of it."

"Why?"

"Because he had a temper that went with it. Mr. Chester saw sufficient evidence of it, that night when you tried to have him arrested, here in the house. Mr. Chester told me about it himself," he added, when the inspector raised his brows. "Just the same as some men have big feet and can't help it, or more brains than others and can't help it, so Bing possesses about four times the strength of an ordinary man, and can't help it. And he's got the temper of a dozen demons, too, when it's roused, and he can't help that, either."

The inspector turned to the banker.

"You believe him to be guilty of the theft, do you not, Mr. Chester?" he asked.

"I have tried not to do so," the banker replied. "But the evidence against him was too convincing."

"Oh, you bankers make me tired!" Clancy said in an aside. "Inspector, I don't like to interrupt you when you have turned your attention to Mr. Chester, but I'm afraid I'll have to do it."

"Well?" queried the inspector, turning toward him with a smile.

"I don't seem to be exactly in my element at this confab. I'm misplaced. I would like to know, and I think I have the right to know, just what this conference is for."

"I'll be quite frank with you, Mr. Clancy," the inspector replied. "Your erstwhile friend, Bingham Harvard, now known throughout the length and breadth of the land as the Night Wind, has almost demoralized our police force. His phenomenal strength and agility in using it, his surprising alertness and swiftness of action, his consummate daring, and last of all his absolute defiance of all authority as represented by the police, have developed beyond the bounds of repression. Do you understand me, Mr. Clancy?"

"I think so; but go on, please."

"The Night Wind must be taken. The self-respect of the entire department demands that he be taken."

"And am I to understand that you have invited me here, in the capacity of his former friend, to obtain information from me to the end that I may furnish you with information that will assist you in taking him?" Clancy demanded bluntly.

"One moment, please."

"Oh, I'll wait. Go ahead."

"He practically ran amuck through four of the five boroughs of the city, and in Hoboken also, not very long ago. He has broken arms, and legs, and wrists, and hands, of well-intentioned police officers, until the count is assuming appalling proportions. His career as a bone-breaker and a joint-dislocator must be brought to an end. It cannot be permitted to go on. That, Mr. Clancy, is the whole thing in a nutshell."

"And so you have taken the field against him—the active field I mean—yourself. Is that the idea?"

"That's about the size of it."

"And you expect me to help you?"

"If you can do so—yes. I call upon you, officially, to assist me. I have that right under the law."

"And I tell you, privately, to go to blazes, Mr. Inspector. I'll see you in ballyhack, first. You've got your answer. Good night. I'm going to get out. You and Chester can put your heads together and cook up whatever schemes you please—but you can't rope me into them. That's flat."

Clancy turned fiercely upon Chester, and added:

"If we bring this thing right down to cases, Chester, you're a whole lot guiltier than Bing Harvard is. You forced him into his present predicament. You made an outlaw of him. You helped this rotten police force, or at least one member of it, to frame up the case against him. You were the first man who actually believed him guilty. Well, you can wash your own dirty linen. I won't help you."

"My dear Tom!" the banker began, but Clancy interrupted him.

"Don't 'dear Tom' me, Chester. Bing has been like a son to you, and you have pretended to love him. No doubt you have done so, in your own way, and after your kind; but, thank the Lord, I'm not that kind.

"Some day, mark my words, you will see the mistake you are making now, and be sorry for it—when it is too late. I have got just this much to add before I leave you: You need no longer include me in your list of friends; not so long as you persevere in your present attitude."

Without another glance in the direction of the inspector, Clancy seized his hat and strode from the room. Very soon the two who remained behind heard the outer door close none too gently. They knew that Clancy had gone.

The inspector—it has been said that he was one of the old school detectives—smiled complacently when Clancy took himself off.

"That is as it should be, Mr. Chester," he said mildly. "It is exactly what I calculated upon. Mr. Thomas Clancy is a loyal friend. He declines to take the side of the police in this affair. But what he does not know now is that he will be of much greater assistance in the part he has selected to play than he would have been had he accepted the suggestion I made."

"I am afraid I do not understand, inspector," Chester said.

"Clancy has been keeping himself in the background. In the mean time I have made some inquiries concerning him, and his former friendship for Harvard. Now, when he has gone from here under the stress of what has occurred in this room, his first thought will be to find some means of warning the Night Wind—of putting Harvard on his guard against *me*."

The banker nodded.

"It is precisely what I anticipated, Mr. Chester; what I figured upon. You may be assured that, from the moment your outer door closed behind Thomas Clancy when he passed out just now, my men will not lose sight of him. Ultimately, he will be the one who leads us to the prize."

"How?"

"Harvard will, sooner or later, consent to meet him for an

interview. It isn't likely to be at Clancy's house, for I doubt if Harvard would consent to go there. It is likely to be in a room that is temporarily occupied by Harvard. In that case we will get him."

"What more did you wish to consult me about, inspector?" the banker asked.

"Nothing more. My sole idea in making this appointment for to-night was to accomplish exactly what has been done. I will ask you this, though: Are you honestly convinced of Harvard's guilt?"

"I suppose I am. There are times when I doubt, but, always, I am confronted by the evidence that Rushton found. It seems unanswerable."

"You want him apprehended?"

"As a matter of principle, yes. As a banker, yes. Personally, sentimentally, in consideration of the affection I have had—and in a measure still have—for him, I cannot say that I do. I am torn by conflicting emotions. I would much rather have lost the sum ten times—yes, a hundred times over, than to have had him accused of stealing it."

"You realize, I suppose, that, even if he were not guilty of the theft, he has, nevertheless, made an outlaw of himself since that occurrence?"

The banker threw out his hands in a gesture of repugnance.

"Understand me, inspector," he said with that cold decisiveness which he made use of in financial affairs at the bank, "I don't care one jot or tittle how many police bones Bingham Harvard breaks.

That does not concern me. That is your lookout, not any part of mine."

"Oh, well—"

"If I could bring myself to believe, as Tom Clancy quite evidently does believe, that the evidence of Bingham's guilt *was* what is called a 'frame-up' I would rejoice over the broken bones, and I would be willing to spend almost my last dollar in putting where he would belong the man who did the framing up."

The inspector laughed aloud and left his chair. It was useless to continue the interview. He had gone to the banker's house to keep that appointment apparently alone. Nevertheless, he had anticipated Thomas Clancy's conduct, and had prepared for it.

There had trailed after him another old-timer like himself, whom he had selected for the purpose; a man no longer on the force, but in every way as capable and active as when he had been. *His* duty was to take the trail of Clancy when Clancy should come out of the banker's house.

The fact, therefore, that this man was nowhere in sight when the inspector issued from Chester's residence did not disturb him.

He paused for a moment at the bottom of the steps and looked up and down the avenue, then he turned his gaze across it, toward the park.

A man was leaning against the park wall, directly opposite him, motionless, and with a soft hat pulled well down over his forehead. He had the attitude of one who might be watching the house, and the inspector, after another moment of hesitation, started across the avenue, toward him.

The man did not stir as the inspector approached him. His figure, relaxed as it was against the park wall, with shoulders hunched and hands thrust deeply into trouser-pockets, did not indicate much individuality.

But when the inspector was quite close the form suddenly straightened.

Two arms shot out and seized the inspector's, holding that official rigidly helpless.

The eyes of the Night Wind looked calmly into the eyes of the police inspector, and the voice of the Night Wind said evenly:

"I was waiting for you, inspector."

CHAPTER XIV

BEARDING THE LION

"I AM GLAD that you did wait for me, Harvard," the inspector replied calmly, evidently unmoved by the encounter. "I don't know of anything that could have given me so much real pleasure as this opportunity to talk to you."

"Are you armed, inspector?"

"Yes. There is an automatic in the top pocket of my waistcoat, on the left side."

"Anything more?"

"No."

"Handcuffs?"

"Yes. You will find a pair in my coat pocket, at the right side."

"Will you remain quiet while I frisk you a bit?"

"Yes."

The Night Wind helped himself to the automatic, removed the magazine and emptied its contents upon the ground, tossed the steel handcuffs over the wall into the shrubbery of the park, and then satisfied himself that the inspector had told the truth about having no more arms in his possession. While he was thus engaged, the officer asked:

"Why did you wait for me, Harvard?"

"Because I wished to see you—and to say something to you."

"How did you know I was there?"

"I saw you go in."

"Then you must also have seen your friend, Clancy, eh?"

"Yes. Now, inspector, do you think you are equal to climbing over this wall, or shall I give you a lift? You see, some of your men might happen along, and if we stand here—well, if we are to have a talk, we'd best seek the seclusion of the park."

"Then you might give me a lift, Harvard. I'm not much on the climb. Besides, I have never happened to see an exhibition of your strength."

Without replying, the Night Wind swung the officer around, grasped him beneath the arms, lifted him as if he had been a child, and, with a swing, tossed him over the top of the wall.

"Look out how you land," the Night Wind remarked as he did it; then he followed after, leaping lightly over the barrier—to find that the inspector was still upon the ground holding one of his ankles tightly in the grip of his right hand.

"I turned it," he said. "Lighted on a stone. I don't think it is sprained, but it hurts."

"I'm sorry," the Night Wind said, and lifted him to his feet. "Can you stand on it? Not very well, eh? Or are you faking?" Stooping slightly, he easily lifted the inspector in his arms, and, carrying him as if he were weightless, bore him into the shrubbery, where presently he put him down again.

The place selected was well screened from view from the avenue, though not far distant from it. They could see without being seen.

"I weigh close to two hundred," the inspector said, again nursing his ankle. "How do you do it?"

"It is natural to me. But we will drop that subject, if you please."

"All right. What about Clancy? You told me that you saw him."

"I did not say that we talked together, did I?"

"No."

"We will drop that subject, also."

"You seem to be determined to drop all of them that are of particular interest to me. Perhaps you will tell me just why you waited for me to come out, and what it was that you wished to say to me?"

"I wanted to ask you if it were possible that we could declare a truce that would last long enough to enable me to establish my innocence?"

"I'm afraid that I don't quite get you, Harvard?"

"I spoke plainly enough. I want you to call off your dogs for a time, and give me a chance."

"To do what?"

"I have already told you that."

"It strikes me that you are *laying* them off rather expeditiously, aren't you? Besides, that 'innocent' bluff hardly works with me."

"Inspector"—calmly, but with evident restraint—"do you mean to tell me that, with all your experience in the police department, you don't *know* that the charge against me was a deliberate frame-up, and planted and engineered by that fellow Rushton?"

"I don't know anything of the kind. How am I to suspect such a thing? You talk foolish, Harvard."

"I suppose I *am* foolish to attempt to reason with one of your ilk. You are all alike. Come; I'll lift you back again, over the wall. Your ankle isn't sprained. You will be able to walk with it very soon."

"Wait a moment."

"Well?"

"Don't you know that you can't keep up this sort of thing forever? Can't you understand that sooner or later you'll be caught? And aren't you able to realize that, the longer this lasts, the worse it will be for you?"

"What's the answer, inspector?"

"The answer is up to you."

"Oh, no, it isn't. I haven't got any answer for you, except the old one: That I will never be taken, and that I'll hurt any man who attempts to get me."

"You don't know the last order that has been issued concerning you."

"No. But it doesn't matter to me what it is. A 'dead or alive' order, I suppose."

"Exactly."

"Shoot me on sight, eh?"

"Just that."

"Was it your order?"

"It was my suggestion."

"Aren't you just a little bit afraid of me, right now, inspector?"

"No. You haven't hurt anybody who hasn't tried to get you first."

"Would you have taken a shot at me a few moments ago, if you had recognized me from across the avenue?"

"No. I would have done precisely what I did do. In fact, I did suspect that it was you, by the time I was half way across. I want you to give yourself up. I want you to surrender, and stand your trial. I'll give you my word—"

"*Your* word! The promise of a cop! Your personal word might be good enough, outside of your daily occupation, but I wouldn't believe you under oath in your official capacity. You are all liars, and you are not the least among them, inspector."

The officer flushed to the roots of his hair. It was not pleasant to hear himself so calmly denounced as a liar. The Night Wind continued, before he could speak:

"I did have an idea that you might be a little different from the others. You have been with the department a long time. You know the inside workings of it from A to Z.

"In your heart you know that the evidence, as supplied against me by Rushton, was manufactured, every scintilla of it. You know that he had to have a goat, and that he selected me. I know that you know it, because I know that you've got the brains to know it. Moreover, you must know Rushton for a consummate scoundrel.

"Oh, you need not reply, inspector. I wouldn't believe a word you might utter—now. Let it all go as it lays. But I'll put you wise to one small fact that has escaped your attention, provided you care to hear it."

"Well?"

"Rushton, and you, and the bunch of you that trail along behind, are driving me deliberately into a mood that isn't healthy for those who hunt me. I figure that already I could be tried on enough indictments for 'interfering with an officer in the discharge of his duty' to send me away for the balance of my life."

"But I have already told you—"

"And you lied when you told me—Keep still. Sit quiet, inspector, or I'll send you to headquarters in an ambulance.

"Now, listen. I had determined to see you, and to make this one plea to your better sense and judgment. You have elected to despise it, and me. All right. Let it go at that.

"The one small fact that I called your attention to, a moment ago, is this: Henceforth I shall hold you equally accountable with Rushton for making an outlaw of me. *And, inspector, if it must go as far as that, I have made up my mind to have the game as well as the name.*"

"Just what do you mean by that, Harvard?"

"I mean this: The next time that Rushton gets up against me, after his arm has mended, I'll break his neck instead of his arms and legs."

"You mean that you'll kill him?"

"Men as a rule do not walk about the streets with broken necks, do they?"

"That would be murder. You'd go to the chair."

"Oh, no, it wouldn't be murder. It would be justifiable homicide, from my point of view. And as for the chair—well, there is the old recipe about cooking a hare."

"You don't suppose, do you, that you can continue to defy the twelve thousand men of the New York police department in the way you have been doing it? You talk like a fool, Harvard."

"I have talked enough, anyhow. I've only one more thing to add. You are now out on a self-imposed assignment. You detailed yourself to take my trail. Let me advise you to get off of it, right now. That's all."

The inspector smiled. He thought he had made a point.

"So you did talk with Clancy, after all, eh?" he said.

"No; I did not talk with Clancy. He did not see me, although I saw him."

"He heard me say that I had given myself this assignment."

"And I guessed it. Shall I tell you how?"

"Yes."

"I have been out of the city, as you doubtless have heard—to Chicago, and a few other places. I landed in New York only a few hours ago, and I went straight to Mr. Chester's house, determined to have one more interview with him before I was driven quite entirely to the bad. I intended to suggest to him something very much like my suggestion to you."

The inspector laughed openly.

"You would have received from him very much the same reply that you got from me, Harvard," he said.

"Yes, I understand that now. But I had determined to make the effort, anyhow. Whatever may happen hereafter will be your fault, inspector. The blood, if there should be any, will IDC on your head. But that isn't what I started to tell you."

"It was something about how you happened to guess that I had assigned myself to your case, wasn't it?"

"Yes. If you had been five minutes later in arriving at Mr. Chester's, you would have found me inside—unless Clancy had warned me that you were expected. Even in that case I might have waited for you. I saw Tom go in, and had been considering for a long time whether I would follow him or not, when you appeared. I made rather a shrewd guess as to what was going on then. I was pretty certain of it when I saw you pause to give directions to the fellow that trailed you.

"Tom Clancy didn't stay very long after you got there, did he? My idea about that is that you wanted him to act as a decoy, to help get me, and that he turned you down; also that you rather suspected that he might do that very act when you proposed such a thing; and that you figured it out that he would try to warn me of what you were up to. So, inspector, you brought the man along to trail *him* when he should leave the house. And, so, when the fellow did take Tom's trail, I took his—and him also."

"What do you mean, Harvard?"

"Nothing much. I slipped up behind him, took him by one arm, and led him in the opposite direction for two or three blocks. Then I told him to take a good and sufficient look at me so that he would recognize me the next time he saw me—and I let him go. I shouldn't wonder if he's running yet. That's the way he started."

"You did not hurt him, then?"

"No; not unless his feelings were injured. You know, now, how I did my guessing. How is that ankle?"

"I don't believe that I can use it."

"We'll try it, anyhow," the Night Wind said, bending suddenly forward and seizing the inspector.

He lifted him to his feet, turned him about, and gave him a sharp push so that the officer was compelled to run down the gentle grade before him; and the ankle supported him all right.

But the inspector was furious at the indignity.

As soon as he could recover from the impetus that the Night Wind had given him with the shove, he turned about, his mouth opened to say something of what was on his mind.

But he did not utter a word—for the very good reason that there was no one there to speak to.

The Night Wind had disappeared.

Chagrined, crestfallen, grateful that there had been no third party present to witness his discomfiture, angry with himself, but, more than anything else, thoroughly enraged at the Night Wind, he made his way slowly to one of the park paths, and followed it until he arrived at a gateway. Then he went to his own home, and to his bed, determined that nobody should be made the wiser concerning his experiences of that night.

But Bingham Harvard had no intention of letting the inspector off so lightly.

Before he left the park he wrote an identical message upon the backs of several postal cards. One he addressed to the commissioner; the others were sent to lesser officers of the department. The message was this:

> The Night Wind's compliments. Ask Inspector Blank, of the detective bureau, concerning what happened to him last night in Central Park, opposite the residence of Mr. Chester.

The Night Wind did not break any of the inspector's bones, but he did that which went far toward breaking his spirit and his pride, and which, incidentally, made as bitter an enemy of him as Rushton was already.

Incidentally also, although quite illogically, it would seem, the Night Wind's act turned some of the inspector's wrath upon Katherine Maxwell; and quite possibly there was something of telepathy in the resentment he felt so suddenly and inexplicably toward her.

The fact of meeting and talking with the Night Wind; the assurance of the man's phenomenal strength of muscle; his remarkable physique; his engaging personality, all reminded the inspector in some extrinsic way that he and Katherine Maxwell were known to each other, and he was convinced that it was quite possible that the woman detective might have fallen under the Night Wind's almost magic spell, as the inspector had so very nearly done himself.

Anyhow, he decided to send for her, peremptorily, the following morning.

Also, he immediately got busy with the telephone, and during the conversation that followed with the officer in charge at headquarters, the names of Thomas Clancy and of Bingham Harvard were frequently repeated.

CHAPTER XV

OUTSIDE OF THE LAW

BINGHAM HARVARD CROSSED the park to the west side and made his way swiftly to that house where, not so very long ago, although the time now seemed long, he had protected his friend, Tom Clancy, from the footpads.

Light gleamed from the windows of the second floor, and knowing that room to be the private library and lounging place of his friend, Harvard ran up the steps and pressed the button of the electric bell.

At the same time he put two fingers to his lips and gave utterances to the same shrill whistle which had been their favorite signal to each other in the good old days of college, when they were inseparable companions and chums.

Within two minutes the door was thrown open and Clancy, clad in pajamas and slippers, appeared at the threshold.

"Bing, old chap!" he cried out, with instant recognition, and the two clasped hands.

"Thank Heaven you have come to see me," Clancy went on, with enthusiasm. "Come inside. We'll have a jolly old chin together. I'd rather see you than to have cleaned up a million downtown."

"I'm glad to see you again, too, Tom," Harvard replied heartily; and he stepped inside the vestibule, behind that half of the outer door which was closed. "But I can't go inside. It won't do. I shall remain only a minute or two."

"Now, look here, Bing—"

"I didn't come here to compromise you, Tom. You ought to know that you cannot hobnob with me and not get yourself into trouble with the police. Your experiences to-night ought to assure you of that much."

"Rats! A lot I care for that bunch."

"All the same, old man, the police of New York city is not a good proposition to be up against. If they can't get you one way they will another. There, now! Don't say another word."

"Then what in thunder did you come here at all for?" Clancy demanded.

"To see you. To thank you for what happened to-night at Chester's house—for I think I have guessed rather clearly what did happen there. You believe in my innocence. I feel assured of that; and, Tom—"

"Say, Bing?" Clancy interrupted him.

"Well?"

"If you don't step inside the hallway, so I can close the door, I swear I'll bang it in your face."

Harvard shrugged his wide shoulders, smiled, and stepped inside the hall. Clancy closed the door. Then he turned about and began leisurely to mount the stairs, but he talked over his shoulder at his friend as he did so.

"Come on up to my den," he said. "We can talk it all over there. You've got to come."

"I ought not to, Tom. Wait a moment, until I tell you something."

Clancy paused and turned.

"Well?" he said interrogatively.

"I really ought not to remain in your house a moment longer than is absolutely necessary," Harvard replied. "I'll tell you why."

"Go ahead, then. It's a fool reason. I know that much before you begin. But I will hear it."

"You may have wondered how it happens that I know of your presence at Chester's to-night."

"I have long since ceased to wonder about things that concern you, Bing," his friend replied, with a smile. "But—go on. What's the rest of it?"

"I was there, outside the house, when you went in. I had determined to have an interview with Chester myself to-night. I hesitated after you entered the house, and I am glad I did so, because, not long afterward, I saw the inspector who had charge of the detective bureau down-town also go into the house."

"Correct. But what of it?"

"I decided not to go in at all then. But I waited. There was a 'shadow' with the inspector. They talked together for a minute before the inspector went inside. I thought I understood things then. A little later I knew that I did."

"Say, what are you trying to get at?"

"You will have to listen to me where you are, or else I will go away now, without completing what I came to say," Harvard said with decision.

"Oh, well, have it your own way, Bing. You always did." Clancy swung one leg over the balustrade.

"You come out of the house first. That second man, whom I have called the shadow, started to follow you. And he would have done it; he'd have been standing outside your door right now, waiting and watching, if I had not led him aside, told him who and what I am, and persuaded him to abandon the idea."

Clancy chuckled.

"Which hospital did you send him to?" he asked, grinning.

"I didn't hurt him. Somewhat later, the inspector came out. I was across the avenue, and he came over to me."

"Eh? Knowing you, he crossed over—"

"Oh, he didn't know me at first. I took him into the park, behind the trees. I said some of the things to him that I in-tended to say to Chester. I wanted them to give me a chance, but I was soon assured that I would not get one. I think he went straight home when we parted."

"Then what—"

"This is the point, Tom: The inspector didn't lose any time when he got home in communicating with headquarters. Now, if I have guessed correctly about you, he has got an idea that you will make an effort to get into communication with me at once."

"As I should have done—only, the Lord only knows how I would have accomplished it if you hadn't come here yourself."

"Well, he's just about doing that very thing now—telephoning to headquarters. Inside of half an hour there will be at least two men from the central office stationed outside of your home, and hereafter you will not take a step that is not observed.

"If I stay here now they will see me go away, and even if they should not make an attempt to capture me to-night you would be compromised. So, you see, I ought not to remain a minute longer than is necessary to tell you what I came to say."

"Bing, look at me." Clancy swung his leg clear of the rail. "Did you ever know me to funk, in the old days?"

"Never, Tom."

"And you're the very last one that should expect such a thing of me. I don't care a hang if the whole New York police force is waiting outside of my house. We will find a way to get out of it all right when the time comes."

He turned without another word and mounted the stairs to the second floor; and Bingham Harvard, alias the Night Wind, followed him.

The room into which Clancy conducted his guest was exactly such a one as a man of his temperament would be supposed to enjoy. Heavily laden book-shelves lined the walls which otherwise were covered by well selected engravings, paintings, and a various collection of curios and keepsakes, autographed photographs, antique and modern weapons, mounted heads, and what not.

A bag of golf clubs stood in one corner. The room answered to the description that Clancy had given it: A den.

"Help yourself to a chair that suits you, Bing. You don't smoke, I know, but I'm going to. Now, what's on your mind?"

"First, I would like to hear you say that you do not believe me guilty of the affair at the bank, Tom."

"Huh! I'd punch your head for that, if I dared. Of course, I don't. Neither does Chester, for that matter. He's only *afraid* you are, and his soul is too little to understand the difference between being afraid of a thing and believing in it. You give me a pain, Bing."

"I have broken the law since that time."

"Is that what you call it? The law? Bones, Bing, bones! You're the star anatomist of the world, old man! Gee! I always thought you were a wonder, but now—"

"Nevertheless I am an outcast. An outlaw. A hunted man. There is a price on my head, although it has not been publicly announced. To-day, the edict has gone out to the members of the police force to shoot me on sight; to get me, dead or alive. That is a pleasant thing for a man to have to contemplate, isn't it?"

"Maybe. I don't know. But that isn't what you came here to say to me, Bing. I know you well enough to know that much."

"No. It is not."

"What, then?"

"Will you keep quiet and listen to me through rather a long statement, without interruption, Tom?"

"Sure I will, if I can."

"I have reached the point where I have got to talk to somebody. A hunted man, wanted by the law, is a solitary chap. He has no friends whom he can trust. He gets into the habit of being suspicious of everybody. He—"

"Hold on a minute. I've got to interrupt you there."

"Oh, my remark does not include you. If it did, I would not be here."

"Go ahead, then."

"Tom, this thing fell upon me like a thunderclap out of a

cloudless sky. It is a wonder to me that, under the stress of it, I did not kill those three men who attempted to arrest me at Chester's house.

"One of them I would have killed, had I thought twice about it. But I will get him yet, when the proper time comes.

"When I went from that house that night I realized exactly what I was up against. I knew that, until I found the real thief, I would be a hunted man. I also understood perfectly well that, even if I did find him, I would still be a marked man, and a hunted one, for what I did to those three officers.

"I had money in my pocket, a good supply, of it, which was fortunate. Before I had gone two blocks I had decided what to do in the immediate future.

"I won't bother you with the details of that, or with what I actually did do. It is enough to tell you that for weeks I never occupied the same room twice.

"I went from house to house, from one locality to another, from one city to another to get my rest. I slept in the daytime and went abroad at night for air and exercise."

"You sure got the exercise, all right," Clancy could not avoid remarking.

"I never engaged a room for the day, that I did not first see to it that there was a way to get outside, and quickly, if I should have need to do so.

"Perhaps I was fortunate in my selections, possibly I was sagacious in making them. Anyhow I have not been taken yet, although there have been times when the cops might have got me, hands down.

"I have been to Boston, to Philadelphia, to Buffalo, to Washington, to St. Louis, and to a dozen other cities besides, hoping that I might lose myself, for a time, in one of them. Everywhere I have been recognized, and hounded, and—well, that is a mere outline of what I have endured.

"Through it all I have succeeded in accomplishing just one thing that works a little bit to my benefit."

"What is that, Bing? Excuse me for interrupting, but I'd like to know."

"I have made the police so afraid of me that I am comparatively safe from an attack by one or two of them when I am in the streets."

"And that's no idle dream, mister," Clancy remarked, grinning.

"That is to say, I was comparatively safe until this last order that the inspector has told me about—the 'dead or alive' order."

"You mean that now they are likely to plug you in the back, when you're not looking?" Clancy asked.

"Yes; but I wasn't thinking of that, so much as of the likelihood that some innocent citizen may be mistaken for me by a too zealous cop and shot. I ought to get out of town, Tom, and in a way that will assure the police that I have gone.

"I have decided to do that thing. I would go now, to-night, or to-morrow, or as soon as it could be done, if it were not for two things that I must accomplish before I go. One of those two things I will attend to myself; the other one—the other one, Tom—I have come here to ask you to do for me."

Clancy half rose from his chair.

"You want—" he began. Harvard silenced him by a gesture, and he leaned back again.

"The thing that I shall do myself may not meet with your approval," Harvard continued. "More than likely it will not. If it should not, the fact will make no difference whatever in my determination. I shall do it just the same. If you were in my place, you would 4p it—or at least you would have the spirit to do it."

"Do you care to tell me what it is, Bing?"

"Yes."

"Well?"

Harvard's reply was spoken so deliberately that it was almost gentle. He remarked:

"I am going to kill the man who framed up this charge against me. The man who manufactured the evidence that convinced Mr. Chester of my guilt.

The man who is alone responsible for all of it. The man who, because of what he has done, has brought down a still greater sorrow upon me than I have yet told you."

Harvard got out of his chair and stood upright before his friend. He stretched out his arms. His face was like a mask, straight-lined, pale, handsome.

His eyes were cold and hard and dangerous. Then, very slowly and very distinctly, he said:

"I am going to kill Lieutenant Rodney Rushton with my two hands."

Quietly he resumed his chair.

Clancy stared. Then he nodded his head as if he entirely comprehended. At the least, he thoroughly understood the utter futility of any attempt to dissuade his friend Bingham Harvard from that settled purpose.

Perhaps he recognized the justice of it; that Harvard, being outside the law, must take the law unto himself and administer it.

Presently Clancy left his chair, but without breaking the silence that had fallen upon the two men. He passed out at the door and closed it after him. But he was gone only a moment when he returned.

"Bing," he remarked dryly, "you were evidently right about what the inspector would do when he got home. I just went down to the parlor floor, where it is dark, to take a look into the street. There are a couple of chaps on the opposite side who wear the ear-marks. They've got the brand, all right. You couldn't mistake 'em."

Harvard started to rise. Then he sat down again. Clancy made no comment. But after a moment or two he said:

"Now tell me what it is that you want *me* to do."

CHAPTER XVI

THE NIGHT WIND
PASSES SENTENCE

"**WHAT IS IT** you want me to do?"

Clancy repeated the words in the form of a question, after an interval of silence that followed his announcement of the presence of the two men from headquarters outside the house.

"Just one moment before we go into that," Harvard replied. "I wonder whether those two men out there suspect that I may be here with you."

"What difference does it make whether they do or not?"

"Very little, I'll admit. But it is likely that they do suspect."

"Why so? How could they suspect your presence, Bing?"

"There is the light still burning, for one thing. For instance, the inspector, whether he issued the orders that sent them here over the telephone, or in person, probably remembered what I said to him concerning my impulse to follow you into Chester's house, after I saw you enter; and he is smart enough to assume that I would be likely to come directly to you after I left him."

"Well, what of it? Suppose he did?"

"I can't stay here forever, Tom. You know that."

"All the same you *are* here now, and you can't go outside just now. So just forget all about those cops across the street and tell me what it is that you want me to do for you. We won't think about the manner of your going until the time comes for you to go."

"So be it. A little while ago, when I mentioned that night at

Chester's house, at the time the charge of theft was first made against me, I purposely omitted one circumstance, Tom."

"All right. Let's hear about it."

"There was a woman in the case."

"A woman? Who?"

"A young woman, Tom, a very beautiful woman, and a thoroughly good woman, too. But a sadly misplaced one. I want you to save her—from herself."

There was no pretense in the stare of unfeigned astonishment which Thomas Clancy bestowed upon his friend. At last he said:

"That is a pretty big proposition, isn't it?"

"Perhaps so. I cannot do it myself; therefore you must do it for me."

"Between you and me, Bing, I think I'd much rather tackle the other job. I never did anything in the killing line, but when it comes to a choice between that and saving a beautiful young woman from herself—Say! What the dickens have you been up to, anyhow?"

"Nothing. I'll tell you about it."

"I wish you would."

"On my way to Chester's, that night of the attempted arrest, I met her just before I got to the house. She led me to think that she was not sure of her direction; also that she was, or had been, ill. I walked with her and put her aboard a Madison Avenue car."

"Highly romantic, that. Go ahead, Bing."

"One night, about four weeks ago, I came upon her again, quite unexpectedly."

"Well?"

"I had not forgotten her. I recognized her the moment I saw her, although she was walking ahead of me, and her back was toward me. But I knew her. I thought it strange that she should be alone on the street at that hour. It was very late. I overtook her. I spoke to her."

Then the Night Wind related his experiences and his meetings with Miss Maxwell.

"You are telling me," said Clancy, "not in words, but by implication, that all the while your beautiful and charming young woman belonged to the police force, and was a woman detective who had been put on your trail."

"Precisely that, Tom."

"You have told me another thing—also by implication."

"I don't doubt it."

"That you are in love with her. That is the plain. English of it."

"I suppose it is—only it is a trifle plainer than I have admitted to myself. Now wait a minute."

"Go ahead."

"That night, in front of the house where I had taken a room, she warned me that Rushton was coming, and advised me to get away. Later that same night, when I got out of the clutches of the doctor, she actually saved me from capture.

"When I was sick and helpless, and a dead easy mark, she took me in, cared for me, nursed me, and subsequently kept Rushton occupied while I again made my escape. That was about four weeks ago."

"Bing, what is it that you wish me to do?" Tom Clancy asked with deliberation.

Harvard leaned well forward in his chair. He reached out and laid one hand lightly upon his friend's knee. He gazed searchingly into Clancy's eyes.

"What I tell you now, Tom, I have not until now so much as confessed in secret to myself.

"It is true that Katherine Maxwell has awakened in me that emotion which we call love—and all the while I know her to be a police spy. All the while I know her to be a woman who has sold her beauty and her attractions for a mess of pottage.

"I know that she started out to find me with the idea in her head that I would fall a victim to her charms, and so be easily led into any snare that she might set for me. I know she belongs to that same devilish system which has made Rodney Rushton what he is, and which, sooner or later, if she stays with it, will make her just such another—like him.

"I know that she has been false to the powers that employ her because she has saved me from them, because she has befriended me. Having discovered something in me that was not all bad, she has been a traitor to her own cause. And yet, with all that, and more that I have not told, I am compelled to the confession that she is more to me than all else in the world.

"Curse Rushton! But for him I could have gone to her clean-handed. But for him I might have loved her, and told her so, and won her, and made her my wife—after I had torn her away from that festering blister that they call a police system. Don't you see now, Tom, why I have *got* to kill him with these two hands of mine?"

"I see your point of view, all right. But—"

"There are no buts."

"Wait a moment. You said something about going away, didn't you?"

"I think I did."

"Why don't you go to her first and tell her all that you have told me? Why don't you take her with you? Eh? Why don't you?"

Harvard laughed aloud and bitterly.

"Ask her to go away with a felon? Ask her to become the wife of a man with a price on his head?" he demanded contemptuously.

"But you are not guilty. You are not a felon."

"I will be one—when I have finished with Rushton."

"You can put him and your vengeance against him aside, if you win her, Bing."

"I don't want to win her. I wouldn't marry her if she were the last woman on earth—and, because of the very reason why I would not do that, neither will I put aside the sentence I have passed upon Rodney Rushton."

"What is that reason?"

"Don't you know what it is?"

"If I did know I wouldn't ask."

"Can't you see—don't you know that she believes that I am guilty? Can't you understand that she looks upon me as a thief? Great Heavens, man, don't you grasp the truth that Rushton has forced her to believe that of me in precisely the same way that he convinced others?"

"Has she told you that she believes it?"

"In words—no. By implication, by actions, by a thousand little things—*yes!*"

"It is just possible that you are mistaken about that, Bing."

"It is not possible, I tell you. I am not mistaken. She believes it—and, notwithstanding the fact that she does believe it, she has permitted herself to defend me, to assist me, to help me, to make a traitor of herself for my sake, and all because, woman-like, she has allowed herself to think a little too much of me.

"Don't misunderstand me, Tom. I'm not fool enough to think for a moment that Katherine Maxwell is in love with me. That would be nonsense. But her life down there at headquarters has brought her so closely in touch with the things that are false that she has forgotten what real things are like.

"She has discovered inside of herself some sort of sentimental fondness for me—possibly because I *am* honest—and she has mistaken the imitation for the real."

"Oh, well, I won't argue it with you. What do you want me to do?"

"Find her. Go down to headquarters, if necessary; but find her. Tell her as much or as little as you please of what I have said to you. Make her understand that, in the eyes of the law at least, I have become, or will have become by that time, a murderer.

"Tell her that she is a misfit where she is—that she does not belong there. Tell her that I said so. Find a position for her somewhere in some other calling. Make her resign from that damnable system. *Save her from herself. Save her from herself, for my sake and for her own.* That is what I want my friend Tom Clancy to do for me. That is what I cannot do myself, and must ask you to do in my place."

Clancy was silent.

"Will you do it, Tom?"

"I'll try. I was thinking over the possibilities of it. I'll try."

With clasped hands the two men stood looking into each other's eyes. At last Clancy spoke.

"I wish, Bing," he said wistfully, "that you'd give up that idea about Rushton."

"Give it up? Spare Rushton *now?* Not in a thousand years, Tom. His arm is mended by this time. Spare him? I guess *not!* I am going after him as soon as I leave you, and when I have found him and finished with him—*then*—I shall leave the country for good and all."

CHAPTER XVII

THE THIRTEENTH HOUSE

HARVARD ACCEPTED A shakedown on the couch in Tom Clancy's den, and so caught a few hours of sleep after they had finished their talk.

Accustomed, as he was, to sleeping by day, and being much fatigued by the exertion he had undergone, and had been undergoing every day of the many days that had passed since the night he left Katherine's house to establish the alibi, he slept soundly and well, until Clancy came softly into the room at half past eight to rouse him.

"Your friends are still waiting," he announced cheerily. "That is, I'm not at all certain that they are the same two; but, whoever they are, they're there. Now, what will you have for breakfast after you've taken your dip? I've got that all ready for you."

"I am hungry enough to eat a raw dog, Tom," Harvard replied, smiling. Then, with seriousness, he added: "I wonder if you can appreciate half that it meant to me to awaken and hear a friendly voice, see a friendly face, and feel a friendly presence near me?" Then bitterly: "Oh, the emptiness—the utter emptiness of the life I lead! And all—all of it because of the scoundrelism of one man!"

"There, there, old chap; forget it! Take your swim. Breakfast will be ready by the time you are. I think you will find it more palatable than the morsel you mentioned, too."

"Hold on a minute, Tom. Do the people in the house know that I am here?"

141

"It just happens that there ain't any people in the house, Bing. There is only my particular factotum, who answers to the name of Scipio. I don't think that is his really true name up in Harlem, but it goes here. He's a bully good cook, anyhow, and he has been with me long enough so that I know him to be entirely trustworthy."

They breakfasted together half an hour later.

During the meal no reference whatever was made to the subjects that were uppermost in the minds of both; but at the close of it, Clancy inquired:

"Now, Bing, what are your plans?"

"I haven't had time to make any yet," Harvard replied.

"Don't you think you had better lay up here today and rest?"

"Perhaps, since it is daylight outside. Those cops over there—"

"Will doubtless chase me down-town when I go out."

"Yes; and back home again when you return. I'll have to get out before that."

"Or afterward. Why not stay right on here for a few days and rest up?"

"No. That is out of the question."

"Why?"

"Don't you realize, Tom, that you are harboring and giving succor to a criminal?"

"I don't care a hang—"

"I know you don't."

"It isn't any sure-pop proposition, Bing, that one of those chaps, or maybe a pair of them, won't stay behind when I go out to keep an eye on the house. You sort of had a hunch last night that maybe the inspector thought you might come directly here after your interview with him."

"I think it quite likely that the house will be watched now as well as yourself."

"Then you've got to stay."

"On the contrary, all the more reason why I should go away."

"But if you cannot go without being seen—what then?"

"I'll go anyhow. I must go. I can't stay here. I won't stay."

"How are you going to get out of it?"

"There is a roof on the house, isn't there? And a scuttle to the roof—or something of the sort? I'll find a way out somehow."

"You might blacken your face and borrow a suit of Scipio's clothes, and—"

"And get pinched before I got to a corner. No."

Clancy looked at his watch and started to his feet.

"I've got to go, and that's all about it," he announced. "You will stay on here until I get back, won't you? We will have been able to think up something by that time. Eh?"

"Perhaps. Only I won't make any promises."

"I'll call you on the telephone as soon as I get to my—"

"For goodness' sake, Tom, don't do that!"

"Why not?"

"Don't you realize that police headquarters would know that you had called me up here inside of five minutes after you did it."

"Well, I can call Scipio. I do that frequently."

"Please do not do it to-day, then. If you really wish to do something to serve my interests, take Scipio to the office with you, and keep him there, under your own eyes, all day long. He seemed mightily interested in me while he was waiting upon us. I think he more than half suspects who I am."

Not a word was passed between them about Lady Kate that morning. Harvard was naturally reluctant to bring up the subject again, and Clancy had his own good and sufficient reasons for keeping silent.

So Bingham Harvard presently found himself alone in the house of his friend. For the first time in many weeks he was really comfortable, and, in the main, contented.

The day passed slowly and uneventfully.

Harvard got through it after a manner that had not been his privilege during many a long week. He read, he rested, he slept a little; he spent hours in deep thought upon the problems that confronted him. At five that afternoon—an hour before the time he was normally due—Clancy came home.

"Business first; pleasure afterward," he announced as soon as he was well inside the house.

"To begin, I have sent Scipio away, so his presence won't bother you. I thought up an important errand that took him to Philadelphia—that is far enough for present purposes."

"Yes. What about the 'shadows'?"

"Oh, they have been in evidence all right. I have been followed. I might not have noticed it if I had not been forewarned. I am quite sure, too, that they have kept tabs upon the house as well as on me."

"Sure thing, Tom."

"So I have decided that you had better remain here where you are for a week at the least."

"And I have irrevocably decided that I will not remain an hour after it gets dark outside."

Clancy grinned.

"I expected that answer, and so I have prepared for it," he said. "It was a suggestion of your own that opened the way for it."

"What is it?"

"I'll tell you; but I've got to ask a question or so first."

"Go ahead."

"Having been accused of theft, and having committed several actual infringements of the law since that accusation, I don't suppose it will get on your conscience to any great extent to have another crime or so charged at your door, will it?"

"No; particularly since I am contemplating what most people would call a greater one. What are you driving at?"

"Down the street, to the west of us, there lives a man named Rice. I know him by sight only.

His house is twelve doors from here, and just at the present time it so happens that there is not a soul in it—not even a caretaker. See?"

"Not quite. Go on."

"You said something this morning about roofs and scuttles. I'm going to suggest that you become a burglar. See? My scuttle; that's easy. His scuttle! I have an old crowbar and an ax in my cellar. Catch on, Bing?"

"Yes. It's the house with the windows and doors shuttered, isn't it?"

"Surest thing you know. The only difficulty is that you will have to break out of it as well as into it. More than likely Rice has taken the key to the little door through the shield away with him. But you can manage that somehow."

"Yes. I will be able to manage it."

"So we will take it easy until it gets dark outside. We'll prepare our own dinner, and then, when the time comes, we will—"

"*We* will not. I will. You have got to promise me that you will let me go it entirely alone after I leave the trap-door in your roof. You have got to get back into it and lock it on the inside before I move a step toward the other house. It is a good plan all around, Tom. You are sure that Rice's house is the twelfth one below here?"

"Yes. I know by the relation of the numbers, and I have just counted the doors as I came up the street. But I want to go with you, at least as far as seeing you well inside of the other house."

"Nothing doing, Tom. Hear *my* plan."

"Well?"

"It is going to be a warm evening outside. As soon as you have fastened the scuttle in your roof after me, I want you to take a chair outside on your front steps and sit there while you smoke your cigar. Leave your door open behind you. If the cops want to enter your house, let them.

"If anything happens at the house that is twelve doors below here, you are to manifest the same sort of interest in it that you would show if I did not exist. After you have sat there for an hour or more, put on your hat, lock your door, and go away—and stay away from home all night.

"Give the cops a chance to do the burglar act themselves; that is, to enter your house during your absence, and to search it. Now, while it is light, we will get the tools together and take them to the roof. Those you mentioned will be the right ones— an ax and a crowbar."

While they were in the cellar procuring them, Harvard picked up a hammer and half a dozen wire nails which he thrust into the side-pocket of his coat. The ax he decided to leave behind. The crowbar was a small one, fortunately, and seemed just the tool he needed.

Time slipped away from them more rapidly than they imagined.

They made their dinner of the cold things that Scipio had left in the icebox, and carefully put everything away that they had used when it was finished.

"I'll take these tools to the scuttle now, and leave them at the foot of the steps until I need them," Harvard said then. "Come along up with me."

They mounted to the top floor together. Harvard was about to put down the heavy bar when both of them were startled by hearing the rattle of the electric bell at the front door.

"Let me outside, Tom, and hook down the scuttle after me. Then go down and answer the bell. It is nearly dark. I won't be seen."

Almost before he had ceased speaking he had lifted the trap and climbed outside.

For a moment then he listened.

He could hear Clancy put the hook through the staple inside the scuttle and climb down the steep steps afterward. He heard the door at the bottom of the steps close.

Instantly he produced the hammer and nails from his coat-pocket, and before Clancy could have reached the parlor floor of the house Harvard had driven three of the nails home. The scuttle was fastened down—nailed from the outside.

It was not entirely dark as yet, but Harvard took a chance. He realized that what he had to do must be accomplished expeditiously. There was no time to lose.

He ran across the roofs, counting them as he went, to what he supposed to be the twelfth house below Clancy's. It was not a trap-door that he found there, but one of the hooded kind, that was approached from inside by a regular stairway, doubtless.

Without an instant of hesitation Harvard lifted the heavy bar and smashed in the panels of the door which had been set to open outward.

There was noise, but he paid no attention to that.

Still grasping the bar he climbed through the opening he had made, descended the narrow stairway rapidly, for there was still just sufficient light for him to see his way, and passed another door that was not locked to the hallway of the top floor of the building.

There he paused, startled, and uncertain what to do.

Below him, as he bent over the rail of the balustrade, lights gleamed, and he could hear the voices of several persons who seemed to be trying to talk all at the same time. They were women's voices, and Harvard understood at once that they had been alarmed by the crashing in of the door to the roof.

Here was a dilemma upon which he had not figured.

This was no vacant house. It seemed to be very much occupied indeed.

Evidently he had not counted right when he fled across the roofs. He had stopped at the eleventh house, or he had passed on to the thirteenth—or else Tom Clancy had been mistaken.

But there was no time to waste in idle conjectures. He was in that house and he had to get out of it at whatever cost.

He descended the stairs swiftly.

CHAPTER XVIII

STRATEGY OF LADY KATE

FORTUNE IS SOMETIMES kind even to the oppressed.

The excitement rampant in the house in which the Night Wind had entered so unceremoniously worked to his advantage.

The frightened women—three of them—were huddled together near a telephone in the front room of the second floor. One of them was talking confusedly over the wire. The remaining two were adding to her confusion by hasty interpolations and suggestions. Each one had her back turned toward the open doorway that Harvard must pass.

His aptitude for swiftness and silence had never worked more to his advantage than then. The three women at the telephone instrument neither heard nor saw him when he passed, and he gained the parlor floor and the front door of the house without further trouble.

For just one moment he hesitated after he had closed the inner door behind him. Then, with a jerk, he pulled his hat down over his eyes, hunched his shoulders, and passed outside.

The way was clear.

Whatever alarm may have been given over the telephone, it had, as yet, produced no visible effect.

As he descended the brown-stone steps he saw that the windows and doors of the adjoining house were tightly shuttered. It was evident that he had descended through the thirteenth house.

One hasty glance farther along the street discovered three

men who were apparently engaged in an animated discussion on the steps of a house which he thought was Clancy's. One of the three was hat-less. Evidently that was Clancy.

All this he noticed in the brief interval while he ran down the steps.

Half-way to the corner, as he passed swiftly down the street, he saw a uniformed policeman hurrying toward him, led by a maid who had doubtless been sent out to find him. Harvard stopped, lifted one foot to the second step of the house nearest him, and pretended to tie the lacing of his shoe. The policeman and the white-faced maid passed him without so much as a glance in his direction.

The Night Wind smiled to himself when he thought how puzzled that policeman would be concerning the supposed burglar's method of getting out of the house. The iron bar he had abandoned in the hallway at the top of it; the hammer and remaining nails he dropped into a convenient ash-can as he passed along.

At Clancy's house the man who had rung the doorbell proved to be Lieutenant Rushton. There was one man with him, and another at the bottom of the steps. He explained to Clancy that the inspector had sent him to make some general inquiries concerning the Night Wind. It was thought that he might have called upon his friend during the preceding night—and remained there. They would like to be convinced that he had not done so.

They were convinced.

Clancy invited them to search the house, if they wished. They finally did so, in a perfunctory manner. They rejoined Clancy on the doorstep, satisfied. There was only one circumstance which did not entirely satisfy Rushton.

"The scuttle-trap to the roof had been nailed down," he said to Clancy tentatively. Clancy nodded.

"I wear it that way," he replied. "Scipio, my man, may have done it. Nothing odd about that, is there?"

"But it is nailed from the outside, Mr. Clancy."

"Oh; is it?"

"How did Scipio get back into the house after he had done that?"

"I'll give it up, I'm sure; but I'll ask him."

At the precinct station-house the blotter carried an entry concerning the attempted burglary of that other house—the discovery of the iron bar which the man had used in breaking in from the roof, and his mysterious getaway. Part of the truth was surmised by the police—that the man had succeeded in passing through the house without discovery; but the Night Wind was not associated with the incident.

At half past eleven o'clock that night—four hours or more after the escape from Thomas Clancy's house—the Night Wind settled himself upon one of the benches in Union Square to wait.

He had conducted himself even more boldly than usual that evening since his departure from the house of his friend. He had decided that he would not—could not, in fact—longer continue the hunted life he was leading.

His defiance of the authorities, his aggressiveness when attacked, his swift and mysterious movements, the fear of him that his acts had engendered, his homelessness, the never-ending necessity that he must "keep moving," the uncertainty of consequences with every step that he took, had convinced him at last of the utter futility and hopelessness of further effort if he remained within the environment of New York.

He had made up his mind to end it all that night and to make his getaway.

To "end it all" meant that he intended to find Lieutenant Rodney Rushton before another day should dawn; and the last bold act of his, before he sought that bench in Union Square to wait, had been to seek a telephone booth and to call up police headquarters.

"This is Mr. Knight," he announced when he did that. At

least the officer at the other end of the wire would have so spelled the name, which was really half of the alias that had been tacked upon Harvard. "I wish to speak to Lieutenant Rushton."

The resultant conversation, every word of which on his own part he had thought out with care before he gave in the call, told him where he might find the lieutenant at twelve o'clock that night.

Rushton was to be at headquarters at that hour to report in and out again, and Mr. Knight, if he was so disposed, might present himself there at that time. Mr. Knight, alias the Night Wind, was so disposed.

He arrived at the stone building a few minutes before the stroke of midnight, but, instead of entering in, he waited outside. Nor had he immediate fear of recognition. If there is a place in the world where the "bulls" do not expect to encounter the "hunted," it is within the shadow of that same stone building in Center Street.

There are always shadows at night in which a man may temporarily hide. The Night Wind found such a one, and from the obscurity of it he commanded a fairly good view of the entrance to the building.

To his astonishment, shortly before the stroke of twelve Lady Kate descended from a taxicab—a real yellow one this time—paid the chauffeur, and passed inside. She had been summoned there peremptorily, but the Night Wind did not know that. Her presence merely served to confirm some of the opinions he had formed concerning her.

Barely had she disappeared when Rushton swung into view from the direction of the subway station and entered the building.

The Night Wind had no intention of going inside. His boldness did not carry him that far. But he had had two purposes in mind when he telephoned to headquarters. The main one was to learn exactly when and where he could find Rushton;

the other was to keep the lieutenant waiting, for a time, for the expected caller—to hold him until he would be more likely to come away from headquarters without companions.

The Night Wind figured that Rushton would not wait long, but it did not matter if the interval were an hour, or two, or three. *He* could wait.

Several times he moved away from the concealing shadow and returned to it. A half-hour, three-quarters, then an hour elapsed, and—Rushton came out of the building with Lady Kate beside him.

During a moment they stood together at the entrance talking. Then they moved up the street, side by side, toward the subway station. The Night Wind followed at the opposite side of the street.

Lady Kate went down the stairs into the subway alone. Rushton raised his hat to her and remained where he was. He did not seem disposed to leave there. He lighted a cigar and appeared to wait for somebody or something, smoking vigorously while he did so.

There was one incident which neither the Night Wind nor Rushton discovered, however. Lady Kate reappeared at the other stairway to the subway very shortly after she had disappeared into that one to which Rushton had conducted her.

But she kept herself out of sight by dodging quickly behind the kiosk that covered it, and then by entering what appeared to be a taxicab that was standing at the curb close to her.

The chauffeur sprang down from his perch to close the door for her, and some rapid-fire words were spoken to him through the open window. Then the curtain was drawn, the chauffeur returned to his place, and the cab was driven to another position across the street, from which point Rushton could be seen still waiting beside the other kiosk.

Had the Night Wind observed all this it might have caused him to change his plans for the night. Had Rushton seen them he, too, might have conducted himself differently.

CHAPTER XIX

A NIGHT OF SHADOWS

THE EASIEST MAN in the world to "shadow" is a professional detective. Whether it is self-consciousness, complacency, individual cocksureness, or, what is more likely than all, merely indifference, the fact remains.

Such an idea as the Night Wind shadowing him probably had not occurred to Rushton. Such a possibility never would have occurred to him before that night. But all the while, directly across the street, half concealed, and yet not wholly so, and feeling all the more secure from observation because of the absence of effort at concealment, the Night Wind waited.

So did Rushton—until a man approached him from the direction of headquarters, murmured a few sentences into his ear for which he received merely nods or shakes of Rushton's head in return, and then departed whence he came.

Then Rushton crossed the street—directly toward the Night Wind, who resorted once more to the shoelace occupation, turning his back the while.

Rushton passed on.

At Broadway he turned northward, walking leisurely, as if there were no such word as hurry in i his vocabulary. The Night Wind had no difficulty whatever in following him at a safe distance on the opposite side of the street.

Rushton did not look behind him once. Neither did the Night Wind. Had they done so it is not likely that either of them would have given more than a passing glance at the cab that held far to the rear, and which was driven at a snail's pace by a black man.

If Bingham Harvard could have overheard the words that had been said to Rushton by the man who came from the direction of headquarters to report to him at the subway kiosk, he would have abandoned his purpose for that night. Also, he would have given Rushton credit for being a much more efficient detective officer than he had supposed him to be.

The fact was that Rushton's eyes were everywhere at once whenever he happened to be alone in the street, particularly at night. It had been so with him ever since the beginning of the affair with the Night Wind.

Experience is an apt tutor.

Rushton knew his own guilt in the matter of the frame-up. By analogy he realized that Bingham Harvard must know as well as he did that it had been a frame-up, and that Rushton was the framer. Hence it was only natural that the Night Wind must hate him most cordially, and would, when occasion should offer, seek the best redress possible. Hence, also, Rushton's particular alertness whenever he chanced to be alone in the streets.

So, earlier, when Rushton swung down the street shortly after Lady Kate had entered the big stone building, he peered into that deeper shadow across the way, but without in the least appearing to do so, and he saw—the Night Wind.

One might suppose that he would have taken immediate steps to have the man surrounded and captured, but there were several reasons why he did not do that.

For one thing, he was not entirely certain about the identification. The man who lurked in the shadow across the way had been only dimly visible. For another, it was not likely that the Night Wind would have posted himself in such a place without having prearranged a means of escape if he were seen and recognized. Rushton had long since abandoned the idea that he could be caught in the open.

There was still another reason. He, also, had seen Lady Kate enter the building in advance of him. The propinquity of the Night Wind, if the man was the Night Wind, suggested to his mind that the much-wanted man might be there seeking her rather than Rushton himself.

To have the Night Wind surrounded and taken by a dozen men, under the very shadow of headquarters, would not redound to Rushton's personal credit, and he very much desired to win that personal credit, if it were possible to do so. The incident, he thought, provided the opportunity.

A man less brave than Rushton—and certainly he was not a coward; that accusation had never been laid against him— would have hesitated a long time before adopting the course that he did.

It was to lead the Night Wind, as he was now being led, into a well-laid trap which he, Rushton, must have time to prepare. And so Rushton took chances, just as he had taken them at the time he prepared the frame-up against Harvard.

He had not lost out on that yet; he did not mean to lose out on it if he could help it.

Coniglio, his former side-partner, was at headquarters await-ing him. Rushton called him aside, told what he suspected to be the case, outlined a quickly laid plan that had occurred to him even as he ascended the steps of the stone building, and added:

"If it *is* him, and if he is there watchin' for Lady Kate, he'll likely follow her when she leaves here. When she comes out of the skipper's office I'll fall in beside her 'n' take her to the subway. Then I'll keep an eye on *him*. If he lets her go an' hangs on, then it's me he's after—an' the rest'll be easy. I wanta get him, and get him right—and alive."

Then, in whispered words, he related his quickly laid plan.

"You chase me out to the subway entrance as soon as you have passed the word around an' fixed things," he said in conclu-sion. "If I ain't there, waitin', you'll know that it's all off for to-night. You'll know that it wasn't the Night Wind at all, or that he has gone on after Lady Kate, and that I'm chasin' along just to look on an' see what happens. If I *am* there, waitin' for you, you will know that his nibs is somewhere in sight; that it's *me* he's after, and that I'm goin' to let him think he's goin' to get me."

The one-sided conversation between Rushton and the man whom Coniglio sent to report to him at the kiosk was this:

"Coniglio has everything fixed as you directed, lieutenant." A nod from Rushton. "He wants to know if you have found out for certain that it's the man you thought it was." Another nod. "And if you would not prefer to have two or three of the men trail along behind him than to have them go ahead and get there first." A decided shake of the head. "Also, he hopes that you will go slowly, so as to give him time." Still another nod, and the last one.

Rushton, astute as he was, being so taken up with the matter in hand, did not have another thought of Lady Kate after she disappeared. He had said very little to her during the short walk to the subway stairs. She had barely spoken to him at all.

He knew that she had been summoned to headquarters by the skipper; that she had received what he called a "dressin' down" for something she had done or had failed to do, and that she was likely to go straight to her home after it.

In fact, when he became certain that the man across the way was the Night Wind he did not care where she went.

But Katherine Maxwell had eyes in her head, as well as Rushton and others.

Moreover, her restless glances here and there whenever she was abroad in the streets were stimulated by something that was new and strange to her since the occurrences of the last few weeks.

Unlike Bingham Harvard, when he had made Tom Clancy his confessor, Katharine *had* admitted to herself exactly what that stimulus was.

Her eyes were always searching for just one face, one tall,

straight figure of a man, one quick-motioned individual. They, too, had peered into the shadow across the street, and, being in a still deeper shadow inside the taxi, had made no doubt of the identification.

Julius and his car were never far distant from her at such times. For the sake of policy she had gone to headquarters in a hired taxi, but Julius had followed it and had waited, by her order, near the subway stairs.

The short walk beside Rushton had convinced her that he, likewise, had discovered the nearness of the Night Wind. Rushton's preoccupation where he was customarily loquacious had assured her of that.

From her vantage-point across the street when she was supposed to have gone away she saw the man from the stone building who reported to Rushton, and knew him and put two and two together.

Rodney Rushton, as he strode slowly up Broadway that midnight, showed nerve.

He knew that the man who followed behind him hated him and had the necessary strength of arms and hands to kill him, yet he walked onward leisurely and without once looking back. Nor did he know at what moment the Night Wind might take it into his head to run forward and attack him.

Rushton was a bachelor and lived by himself in a house that he owned, occupying the third story of it for his own uses. The two floors and basement beneath, he rented out. The occupants thereof supplied his meals and otherwise cared for his needs. Just now they were gone away to the country, and he was, therefore, the sole occupant of the dwelling.

It was located in a side street, east of Fourth Avenue and not far distant from Union Square.

He led the way directly to that house, gradually increasing his pace until it became a rapid walk. He felt sure that he was giving time enough for Coniglio to carry out the arranged plans.

Only once he looked behind him. That was after he had

turned into the street where he lived and had gone some distance along it toward his home. An involuntary chill swept over him as he did so; the Night Wind was quite close—barely thirty paces to the rear.

He hastened his steps, came abreast of his home, turned abruptly, and fairly ran up the steps, admitting himself with his key in haste.

Inside the vestibule door, having closed it and turned the key in the lock, he paused a moment. He had to confess to himself that he had very nearly lost his nerve during the last few minutes.

But he recovered quickly. He shook his clenched fist at the closed door and toward the man who was beyond it, and who had stopped, no doubt, at the bottom of the steps.

Then he grinned sardonically.

"Now, you Night Wind, come on!" he muttered. "That's what you're up to. You'll ring the bell in a minute, an' I'll come down an' let you in—an' 'by the great boot in Chatham Street,' mister, I'll let you in for a heap more than you're lookin' for."

He turned, reached the post of the balustrade, and stopped with his hand resting upon it. The doorbell, one of the old-fashioned gong-bells, was already clanging ominously.

Hearing it, knowing who it was that had pulled it, and who, after an instant, rang it a second time, Rushton hesitated.

There was no time for him to determine if the men he had directed to be at his house and in his rooms before his arrival had obeyed orders. He could not know that they were there, but he had no reason to suppose that they were not.

His directions and orders, given through Coniglio, had been sufficiently explicit—and he had given them ample time. Had he not walked all the way to his home in order that they might have plenty of time?

The doorbell rang out a third peal. Hesitating no longer, Rushton returned to the door and threw it ajar.

The Night Wind stepped inside.

CHAPTER XX

THE MAN AFRAID

RUSHTON'S IMPULSE WAS to reach for his gun and to use it with deadly purpose, but for some unknown reason he could not do it. His hand refused to obey his will. In the actual, physical presence of the Night Wind, and alone with him, the crafty policeman, who, with all his faults, had never been known to show the white feather, was suddenly and inexplicably afraid.

Beneath the dim light shed by the gas-jet, face to face with the man he had so cruelly wronged, a sense of panic stole into the heart of Lieutenant Rodney Rushton. It paralyzed his muscles, minimized his forces, belittled his soul.

He was scared. A tremor shook him to the center of his being. And it was moral rather than physical fear that was upon him.

In that first moment of the encounter he forgot all about the men who should be waiting in the rear room of the top floor two flights up. He could see nothing, think of nothing but the man who stood silently before him, looking down upon him in the dim light of the hall, with the oddly significant smile upon his lips, and the cold, almost expressionless, glitter in his eyes.

"You live here. This is your home, is it not?" the Night Wind asked in a calm, cool tone.

Then, before a reply could come, his hands shot outward and he seized Rushton's wrists and held them.

For the mere sound of the Night Wind's voice had brought

the policeman suddenly to his senses. Rushton's right hand had darted toward the pocket where he carried his favorite automatic.

For a moment the Night Wind held Rushton so. Then slowly he loosened his grip, saying coldly as he did so:

"Put up your hands, Rushton—high above your head—precisely as if I held a gun on you, pointed at your heart. That's right. You know, don't you, what I could do to you with these hands of mine? Very well; don't tempt me to do it too soon."

He felt for the pocket that Rushton had tried to reach, removed the weapon, stripped it of its venom' and tossed it the length of the hall.

"Now take me into a room—any room where we can have lights," the Night Wind commanded. "I have much to say to you before we part."

Ah! there was to be a parting, then. Rushton's spirits rose with that remark. He remembered, too, that there would be others upstairs awaiting him who would help him to turn the tables on this man who had disarmed him so easily.

"My rooms are at the top of the house," he replied surlily. His courage was returning. "I let out two floors and the basement. Will you go up there?"

"Yes. Lead the way. Wait a moment. You usually carry handcuffs with you, I suppose. Where are they?"

"In my coat-pocket, on the left side. What do you want with 'em, anyhow?"

"I'll show you. Turn your back toward me. That's right. Now put your hands behind you—so. Click! and it is done.

"Now march. When we get nicely settled upstairs I'll take them off again. It is for your sake more than my own that I have made use of them. I do not want you to attempt to do things which will force me to hurt you. Not yet. Why, what's the matter, lieutenant? Are you afraid? You look it. I never supposed that you could bleach out so white," the Night Wind said.

But it was more rage and shame that whitened Rushton's face than fear. He swore frightfully.

"Take them off *now*, you human devil!" he finished. "Do you suppose—" He stopped. He had nearly betrayed the fact that he believed there were other men in the house who might see him in his present plight.

"Well? Do I suppose—what?" the Night Wind asked him.

"Do you suppose I want to wear my own irons locked on my wrists?"

"Oh! That, eh? I just told you that I would remove them as soon as we were comfortably settled up-stairs. Believe me, you are much safer from me with them on than you would be without them.

"Did you ever know me to hurt a helpless man? And just now you are helpless, aren't you? How are the mighty fallen, Rushton! Come! Lead on! Show me to your own quarters."

Almost foaming at the mouth with rage and the shame of it, but perceiving that he must obey, Rushton complied.

More active than most men of his build and weight, he fairly ran up the stairs, believing, as he could not help but believe, that Coniglio and the others had overheard all that had been said, and were waiting their opportunity to take a hand in the game.

At the landing of the second flight he stopped suddenly, and his heart almost ceased to beat. The doors to both rooms were open, as he had left them some hour earlier. He was suddenly conscious, he did not know how, that Coniglio and the men he was to have taken there with him had been delayed.

Quaking, palsied with fear, overwhelmed by the catastrophe that confronted him, he led the way into the front room, where a jet of gas was burning low.

The Night Wind stepped forward to turn it up to its full capacity; but before he could reach it he paused, his hand arrested in the act by a sound that came to him from the lower hall—the unmistakable clanging of the front doorbell.

His experiences during the past weeks had made him quick to think, and as quick to act, in the stress of an emergency. He turned toward Rushton with a glance of inquiry—and discovered that the police officer was as greatly astonished as himself. And Rushton was so, in fact. Coniglio had a key to the door. Therefore, it could not be he who rang. A closet door in the room stood widely ajar, the hooks upon it and inside the closet weighted down with clothing.

There was barely room inside of it to accommodate a grown man. Yet the Night Wind instantly decided that it was the only way to force Rushton to silence. He seized him, helpless as he was in his own irons, thrust him inside the closet, closed the door, and turned the key that was on the outside; and Harvard could hear the muffled sounds of Rushton's cursings as he darted into the hall to lean over the banister and listen.

The bell did not ring a second time.

There had been only that one peal of it, then silence. He wondered if it would ring again, and waited for the clang of it, trying to decide in the meantime what to do in case it should.

Then entirely different sounds came to him from below— sounds made by the opening and closing of a door, the voices of men conversing in low and guarded tones, the heavy tread of feet upon the stairs.

In that instant of revelation the Night Wind grasped and understood the situation; all but that part of it which concerned the ringing of the doorbell.

But he grasped at once the fact that Rushton had seen him waiting in the shadow down at headquarters, had set a trap for him, and had baited it by purposely leading him that long walk uptown.

Was he trapped? he wondered. Did those men know that he was already there?

Already one of them had reached the landing of the first flight of stairs, and had made the turn. There was no time for the Night Wind to seek a way out of his difficulty. If he acted at all, it must be at once, and entirely without plan or reason.

The man in the lead paused in the hallway just below and spoke in a low tone to the others, and the Night Wind recognized the voice of Coniglio. He had never heard it but once before—that night at Chester's house—but he remembered it.

"We're in time, after all," was what he said. "They haven't got here yet."

Coniglio's foot was upon the first stair of the last flight before the Night Wind made a move. Then, and not till then, he drew back and passed hastily into the room at the rear of the house, which was dark.

He closed the door softly after him, found a key in the lock, turned it quickly and silently, crossed to the two windows, both of which were raised to their full extent, and looked out upon a confusion of back yards from that third-story height.

Somebody in the hall tried the locked door even as he slung one of his legs across a window-sill. He heard louder voices than before, proceeding from the front room, as he lifted himself through the window and lowered his body outside of it, clinging with his fingers to the stone sill across which he had just passed.

He knew that in a moment more those men would have dragged Rushton from the closet, and that then they would batter in the door of the rear room, seeking their prey.

The house was an old one—a relic of past days.

It was one of a row of several that had been built exactly alike a generation or more ago, when outside blinds were preferred to protect the windows.

Clinging to the sill, his feet sought the tops of the blinds beneath him—and found first one, then another of them.

Testing them, he found that they would bear his weight, or at least that part of it which he bore upon them, and he edged his way along, clinging with his fingers to the sill above him until, by stretching out a leg and then an arm, he could touch the open blind of the nearest window of the adjoining house.

He pulled himself along, inch by inch, but moving rapidly nevertheless, and so passed the third house from whence he started. He was between that and the fourth one, with his feet upon the open blinds of the windows beneath, and clinging with his hands to a flimsy lattice over which a rose-vine grew, when he heard the crashing in of the door to the room he had just left.

He knew that in another instant heads would be thrust from the window through which he had made his escape, and he clung tightly as he could to the rose lattice, flattening himself against the building as closely as possible, but bearing nearly all his weight upon the two blinds beneath him.

He could not see, but he could hear the men when they gazed out at the window in search of him.

There was a brief order given for one or more of them to go to the roof, for another or others to descend to the basement and the yard—and he knew; that they had not discovered him, and that they had left the window.

Then he attempted to move one of his feet in the effort to work his way along still farther—and the hinge of the blind upon which his foot rested gave way.

It lost him his balance. He tried in vain to regain it. In the effort he bore more weight than he should have done upon the lattice, and that broke partly away from its fastenings against the house.

Then his left foot slipped from the top of the other blind.

He fell. But, knowing in time that he must inevitably fall, he tried to save himself by jumping backward so that he would alight upon his feet.

All of these casualties happened with the rapidity of the ticking of a watch, and within a second or two after the men who were seeking him had withdrawn into the house.

Apparently nobody heard the noise of his fall, or the crash of it when he struck the bare, hard ground of the yard beneath.

He landed on his feet, as he had hoped to do; but one of them gave way under him and he sank down, conscious of a sharp, benumbing pain, which for the moment paralyzed further effort.

His idea was that he had broken one of his legs somewhere below the knee. But he could not determine for certain as yet.

Fully alive to the fact that a search, more or less thorough, would be made for him by Rushton and the men who had come to Rushton's aid, he lost no time in rolling himself over and over toward a small shed which covered and enclosed the rear door of the house behind which he had fallen.

He remembered that he was three doors away from the house from which he had escaped, and he believed that the men might not make a search for him where he was concealed.

Even in his pain, and it was intense, he smiled grimly to think that he, the Night Wind, who had broken so many bones for others during his brief career, should have fallen a victim to something of the same sort himself. But whether it was a fracture or merely a sprain from which he was suffering he did not know.

He could hear the low-toned voices of the men who sought him when they came out into the back yard, three doors away from where he was lying. He could not detect what they said, but he did know when they reentered the house, apparently having abandoned the search.

The Night Wind thought it strange that he had not aroused the inmates of the other houses. It seemed incredible that he could climb along past them, as he had done, and finally, with more or less noise, fall into the yard without doing so.

But the time was at a season of the year when many people of the city were absent. It was just possible that those rooms past which he had climbed were unoccupied.

At all events, there was no indication that people had been

aroused; and when the men who searched for him reentered the house he became convinced that he was thought to have made another of his miraculous escapes.

Perhaps it was half an hour later—it seemed an age to him—when he dragged himself to an upright position and stood, resting his weight upon one foot, while he leaned against the house door under the shed.

Tentatively he touched his other foot to the flagging, but the instant he attempted to bear any weight upon it at all the pain became excruciating. He realized then that he was comparatively helpless, and also that a strange and new weakness was upon him as the result of the shock of his fall.

But the Night Wind could not remain where he was. That was out of the question.

It was two o'clock by then—perhaps three. Shortly the light of day would begin to appear. The city would awaken. The inmates of the house behind which he had fallen, if there were any, would discover him. The alarm would be given, officers would be summoned, he would be taken, and all his heroic efforts would have been for naught.

But how was he to escape from that yard?

Plainly he could not climb fences, and if he should succeed in getting over one or more of them how much better off would he be?

Should he rouse the inmates of the house? The idea was suicidal—not to be considered.

It was too dark under that shed for him to see the face of his watch; but he reckoned that more than an hour had passed, and that the men with Rushton—possibly Rushton himself—had long since gone away.

With a tightening of his lips in the determination to win out at any cost, he decided to adopt the only course that was at all possible: To hammer against the door upon which he leaned, to rouse the people in the house, to make whatever excuse he might for his presence there, and to get away, if it could be done.

His weight was still against the door when he came to that decision. He had begun to straighten himself. Then, without previous warning, for he had heard no sound, the door came open behind him and he fell backward into a dimly lighted hall.

Strong arms grasped him and held him, and raised him, so that he stood again upon his one good foot.

In the light shed by a single gas-jet he could see the sleeves that covered the arms that supported him. And he saw that they were blue, with small, gold service stripes on the cuffs, and he recognized from what he saw the uniform of a policeman.

His muscles stiffened. He was far from helpless even yet. More bones might be broken by his strong hands before he could be made a captive.

Fury at the predicament into which he had so calmly walked overwhelmed him. In just one instant more all the pent-up rage within him would have burst its bonds, and indeed the effort for the greatest battle of his life was on the point of beginning, when a second figure stepped in front of him under the hall light, and the strength and power of resistance went out of him as suddenly as the current may be shut off from an incandescent light.

It was Lady Kate.

Her expression as she looked into his eyes was calm, scrutinizing, uncompromising; and yet behind it all there was something more which he could not read or understand.

A police shield glistened upon the bosom of her jacket.

"You are under arrest," she said calmly, as if there could be no doubt about it. "Resistance will be useless. You cannot escape—now."

There was something in that "now" as she pronounced it that attracted the Night Wind. He could not have explained what it was. But he shut his lips tightly together and did not reply.

Katherine's voice added, addressing the man behind him, who held his arms: "Take him outside, officer."

"Wait!" The Night Wind found his voice. He spoke coldly, slowly, impersonally, directing his remarks to space above Katherine's head. "I am practically helpless. I cannot walk. One of my ankles "

He stopped.

The powerful arms that were clasped around his body beneath his own lifted him from his feet, and he heard Katherine's voice again. She said:

"Let the officer carry you outside. Do not struggle. It will be useless."

For just an instant he hesitated to obey her. Then:

"Go ahead," he said. "I cannot fight against a woman." And to himself he added bitterly: "As well give up now since *she* wins the credit of my arrest."

There was one other person present at the scene—an aged man, clad in bath-robe and slippers, and looking greatly perturbed; evidently the man who lived there. But the Night Wind beyond one glance barely noticed him.

They passed through the basement into the area under the front steps. A door closed behind them, after Katherine had said, past it, to the old man:

"Good night, and thank you, sir. If you do not mention this affair it will not be necessary for you to appear at court. I advise you not to speak of it."

Then, when the door had closed, her whole manner changed.

The Night Wind saw her unfasten the shield and remove it quickly from her jacket. The arms of the man who held him were unclasped, and Harvard reached out and clung to the grated iron door for support. The man himself stepped in front of him—and he recognized Black Julius, arrayed in a policeman's coat.

"Quick now, Julius!" Katherine ordered.

Julius tore off the coat, rolled it, seized another that he had left in the area when he donned it, and, with the rolled coat under his arm, darted into the street and disappeared.

Utter amazement paralyzed such speech as the Night Wind might have uttered then.

Katherine turned her back upon him, and they stood thus in utter silence until the purring of an approaching motor-car smote upon the Night Wind's ears.

CHAPTER XXI

"LADY-KATE-OF-THE-POLICE"

"**I GUESS I'M** all in," the Night Wind said, when he leaned back against the cushions of the fake taxi-cab which Katherine Maxwell used so mysteriously and adeptly. For Black Julius was driving the car which he had heard approaching, and Katherine was now inside of it with her captive. "Where are you taking me, Miss Maxwell—to headquarters?"

She made no reply. He half turned his head to look at her. The car had started on again as soon as the two were seated inside of it.

It was Katherine's profile that Harvard saw clearly outlined against the uncurtained opening beside her.

How perfect it was, he thought. Cameolike in its clearness and daintiness.

He was silent also after that, regarding her intently the while—until she turned and faced him.

Her eyes were sparkling with a suggestion of anger. She resented the injustice of the last two words he had uttered. He should have understood her recent conduct better than that.

"*I* am taking you," she replied to him slowly, "nowhere at all. I shall drop down very soon and leave you. Julius may take you afterward wherever you wish to go—unless it should occur to you to follow some advice that he will give you in that particular."

She turned her head away from him again. Once more he studied her profile.

"Why don't you take me to headquarters and turn me over to the inspector or his representative?" Harvard asked after another pause. "I am practically helpless now, you know. You may as well do it."

"I am wondering myself why I do not do that very thing," she retorted without turning toward him again.

"Well, why don't you do it?"

"Possibly for the same reason that you did not murder Lieutenant Rushton when you had the opportunity a little while ago," she replied coolly.

"Because I do happen to be helpless, eh?"

"Probably."

"Well, I'm not helpless, Lady-Kate-of-the-Police. Not quite. I have got the full use of these yet." He stretched out his arms, but she paid no heed to the gesture.

"Why do you address me by that hateful name?" she demanded, still with her head and eyes averted.

"It fits, doesn't it?"

"Yes. I *am* called 'Lady Kate' down there; and I *am* of the police. You know that."

"Yes, I know it. You seemed just now rather proud of your badge of authority."

"I hate the name," she said, ignoring the latter part of his reply.

"Oh, in that case I will not use it again. I supposed you liked the name."

"And I am beginning to—you are making me do it—hate *you,* I think."

"Really? Believe me, it will be much better for both of us that you should."

"Why?" She turned and faced him again with that question.

"Because it will render your bounden duty so much easier—and pleasanter."

For a moment she regarded him in utter silence. Then she asked slowly:

"Mr. Harvard, have I not served you? Have I not warned you when there was danger threatening? Have I not been your friend?"

" 'Whom the gods would destroy they first make mad,'" he quoted, smiling at her.

He knew that for the moment he was near to acting the part of a cad, but he also knew what she did not—that he was doing it more as a matter of self-protection than to offend her in any way.

"You are ungrateful and you are insufferable," she retorted angrily, and rested one of her hands upon the latch of the door. She had kept watch of the passing scenery; he had not.

The cab came to a stop just as she opened wide the door. She stepped outside and slammed it shut again, and did it so quickly that Harvard had not time or opportunity to interfere.

"Wait, please!" he called to her.

Katherine paid no heed to him. She knew that he could not follow. In that far, she took advantage of his condition.

She stepped forward out of his range of vision, and spoke hastily and in a low tone to Julius. Harvard tried to hear, but he caught not a word of what she said to the black. He was greatly puzzled by all that had happened so recently. There were a hundred questions that he wanted to ask.

He pulled himself along the seat to the side of the cab she had occupied and thrust his own head through the open window. She was already moving away, and Julius had started the vehicle forward.

"Katherine?" Harvard spoke the name softly and with the same half -tender enunciation he had been accustomed to use while he had been under her care and Julius's when he was ill. Then, as softly, but in altogether a different tone, he added: "Wait, Julius."

Julius stopped the cab again. Katherine half paused, seemed

to hesitate for the fraction of an instant, and would have continued on her way if Harvard had not spoken to her yet again.

"Please, Katherine," he said.

She turned her face toward him, but she did not advance.

"Please come closer," he entreated.

She complied. She came to the window and stood quite near to him, but she did not speak. Neither did he for a moment. Then:

"Forgive me—if you can," he said. "But, if you would please me most, forget me."

Harvard withdrew his head from the window, and would have said no more. Indeed, he leaned back again upon the cushions and closed his eyes, believing that she had gone.

But the cab did not start forward, and he opened them again to discover why. Katherine's face was still at the window. Her eyes were gazing into his with an expression that startled him.

But the moment she discovered that he was looking at her their expression changed, and she stepped hastily away from the open window. Nevertheless, she spoke to Harvard through it.

"I hope that you will decide to follow the advice that Julius will give you," she said. "Good night."

"Wait!" he called to her.

"Well?" she made answer, without turning her face toward his.

"This is good-by," he said. "I don't know where Julius is taking me; but, wherever it may be, I will go gladly and without further question.

"There is much that I now wish I had said to you, Katherine; but perhaps it is for the best that all of it shall remain unspoken. As soon as I am able to travel I shall go away. I have no idea where, but I shall go—after I have performed the one last act of justice that my own fault defrauded me of tonight. But I prefer not to think of that now." He was speaking rather lamely and haltingly. When he stopped altogether, at that point, and she did not reply, he went on again:

"I want to thank you for all that you have done for me, for all that you have been to me, and for all that you might have been, Katherine.

"God! Do you wonder that, when I think of it, I want to kill that hound who has spoiled my life? Go, now! Don't answer me. I'd rather you would not. Good-by, Katherine; good-by."

He closed his eyes to shut out the vision of her.

He did not know that for an instant after he had ceased speaking she stood very still; that then she turned and stepped quickly to the window again. But he heard the words she spoke to him—just one sentence, uttered very rapidly:

"I shall see you again when you least expect it."

"No, no! Not that!" He started forward in his seat to reply. But she was gone; and she had so managed her going that he could catch no glimpse of her. Evidently she had also signaled to Julius, for the cab started forward; and the speed at which Julius drove it reminded him of that wild night, not so very long before, when they had shot over the length and breadth of the greater city, establishing an alibi.

Once, somewhere in the lower part of the city—Harvard was giving no attention to localities as they flew along—he touched the signal button, and the big black guided the machine to the curb and stopped. He leaped down, too, and came to the window.

"I am not used to going into things blindfolded, Julius, and I want to ask some questions," Harvard said.

"Very well, sir. I hope I can reply to them. Will you ask them now?" the black replied.

"Indeed I will. In a moment. This confounded leg of mine is—well—bothersome."

"We will have it properly attended to before very long, sir."

"Oh, will we? Good. Where are you taking me too, Julius?"

"Miss Kitty asked me not to tell you until we got there,

sir—unless you really, sure enough, insisted upon it. And I reckon that she just nacherly hoped that you wouldn't insist, Mr. Harvard."

"Oh! All right, then. Never mind, if that is the case. I don't want you to disobey orders. I hope there's a doctor there. This leg is beginning to get on my nerves. It feels like a pillar of stone that a buzz-saw is trying to annihilate. It doesn't hurt; it just bothers. Go ahead, Julius. I wish, though, that you would wait here long enough to explain how it happened that Miss Katherine found me in that back yard."

Julius complied. He began by telling how Lady Kate had seen him hiding in the Shadow of Centre Street, and that they had trailed him in the cab when he had followed Rushton, and had seen him go into Rushton's house.

Believing then, that Coniglio and the others had not arrived, she had sent Julius to the corner to watch for their approach; and, being warned of it, she had rung the doorbell once to put Harvard on his guard.

Then Katherine, with Julius beside her, had waited outside the house, in great anxiety, until the men from the central office had gone away, and Rushton had gone with them.

Lady Kate was certain that Harvard was still somewhere in the rear of those houses, and she felt equally assured that he had been hurt; for otherwise he should already have made an appearance.

Then the old man had appeared, tottering along the street; and Katherine, having pinned the police shield upon her jacket, approached him while he was opening his door, and told a tale which she made up for the occasion.

The police coat and shield which Julius wore were regular "properties" which he always carried with him in the car, to use in case of emergencies—and that was all that Julius could explain about it. "Some day, maybe, Miss Kitty will tell you all about it, sir," he said, in conclusion.

"And now, sir," he added, "I think it would be well to draw

the curtains; and both doors can be locked on the inside. I think I would do that, too, Mr. Harvard. The ferry-boat is coming into the slip."

"Wise Julius. All right. I will do both. What ferry is it?"

"Christopher Street, sir."

"Oh! Hoboken at the other end, eh? They would like to see me over there, Julius. I was there, 'alibi-night' after you left me. Remember that night—eh?"

"Yes, sir." Julius grinned. "That was surely a great night, Mr. Harvard."

Harvard's whole body was racked with pain. He lifted the injured leg to the seat in front of him, then replaced it upon the floor; then repeated the same performance time after time. He was beginning to understand what he had made others suffer when he had broken their bones with his strong hands.

Then he fell to thinking of Katherine again, and of the last words she had spoken to him at parting. She had said: "I shall see you again when you least expect it." He wondered what she had meant by that statement.

Nobody molested them or disturbed them, or offered to do so.

When they left the boat he closed his eyes and settled himself more comfortably against the cushions.

At last, when they were rolling through the residential section of outlying Hoboken, tired and exhausted nature asserted itself, despite the physical pain and discomfort. With one more mur- mured repetition of that last spoken sentence of Katherine's, "I shall see you again when you least expect it," Bingham Harvard fell asleep.

CHAPTER XXII

DISCHARGED

"WELL, DOCTOR?"

"We will soon have you out of this, sir," was the reply. "Your ankle looked bad at first. I was shocked by the appearance of it. But it turns out to be a strain rather than a sprain. There is a vast difference, sir."

"So I have heard. Well, get me fixed up as soon as possible. I'm not forgetful of kindnesses. I have the means, and I will be generous in the matter of payment for your services. There—you need not resent that, as you seem disposed to do," the Night Wind added, when the man he had addressed as doctor raised his head quickly.

The doctor was almost as black as Julius, and strangely like him in all but years. He was much younger than Katherine's faithful servitor. In fact, he was Julius's brother, many years younger, a practicing physician when not administering the gospel, which duty he performed every Sunday at a near-by "colored church."

Harvard had been accepted as a guest in his home, and a patient; and because that home was close to the edge of the colored belt in the outlying districts of one of the New Jersey cities, he felt, for the present, at least, quite safe from the activities of the police.

"How did Julius tell you to address me, doctor?" Harvard asked presently.

"As Mr. Binghampton, sir."

"I suppose you know that it is not my right name, don't you?"

"It is the only one that has been given to me to use, sir. It is quite sufficient."

"Don't you know my right name?" Harvard persisted.

"It may be that I have heard it. But, then, I hear many names. You were introduced here by my brother as Mr. Binghampton."

"Oh, well, that's all right! I like and admire your pluck in taking me in, and I am grateful, too. But, all the same, I can't stay here with you and permit you to run the risk you are taking unless I am assured that you fully understand just what that risk is—and exactly what it might mean to you if I should be caught here in your home. So, doctor, don't you see? We had much better be entirely frank with each other."

"Very well, sir; I *do* know who and what you are supposed to be. Does that satisfy you?"

"Not entirely. Julius said that you were a doctor, and a minister of the gospel, as well."

"I am."

"Well, I can't permit you to tell a lot of lies on my account, and to do things that are going to get on your conscience and make you unhappy. That isn't playing fair. Do you know that in New York, and some other localities, too, I am called the Night Wind?"

"Yes."

"And that there is a price on my head—figuratively, at least?"

"Yes."

"Dead or alive?"

"Yes."

"Well, suppose the bell at your front door should ring. Suppose you should find, when you opened it, an officer of the law waiting outside—one who had traced me to this house. You would be compelled to lie to him, wouldn't you?"

"I am going to speak rather plainly to you, Mr. Binghampton," was the slow reply, with especial emphasis on the name. "I hope you will not be offended."

"Go ahead, doctor."

"All matters connected with this house and the people in it are strictly and entirely my own affair. My relations to you and yours to me are purely professional. It is an unwritten law, but a wise one, that patients must obey their physicians.

"My one order to you, sir, is this: that you pay strict attention to the business of getting well, and concern yourself with nothing else. Just now you may amuse yourself with any of those books that happen to interest you. I have professional calls to make, and you will be alone until I return."

With a low bow and a smile in his eyes, the doctor left the room.

The "business of getting well" went along more expeditiously than either the colored doctor or his patient had dared to hope. No complications interfered with the rapid recovery of the Night Wind. The ice-packs to which the strained ankle was constantly subjected very quickly reduced the swelling, scattered the discoloration, and restored to their normal condition the inflamed tissues and strained tendons and nerves.

"You are physically so wonderful, and your constitution so perfect," the doctor told him on one occasion, "that you recover from injuries like a cat."

Nevertheless, a week passed by, then another, and then a third one, before the doctor would consent that any severe test be applied to the injured ankle; and in the meantime Harvard had sentenced himself to complete silence concerning the one subject upon which he most desired to be informed.

Not a word or a sign of any sort had been received from Katherine, or even from Julius, since that early morning when Harvard was taken to the doctor's house; and the patient had schooled himself to ask no question about either of them.

He had hoped that the doctor would volunteer something

of the sort, but time proved that the physician seemed as little disposed to do that as his patient was to interrogate.

There came a morning when Harvard had been under the doctor's care more than three weeks—when he could bear the silence and the anxieties that filled it no longer.

The doctor often sat with him at his request; and on the particular morning in question, when he cast aside the paper he had been reading and would have left the room for his daily round of calls, Harvard stopped him.

"You can spare me five minutes more, I hope," he said.

"Certainly, Mr. Binghampton."

"How much longer must I remain with you before you are quite willing that I may go?" Harvard demanded quietly. "I have systematically, and every day since it began, followed your directions as to exercise."

"I think that I can discharge you by the morning of the day after to-morrow," the physician replied, smilingly.

"Why not to-day?"

"Are you particularly anxious to go away today?"

"N-no, I think not."

"In that case your last question needs no answer."

Harvard hesitated a moment. Then he asked abruptly:

"Have you heard from your brother Julius since I have been here?"

"Not a word."

"Have you communicated with him, or with his employer?"

"With Julius—yes. Every day."

"And have received no replies from him?"

"None."

"Why is that?"

"It was so understood between us in the beginning. My short reports are ambiguous, misleading, and unsigned. I send them to New York to be mailed. They are sent to a name and address which have no direct associations with my brother."

"I see. I suppose you have agreed to notify him when I was on the point of leaving you?"

"Yes."

"And that fact, instead of my condition, leads you to fix the time for my departure the day after to-morrow, instead of to-day. Is that true?"

"It is."

"Have you an idea that Julius will come to see me before I go away?"

"I think he will do so. And I do not think he will come alone, Mr. Binghampton."

"Oh, thank you, doctor. I will try to be patient."

When left alone to himself, Bingham Harvard was anything but patient.

The doctor had barely driven away from the door in his little runabout before Harvard was up and doing, arranging for his own going, before the doctor should return.

There was not much arrangement to make. Clothing he had none, save that in which he was clad, and a few other articles which had accumulated during his stay.

A fortunate circumstance, entirely accidental, but equally providential, had supplied him with more than sufficient cash for his needs at the time when his misfortune fell upon him. But that is a subject for later discussion. It suffices that he was still well supplied with funds.

Only once had the supply he carried been out of his possession. That was when he was ill, after his experience in the river, when Black Julius had undressed him while he was delirious. But Julius had faithfully folded his clothing and put it away. Nothing it contained had been disturbed.

So when the doctor left him and he began preparations for his immediate departure, there was little for him to do save to write two letters, one to Julius, one to the physician—which latter one contained a yellow-back bill of ample denomination.

He left no word for Katherine.

It was chiefly because he desired to avoid a meeting with her that he determined to depart without leave-taking.

Without admitting the fact to himself, he resented her utter silence since he had been under the doctor's care; and he succeeded in convincing himself that he was glad that she had kept herself aloof and silent.

Harvard disliked going abroad in the daylight, but he had to do that in order to avoid the doctor, who would return at one in the afternoon, and who might not go out again unless he happened to be especially summoned.

The letter he left for the doctor was one of gratitude and appreciation. From the one addressed to Julius one paragraph may be quoted:

> "I must forward my expressions of gratitude to one other person, through you, because it would be unwise for many reasons to send them direct. I desire you to say for "me that I fully and thoroughly appreciate all that has been done for me, and all the kindnesses that have been extended to me. Say, also, that I shall go far away very soon—just as soon as I have performed one duty which still remains to me. If I am ever taken, which I doubt, no act of yours, or of the person to whom I refer, must be performed, or even considered, which can reflect upon or compromise either of you. I am very much in earnest in making this request."

At eleven o'clock that morning Bingham Harvard quietly departed from the house that had sheltered him so thoroughly.

His going was unobserved.

It was the first time he had been outside the door since Julius took him there. It was the first time he had been abroad in the streets in many a day.

There was more than a three-weeks' growth of beard on his face, which he had carefully trimmed to a Van Dyke point, and he believed that if he used ordinary care and caution he would be able, for a time at least, to avoid recognition.

He had become the Night Wind again—or would be so as soon as night should fall—and in that character, when darkness should settle over the world, there were two acts for him to perform—two acts upon which he had irrevocably decided.

Lieutenant Rodney Rushton must yet be dealt with. In not one jot had the Night Wind altered his determination concerning him. He meant to find Rushton before another night should pass, and when he did find him there would be no mistake about the outcome of the meeting.

The second act upon which he had decided was simple. He intended merely to go away—very far away—never to return.

He had been gone from the house of the doctor less than an hour when Katherine Maxwell's imitation taxicab, with Julius driving, stopped at the door, and "Lady-Kate-of-the-Police," as the Night Wind had several times addressed her in mock derision, got out of it and passed through the gateway toward the house.

CHAPTER XXIII

TOM CLANCY'S ACTIVITIES

THREE WEEKS IS a long time for a character like the Night Wind to have disappeared utterly from the face of the earth.

Anyhow, the department of police of New York City thought so, and, generally speaking, was glad. Some of the higher officials thought so, and were not sorry. The inspector at that time in charge of the detective bureau thought so, and was secretly elated.

Rushton thought so, too, and was honestly disappointed—because, being entirely sound and fit again, and his egotism being so great, he never doubted his ability sooner or later to "get" his man. That last experience at his own house had made him all the more eager.

Had he known that "his man" was even then planning, warily and craftily, how to get *him*, it is possible that he might have experienced some misgivings concerning the final outcome of events.

Thomas Clancy had been summoned to headquarters the day following Harvard's escape across the roofs and through the thirteenth house.

He had admitted stoutly and defiantly that he always had been, and still continued to be, Bingham Harvard's friend; that if he had been given the opportunity he would have taken the Night Wind into his house at any time. But the opportunity had been lacking. The police knew that much, and Clancy was sent away with a warning against harboring felons.

Clancy went to see President Chester of the bank, mad clear through.

"I want you to come out positively, in a public statement over your own signature, that you know Bing Harvard to be *not guilty* of the charge against him," he told that much-disturbed and mentally harassed official.

"But I can't do that, Tom," Chester replied.

"Don't you *know* that he is not guilty?"

"No. I do not. And, considering the wild acts he has committed since then, considering the fact that he has made a veritable demon of himself, breaking bones and demoralizing the entire police force, defying all authority, and flying in the face of the law, I am convinced that he *is* guilty."

"Oh, you are, eh? What else could he have done, I'd like to know?" with fine scorn.

"He might have given himself up and stood his trial."

"Yes; and been railroaded to prison for thirty years, more or less."

"Probably—if he were proven guilty. But if, on the other hand—"

"Oh, there is no other hand in a dead-open-and-shut frame-up, engineered and managed by the 'system,' when it needs a victim. You know that."

"I do not know it. I do not believe it. I have known Lieutenant Rushton a long time. He has performed many services for me."

"He is a double-dyed, black-hearted scoundrel! That's what *he* is!" Clancy interrupted. "And if I know Bing Harvard—and I think I do, some!—he'll get that uniformed rat before he's much older, and hand him what's coming to him. Bing will take him in his hands some day and break him in two. If he doesn't kill Rushton for what Rushton has done to him—well, I'll miss my guess."

"Oh, I hope not."

"I suppose if Bing were your own son, instead of being merely a person whom you professed to love like a son, you'd act in precisely the same way, wouldn't you?"

"I certainly would, Tom."

"Honestly, Chester, I begin to think that, in your complacent unctiousness, you're almost as great a scoundrel as Rushton. The only difference is that you don't know it, and he does."

"You would not say such things to me, Thomas, if you were not beside yourself with excitement and concern for your old friend. I can honor you for that, but your father's son must not come here to insult me."

"No. That's so. I beg your pardon, Chester. You are upright, and honest, and conscience-stricken, according to your lights— but your lights are turned down mighty low."

"I think, Tom, that we had best close this discussion," the banker said.

"All right. I've got to ask you another question, though."

"What is it?"

"Have you made any effort to discover who else beside Bing might have got that wad out of your bank?"

"No. There has been no need. Rushton's evidence was clear enough."

"Sure! For you! And for him! And for the system! I'll tell you something, Mr. Chester, that you didn't know. *I have.*"

"Have done what?"

"I have made that effort. I have taken those steps. See?"

"No, I do not see."

"Well, I'll tell you, then, so you will see. I have made some money down here among you licensed con-men. I'm not exactly a poor man; I'm a good ways off from being that, in fact. And I want to tell you this, Chester: I'll spend every last dollar of what I've got before I'll let go of this thing. And just as sure as there is such a thing as justice in this world, I'll nail you, and your complacency, and unctiousness, to the cross of retribution and remorse before I get through with you."

"You are talking wildly, Tom."

"No, I'm not. I'm talking sense. You're just as likely to be the thief, yourself, as Bing Harvard is. I'd sooner think you were it than that he is."

"Thomas Clancy, I will not submit "

"Yes, you will—for another minute or so. I'm almost through."

The banker sighed, rubbed his hands together, and leaned back resignedly.

"I came here to tell you," Clancy continued, "that I've got an eye on every man-jack of your bunch in this bank, your august self not excepted. I have engaged an agency that never lets go, and I have instructed the main guy to go the limit. I'm doing that for Bing, because he isn't in a position to do it for himself."

The banker started from his chair, angrily. His face was flushed. This last indignity from the son of his old friend was more than he would bear.

"I must ask you to leave my office and the bank, Mr. Clancy," he managed to say, coldly. His face changed from florid to waxen hue. "I shall instruct the cashier to request that you withdraw your account, also."

Clancy grinned.

"I did that some time ago," he said.

"You have no business to put detectives on the trail of my employees."

"Haven't I? Well, I have done it, just the same. I've had some interesting reports, too. And before you are very much older, I'll have others that will be still more interesting. Put that in your pipe and smoke it, Chester."

"Will you go, or shall I summon—"

Clancy interrupted the banker by laughing aloud.

Then he swung upon his heels and departed, still smiling.

The interview had interested him. It had roused to further effort the fighting qualities he possessed; and, as his name implies, he was well equipped in that respect.

All that happened the day following his summons to police headquarters; the second day after Bingham Harvard's mishap.

An hour later, after his interview with Chester, Clancy sought the red-headed chief of the detective agency he had employed, and remained for a long time in consultation with him. At the close of it he said:

"Remember, I want my message delivered to Harvard as soon as you can do it. If you or one of your men gets a chance to speak to him, anywhere or anyhow, tell him that your agency is working in his interests, and that I've just *got* to have just one more talk with him. If he should mistake your man for a real cop, and break an arm or leg for him, I'll pension the fellow for life, if necessary. Now, get busy, and find the real thief."

"There are a lot of other charges against Harvard now, besides the theft from the bank," the head of the agency said dryly.

"Sure there are! But do you suppose for a minute that any jury on earth would convict him for breaking the bones of a few cops, after it has been proved that he was innocent of the first charge, and that the whole case against him was a deliberate frame-up?"

Clancy began that night an undertaking that was purely his own idea.

Formerly he had been a "home-body," preferring his own room, his books, his cigar, and restful quiet, to the social attractions of clubs and friends.

But thereafter he took to being abroad on the streets late at night, wandering hither and thither, in every part of the city where there was the slightest hope that he might encounter his friend.

And always he carried with him a bulky envelope which he intended to thrust into Harvard's grasp the moment they did meet. The contents of that envelope would have excited the envy and the ambition of the most accomplished footpad in New York. That was one reason why he wished to see Harvard again. He had forgotten to force upon him a goodly supply of cash, and he honestly believed Harvard needed it.

But three weeks and more passed and there was nothing doing.

Clancy began to grow thin. He did not neglect his business, but he was always very tired when he went to it in the morning, and really felt like work only when night fell and he could resume his ceaseless search.

Besides, he wanted to find Katherine Maxwell without seeking her, at the police department, if he could.

Several times he encountered Rushton, whom he now knew by sight. On one of those occasions he was aware that Rushton trailed after him, and he was very much delighted by the circumstance.

Then, one morning, on his way down town, he stopped at police headquarters.

It happened—he was totally unaware of it, of course—that it was the very same morning when Harvard made his clandestine departure from the colored doctor's house in Jersey—about an hour or a little more before that event.

He sent in his name to the inspector, and waited, seated upon a chair against the wall where several others also waited. Presently Rushton came out of the private office and approached him.

"The inspector is engaged just at present. He assumes that you're in a hurry, Mr. Clancy," Rushton said. "Is there anything that I can do for you?"

"Your name is Rushton, isn't it?" Clancy replied, rising, pretending that he did not know the lieutenant.

"Yes."

"Well, there isn't anything that you can do for me, thank you just the same."

The insolence that he managed to convey in those few words was totally lost upon the lieutenant.

"You're the Night Wind's friend, ain't you?" he inquired.

"Yes," Clancy replied, resuming his seat upon the chair.

"Seen him lately?"

"No. Have you?"

"Nobody has."

Just then the door of the private office was opened. A woman came out. She wore a veil that partly concealed her features, but Clancy instantly decided that she was Katherine Maxwell. He was astonished when she crossed directly toward him, and with the evident intention of speaking. He heard Rushton say to her:

"Hello, Lady Kate! I'd like a word with you before you go out."

But she paid no attention whatever to that officer.

Instead, she stepped a little to one side and passed him. Then she spoke directly to Clancy.

"You are Mr. Thomas Clancy, are you not?" she asked.

"Yes," he replied, rising quickly from his chair, wondering how it happened that she knew him.

"Will you—" she hesitated, and turned her eyes for an instant toward Rushton, who was loitering near enough to overhear what might be said. She went on, but with an evident change from her original intention—"kindly step this way a moment? I have something to say to you."

Katherine moved aside a short distance, Clancy beside her. Rushton scowled and followed. She turned upon him:

"The inspector wishes to see you at once, Lieutenant Rushton," she said. "He asked me to tell you. After that he will see this gentleman."

She waited in silence until Rushton had gone. Then she turned again to Clancy.

"I wish very much, indeed, to have a short talk with you, Mr. Clancy," she said, without preface. "I cannot stop now, even if there were opportunity and this the proper place to take advantage of it. You are Mr. Bingham Harvard's friend, are you not?"

"Yes. And you are—" He came to a stop.

"I am Miss Maxwell. You have already seen enough to know *what* I am. Will you do me the kindness to call at this address this evening at nine?" She gave him a card and turned quickly away before he had an opportunity to reply.

That she must have gone directly from headquarters to the home of Julius's brother in Jersey, we already know.

The door had just closed behind her when Rushton came from the private office to conduct Clancy to the presence of the inspector.

CHAPTER XXIV

FIGHTING BLOOD IS ROUSED

"YOU WISHED TO see me, Mr. Clancy?" the inspector greeted him. Rushton remained in the room, near to the closed door.

"Yes." Clancy glanced in the direction of the lieutenant. "Alone, if I may."

The inspector nodded. Rushton passed outside, his face a thunder-cloud.

"I wanted to ask you a few straight-from-the-shoulder questions about Bingham Harvard, inspector," Clancy said, as soon as the door had closed behind Rushton.

"Fire away. I can give you five minutes—if you will make them interesting."

"Do you believe him guilty of the original charge against him?"

"Sure. We all do. Is that all you came here to ask me?"

"No. It is only the leader."

"Go ahead, then. Only I might as well tell you, before you go any deeper into things, that if the Night Wind had never seen Chester's bank, and had done what he has done since then, it would get him about all the rest of his years up the river."

"Maybe. But that isn't the point."

"What is?"

"Suppose that some day, before very long, I should bring to this department incontestable proof of his innocence, and of the guilt of another—proof that you would have to admit—just suppose all that."

"It's a little bit difficult, but I'll try. Go on, Mr. Clancy."

"Would this department—you, for instance—be willing to call off all the rest of it—all of that part of it which relates to resisting officers, and all that?"

"Is that your straight-from-the-shoulder question, Mr. Clancy?"

"It is one of them."

"I'll answer it. No; we would not. I'll put that guy where he belongs, if it takes me all the rest of my time to do it. I'll get him what's coming to him! Is that all you wanted to know?"

"Yes," rising:

"All right. I'll give you a word of advice before you go out."

"I suppose I ought to thank you, only I'm not quite sure that I want it."

"You can take this, or leave it, just as you please."

"Very well."

"It is known down here just what your attitude is toward the Night Wind. *I* know, moreover, that you have engaged the services of a certain agency to establish his innocence, and it is not supposable that you, or that agency, will be overparticular about the means employed to do that.

"I suspect—I don't *know,* but I've got a decided hunch that way—that you wouldn't let anything slip past you that might give you an opportunity to befriend and aid the Night Wind. My advice is that you drop all such ideas, and keep your hands off of this business.

"Why? Because the very first moment that I find out that you are aiding, abetting, or giving succor, or assistance to that crook, I'll clap *you* behind the bars, Mr. Thomas Clancy, and I'll send you just as far as the law will let me. That's all. Now, get out of here and don't come back. I don't want your kind in the place."

Clancy stopped at the door, pale with anger, but self-composed for all that.

"Your advice seems good, after all, inspector," he said with deliberation, "principally because it warns me against another possible frame-up, with Thomas Clancy for the victim. You'll get me, if you can, but look out that I don't find a way to get you first. I'm a pretty good fighter myself, inspector. Good morning."

Instead of going directly to his office, where he was already overdue, he told his chauffeur to drive to the detective agency, where the red-headed man with a national reputation ruled supreme. Luckily he found his man there.

"Well," Clancy said to him, as soon as they were alone, "three weeks and a half makes twenty-four or five days. How about it, chief?"

"Nothing doing yet, Mr. Clancy."

"No trace of him?"

"Not a trace."

"And promising clues?"

"I might lie to you and say yes, only that isn't my method."

"What is your opinion about the whole business?"

"I think he must have got a bullet in him, or have hurt himself, and is laying up somewhere for repairs. That is the only logical way in which I can account for the present situation. On the other hand, he may have chucked up the sponge, and lit out for China, or Honduras, or another place that's even hotter."

"Keep on trying, chief."

"I'm doing that; only it is costing you a pretty penny, Mr. Clancy."

"That is my own lookout. I'll call you when I think you have gone far enough."

"You're on. I'd like to have a few more employers like you."

"In the meantime, chief, and just to keep you busy, I have discovered another outlet for your superfluous energies."

"Good. What is it?"

"It happens to be the inspector of police, who is at the present time the acting head of the detective bureau at police headquarters," Clancy announced coolly.

The red-haired gentleman uttered a prolonged whistle. It was the nearest he ever came to expressing any astonishment he happened to feel.

"What about *him?*" he asked, presently.

"I want to 'get him,' that's all—and get him good and hard."

"On what?"

"On anything that happens to be lying around loose. I don't care what it costs, only get him. Find something on him that I can take to the mayor, and *prove.* I'll do the rest."

"That's rather dangerous fire for an outsider to play with, Mr. Clancy."

"I'm not playing with it. I'm heating some irons in it; and I want them white hot. And while you're about it I want you to get something on Detective-Lieutenant Rushton, too. Got that?"

"Yes."

"Now, who is the young woman over at headquarters whom they call Lady Kate? Her last name is Maxwell. Who and what is she?"

"One of the regular bunch over there. That is all I know about her. After her scalp, too?"

"Not yet. Find out something about her, though, if you can. I'd like you to telephone me at my office, by or before five o'clock this afternoon, all the information you can pick up in the meantime concerning her. Will you do that?"

"Yes. And I know a way that will produce all that is being given out about her, before that time. I ought to be able to get it to you by two or three o'clock."

"All the better. Now, there is one more thing, chief."

"You're loaded to the muzzle to-day, Mr. Clancy."

"I generally am when I get my mad up. Did you know that you've got a leak here in your office?"

"The best of roofs will leak at times, if strained; but leaks can usually be stopped. Where is this one, if you know?"

"I don't know where it is; I only know that there is one. The inspector you are going to nail for me is wise to everything that you are doing in my behalf, and knows exactly why I have engaged you. You'd better find a way to stop that leak, if you want to stay on my pay-roll."

"I'll stop it," the red-haired gentleman assured him.

Just before three o'clock that afternoon Clancy put the telephone receiver to his ear in response to a call. The red-haired man was on the wire.

"Stop here on your way up-town," he said, when assured that it was Clancy who answered. "I'd rather tell you what I have to say here."

"I'll be there within an hour," Clancy replied.

He hurried through the remainder of his business for the day, and left his office much earlier than usual. Within the time specified he was again in consultation with Red Hair.

"I have found the leak, and stopped it," the latter told the broker. "I guessed where it might be, when you mentioned it, so I made it work both ways. I got all there is to get about Lady Kate, from the same source. There isn't much, but it is interesting as far as it goes."

"Go ahead, then. Let's have it."

"Katherine Maxwell is the only name she is known by down there. They haven't been able to nail any other monniker to her. She blew in a little less than a year ago and wanted a job as a detective. Her looks and her wit passed her up.

They happened to need somebody of her description at the time and gave her a trial. She made good and was taken on probation. She made good again and was taken on regularly. She gave as her address No. —— West Eleventh Street.

"Later, the inspector whose scalp you're after gave her a special assignment. The Night Wind had seen her and spoken to her, without knowing that she was connected with the police, so she was given leave of absence from headquarters and detailed specially to get him.

"Three weeks ago, or about that time, Lieutenant Rodney Rushton went to the inspector with a special report concerning her, and he tried his best to have her special detail changed so that she would have to work under his orders, and, failing that, to have her fired.

"My informant tells me that she accepted the apparent change of masters without a murmur; but the odd part of it is that from the moment she was told to serve under the direct orders of Lieutenant Rushton not a soul connected with the department has seen a sign of her until to-day.

"She was not at the address in Eleventh Street. She has not been at another address further uptown which, it seems, was known to Rushton.

"Rushton has been about crazy about her; the inspector has been puzzled and disturbed, and yesterday the quiet tip was given out among the men to look for her. They had begun to think down at headquarters that the Night Wind had made away with her, or carried her away forcibly—or that she had run away with the Night Wind.

"This morning, apparently not very long before you got there, she blew in at headquarters, was atf once admitted to the inspector's private office—and she handed in her resignation on the spot.

"It seems that the inspector tried to induce her to remain; that Rushton was called in, and added his efforts to the inspector's, and that they might just as well have saved their breath.

"She handed in her shield and everything that goes with it. She repudiated the back pay that was due her—refused to accept an order for a cent of salary, and walked out of the private office with her head in the air.

"Outside, in the receiving office, she encountered somebody who was waiting to see the inspector—and who, I suspect, must have been you—and stopped a moment to speak to him. Rushton was summoned hastily by the inspector; and so it happened that when Miss Katherine Maxwell left headquarters she was followed and shadowed by two of the best men they have got down there.

"In a word, Mr. Clancy, she is under suspicion, and the inspector means to keep himself informed of every move she makes, no matter what it may be, just as long as the Night Wind is at large. That's all."

Clancy was silent for a time before he replied. Then he nodded his head sagely and said:

"You seem to have covered the ground rather thoroughly in the short time you had to do it, chief."

"Well, it is sometimes quite necessary that I keep myself informed of what is happening on the inside of the system. I have a method and a means which I use only in extreme cases. This looked a trifle extreme to me, so I used it."

"Looked extreme? Why, if you don't mind telling me?"

"Because, Clancy, I've got a hunch that the same Miss Maxwell, for reasons unknown, is disposed to be entirely friendly to Bingham Harvard, esquire, alias the Night Wind."

"I have an engagement to call upon her this evening," Clancy told him.

"In that case, my friend, I should advise that you use an aeroplane to take you there, for the very good reason that both of you are under surveillance," was the emphatic reply of the red-haired gentleman.

CHAPTER XXV

SHADOWS ON THE TRAIL

THE NIGHT WIND went directly to New York. He made the journey at midday, and he used no precaution whatever to avoid such police officers as he was obliged to pass on the way there.

Possibly the very directness of his effort and his utter indifference to recognition were the principal safeguards. Certain it is that he passed unnoticed among the people, official and otherwise, with whom he came in contact.

He knew himself to be as strong, as agile, and as competent as ever he had been to take care of himself, and to render it extremely unpleasant for any person who might choose to attack him.

Nobody looked at him a second time.

Three weeks and more is a long interval for any person to remain in the limelight of the public eye in the great city of New York, and the Night Wind had not been seen, had broken no bones, had committed no "outrages" against the uniformed guardians of the city during that time.

For a week or more he had been quite capable of dispensing with the doctor's services. He had known that, but he had waited, nevertheless. He wished to be entirely fit before he did depart. And during that interval he had indefatigably exercised and trained himself, until he knew that he was thoroughly in condition.

He had reviewed his own career with its promises, its partial fulfillments, and its failures.

He had brought to mind, with diligence and care, every good and kind act that had been bestowed upon him by his benefactor, President Chester, of the Centropolis Bank.

Bingham Harvard had loved Mr. Chester; he loved him still; loved him as if he were indeed a real father—as in fact he had been in very many ways. He knew, in his heart, that Mr. Chester still loved him; that the banker's soul was as sad as his own because of what had happened—sadder, in fact, because the man of finance honestly believed him to be guilty of the theft that had been charged against him.

That was the real cross that Harvard had to hear—that Mr. Chester *did honestly* believe him guilty. If all the world besides, save possibly one exception, had believed him guilty, and President Chester had still faith, it would have been different.

And one man, only one, was responsible for it all—Rushton.

"And Rodney Rushton must pay!"

That was the burden of the Night Wind's thought. Rushton *must pay*.

How he had thought over it, worried over it, argued with his own conscience about it, studied it from every viewpoint that he could devise! And always he had been brought back to the same self-statement:

"Rodney Rushton must pay!"

For he believed that there was another one who, like Mr. Chester, thought him to be guilty—and that, he realized, had developed into a heavier cross than his benefactor's defection.

True, that other one had befriended him, had warned him of dangers, had nursed him and cared for him through his illness, had aided him to escape from his enemies when he was helpless—yet he believed now that all the time, and through it all, she had thought him to be a thief.

For that, too, Rodney Rushton must be made to pay!

The Night Wind knew, when he left the doctor's house in

Jersey, that he was going to New York to kill Rushton. He knew, while he rode through the tunnel, that he was on his way to kill Rushton. The iron wheels beneath him clanked it. The rush of air through the tubes moaned it.

Just before he left the house of the doctor he held his hands out in front of him, viewed them with a smile on his lips, and he had said aloud:

"I will kill him with these!"

He knew that he could do that easily.

Never once in all the time he had been a fugitive from the distorted law had be borne a weapon. He needed none. His hands, his muscles, his nerves, his compelling will to accomplish, were surer weapons far than any that had ever been wrought by mechanical skill. Rushton would wilt and wither beneath them as a blade of grass is blighted by intense heat.

So that was the Night Wind's errand to New York.

Katharine crossed the river at the same time he did.

She was above it. He was beneath it. She was bound for Jersey. He was leaving New Jersey for New York. She was on her way to save him from himself—for the colored doctor was an observant man and had faithfully reported certain misgivings that he entertained—and Harvard was on his way to commit the forbidden crime.

So they met and passed, unknowing and unknown, she above the river, he beneath it.

The doctor arrived at his home but a moment after Katherine got there. They found the letters that Harvard had left behind him. The denomination of the yellow-back bill, enclosed in the envelope to the physician, astounded them both and dismayed Katherine.

In his letters the Night Wind told nothing of his purposes or future plans, save that definite one of going away.

But Katherine knew; the doctor knew; Julius knew. And all three were alike helpless to prevent what then seemed to have become the inevitable—the execution of Rodney Rushton.

Katherine read and reread the letter that was addressed to Julius. She understood perfectly well that it had been intended for her more than for her servitor.

"What should she do? What could she do?" she asked herself, over and over again, knowing all the time that there was practically nothing that she could do.

The only thing certain about it all was that Lieutenant Rodney Rushton, of the New York police, was doomed beyond recall if he should fall into the hands of the man he had so grievously wronged—Bingham Harvard, alias the Night Wind.

Katherine remained only a short time at the house of the physician. Then she had Julius drive her to the tube, and left him.

In the tunnel, across the car, and at the opposite end of it, she discovered a face that was vaguely familiar; and presently she remembered that she had seen it only once before—at police headquarters in New York.

She knew then that she was being followed.

For some unknown reason the knowledge gave her courage. It gave an added zest to her undertaking. More than anything else, it classed her with the man she wanted to save from himself.

Furtively, she looked for another face also, for she understood that there must be two men on her trail. She did not find it, but she assumed that it would be in the other car. And she was correct.

She had taken a train that brought her to Thirty-Third Street, in Manhattan. As well there as elsewhere. She left it without so much as a glance backward. She did not care to inform those men that she knew herself to be followed.

Katherine went directly to the house in Eleventh Street and packed the few articles that she cared to have removed. She gave directions concerning them, and passed outside again. Her "shadows" had been changed in the meantime, but she understood perfectly well that she was followed from there to that other address where she had lived and where she had once cared for Bingham Harvard, the house in the Seventies.

Julius had already received instructions concerning the disposition of her belongings at that place. But it was the address that she had given to Clancy that morning at headquarters, so she decided that she would go there and wait. There was nothing else for her to do—and she could rest, and think, while she waited.

Katherine mounted the steps and entered the house without a glance backward. She passed into the house and closed the street door. There was no thought that those men would attempt to follow her inside. They would be content to await her reappearance.

There were three flights of stairs to ascend before she could reach her own quarters—which, as a matter of fact, she had abandoned some time ago. She had not been there at all during the past three weeks.

But her effects were there still. Nothing had been taken away as yet.

She thrust her key into the lock of the door and opened it. The odor of a cigar tanged in her nostrils. The burly figure of a man sprang from a chair near the window and confronted her.

The man was Rodney Rushton.

CHAPTER XXVI

ANOTHER BLUFF

KATHERINE STARTED BACKWARD, more frightened than she would have admitted.

"You?" she cried out. Then, recovering, she demanded: "Why are you here? How did you get inside?"

"I'll answer your last question first, Lady Kate," Rushton replied with easy insolence. "I ain't been a detective an' monkeyin' around with crooks all these years for nothin'. I can find a way into a house when I want to—an' I happened to wanta git in here. See?"

"But why? You have no right to come here." She remained near to the door, which she had not closed. She observed with satisfaction that Rushton kept his distance. She recovered from her fright. It was barely more than three o'clock in the afternoon.

"What would bring me here, I ask you?" Rushton retorted. "I came to see you, of course. An', say, if you think that you can play fast an' loose with me, as well as with that bunch downtown, you may as well get over it. You can't."

"Play fast and loose with you? What in the world do you mean?" She was fast becoming angry, and her right hand sought the concealed pocket where she carried a weapon.

He saw the act and leered at her.

"Oh, you needn't reach for your gun," he said, with an open sneer. "I ain't goin' to hurt you—or try to. That ain't my lay. But there are some things that I'm goin' to say to you, an' you've got to hear 'em."

"Very well. Say them—and go."

"Shut the door, an' I will."

"I prefer to leave it open. Do you know that there are two officers outside in the street, who have followed me here, and that I can easily summon them if I care to do so?" she said.

Again he leered at her.

"Of course, I know it," he replied. "You ain't takin' a step just now that ain't watched an' counted. An' you can summon 'em, if you like. Much good it'll do you. I'm their superior officer. They wouldn't stay around long if they found *me* here."

"Say what you have to say, then, and go away," she answered him.

"Well, it's this: You ain't fooled me none, you can bank on that. You ain't fooled any of them very much; not so's you could notice it. The whole bunch down-town is onto your curves, Lady Kate, but they ain't wised-up quite as particular as I am."

"I don't in the least understand what you are talking about," she retorted.

"I'm talkin' about this Night Wind business, an' you know it. I just got wise to the fact to-day that a woman policeman and a big, black cop—who was a fake, of course—went into a house three doors from mine one night, not so very long ago, an' pulled a chap that had hurt his ankle, or something, outa the back yard.

"I run into the old man that lives there to-day, an' he told me all about it; an', say, mebby you think I didn't tumble to who that woman policeman was, and to who the guy with the game ankle was. Mebby you think I'm just a plain fool, but I ain't. I ain't got on to the black cop business yet, but I will. You're goin' to tell me—or else I'm goin' to clap the irons onto your dainty white wrists, and take you down to headquarters, a prisoner. Think it over, Lady Kate. You're up against it this time, an' you've got to come to terms, or I'll know the reason why."

"What terms?" She recognized his power and thought to temporize.

"These terms: You've got to give the game away. You've got to give the Night Wind away. You've got to lead him into my hands, as you agreed to do in the first place. I don't know what you are to him, or what he is to you, but there's something between you, take it from me? You're hand in glove with him, and you know it. You know where he can be found at this minute, too, an' I know that; an' by the great boot in Chatham Street, you've got to tell *me*."

"I do not know where he is," she replied to him steadily.

"If you was a man I'd say something that ain't exactly polite to mention to a woman, Lady Kate."

"I do not know where he is. I have no idea where he is. I am as ignorant about that as you are. If you had asked me yesterday, perhaps I could have told you. But now I do not know."

"That ain't true."

"It is true."

"Well, we'll pass that up. You can find him."

"I don't think so."

"You can, if you want to. You have found him before when you wanted to; you can do it again if you want to. If it hadn't been for you, we'd have nailed him that night at my house. And now—"

She took one step nearer to him and interrupted.

"If it had not been for me that night, Lieutenant Rushton," she said, "you would not be here now to insult me. Don't you know that he followed you that night to kill you? Don't you know that he means to do so yet, if the opportunity is found? Hasn't it occurred to you that I followed after you that night more to prevent him from killing you than for any other reason?"

"Huh?" he exclaimed. "You can't pull the wool over my eyes that way. You didn't do it on my account; you did it on his. I ain't a boob, Lady Kate. You didn't go into old man Kramer's back yard an' pull him outa *there* on *my* account, did you? You didn't take that nigger in there to carry him out on *my* account, did you? An' what I wanta know right now is who was that nigger? He wasn't any cop; I know that much. Who was he? Where's he at? There's somethin' comin' to him for puttin' on a cop's coat an' shield, an' flashin' 'em on that old man."

Katherine was silent.

"I s'pose he was just a coon that you picked up somewheres an' slipped a five-spot to do the job," Rushton went on. "We'll pass that up, too. But on the other proposition you've got to come across. You've got to deliver the goods. Now, how about it? Are you goin' to do the act, or shall I pinch you an' take you down-town?"

Katherine was in a quandary. She did not know whether Rushton was in earnest, or if he were merely bluffing. She did know that he was reckless enough to carry out his threat, if he elected to do so. While she hesitated he added:

"I ain't sure but what you might be sent up the road yourself for what you've done, Lady Kate. I'm pretty sure that you could be. An' you're goin' to the skipper the way you did an' resignin' this mornin' don't help the case none. Now, what's the answer?"

"Go ahead and arrest me, if you think you have the right to do so," she defied him. "Where is your warrant? You will have to get one first, won't you?"

It was Rushton's turn to hesitate. Then he grinned at her.

"Called me, didn't you?" he said. "Well, we'll let it go at that—for this time. But you've got to come across; don't forget that. I ain't foolin', Lady Kate. On the level, now, you're interested in that chap, ain't you? An' you're more'n likely to see him again, ain't you?"

Katherine gazed steadily into Rushton's eyes for a moment before she replied; then she said slowly:

"On the level, as you put it, I am somewhat interested in him, and for the reason that I do not believe him to be the man you say he is. Also on the level, Mr. Rushton, I regard it as extremely unlikely that I will see him again. If he does one thing which I know he firmly intends to do, I shall wish never to see him again; and if he does do that thing, or attempts to do it, you are likely to see him yourself before I do."

"Huh! That means, doesn't it, that he is goin' to croak me—if he can?"

"Yes. That is precisely what it means."

"An' would *you* care, if he did?"

"Of course, I would care."

"For me or for him?"

"For both of you."

"You helped him to get away that night, over Kramer's, didn't you?"

"That is a question which I decline to answer, Lieutenant Rushton."

"Well, you done it, anyhow. An' you could be sent up for it. But I ain't sayin' a word about it. An' I'm goin' now. I'm willin' that you should take time to think over what I've said, an' if you can see your way clear to help me out on this deal, an' get that Night Wind guy what's comin' to him, you won't lose nothin' by it, I'll tell you that."

"Very well," she replied calmly. "I will think it over, as you suggest."

"Good!" he beamed upon her. "Say, I'll do you a favor if you want me to. I'll send them fellers out there a-kitin' about their business. I'll take the job off their hands by tellin' them that I'll keep tabs on you myself; an' then, when they have ducked, I'll beat it, too. Want me to do that for you, Lady Kate, just to prove that there ain't no hard feelin's? I will, anyhow, whether you want me to or not," he added. "An' I'll go away an' leave you right now, if you'll shake hands. Eh?"

She extended her hand limply. He took it, held it for a moment, started to say something more, thought better of it, dropped the hand, and passed out through the still open door.

"So-long, Lady Kate," he called back to her from the hallway, and was gone.

CHAPTER XXVII

A COMBINATION OF FORCES

KATHERINE TURNED HER eyes to the clock upon the instant that she closed the door upon Rushton's departure.

She did not for one moment believe what he had said about sending the two shadows away. She knew the man who had just left her better than that.

She knew him to be crafty, keen, tricky—and intelligent, after a fashion. What she did believe was that he would, if he could, send the two men away; but that he would remain behind himself, not to desert his post, but to cling to it with all the tenacity he possessed. She believed that he would follow her and spy upon her if she should venture outside; or, if she did not go out, if she remained at home to keep the appointment she had made with Thomas Clancy, Rushton would without doubt stick to the task he had assigned to himself.

Consequently, Rushton would know of Clancy's call. More than likely he would interrupt it. There was no telling or guessing what he might do. He was capable of going to any extremity.

The hands of the clock pointed to ten minutes past four.

For a moment she bent her head in perplexed thought. Then she crossed rapidly to the telephone, seized the directory, and ran rapidly through the pages. Two numbers she jotted down upon a pad of paper; then she took up the telephone itself.

The first call she gave was unfruitful; but she was told that

Mr. Clancy had been gone an hour from his office, so she called his house number.

It was Scipio who responded to the call. He informed her that his master had not yet returned from business, and that possibly he might not be at home until late in the evening. He might call up at any moment and say that he was not coming.

If he did so, would Scipio give him Miss Maxwell's telephone number and ask him to call her up at once? Scipio would.

After that Katherine paced the floor for nearly half an hour—and then the bell of the telephone rang out sharply. Thomas Clancy, at the other end of the wire, announced that he had received Miss Maxwell's message through his servant.

"Mr. Clancy," she told him, "it is important that I should see you at once, instead of at the appointed hour. I do not care to be explicit over the telephone, but if you will tell me where I can find you within the hour, I will go to you. I prefer not to have you come here."

Clancy replied:

"It is now half past four o'clock. If you do not object to an early dinner, or to dining with me, suppose you meet me at the Kelsey at five-thirty. Will that answer?"

"Perfectly," she replied.

Thomas Clancy conducted his guest to a table at one of the windows, which he had already reserved. He had made the selection carefully, with a view to as much isolation as was possible in that room. The hour being early, there were comparatively few people in the great dining-room.

"I missed my luncheon to-day, Miss Maxwell," he told her, as they seated themselves. "As a consequence, I am not sorry to eat an early dinner."

"And I have not thought of eating since my breakfast," she replied, "so we are agreed as to that. I assume, Mr. Clancy, that you are somewhat mixed in regard to your opinion of Lady-Kate-of-the-Police, are you not?"

"Frankly, Miss Maxwell, I had not formed one—until two minutes ago. What that may be you need not ask."

"I think," she said, "that we had better avoid all commonplaces and pretty speeches. I asked you to come to see me tonight because I had a request to make of you. I changed the place of meeting and the hour because two men from the central office have followed me to-day and were waiting outside of my home at the time I telephoned to you. Even now they—or another one who has taken their duties off their hands—may be watching us through this window. The reason for this espionage is that I gave in my resignation at the police department this morning. It is thought down there that I have shown too much friendliness for a man whom we need not mention by name."

"I understand you," Clancy replied. "I, too, am watched."

"The things that I am telling you now are not what I intended to say when I asked you to make the appointment," she went on. "In the light of all that has happened since then, they seem necessary."

"Please be quite frank with me, Miss Maxwell," he said. "I will promise to be the same with you."

"Thank you. Lieutenant Rushton was inside of my apartment, waiting for me when I went there to-day. I had not been there in three weeks and had not intended to go there to-day. It was merely the result of circumstances that I did go there. The lieutenant had used false keys to get inside. We had rather a stormy interview at first; it ended, however, under a flag of truce—temporarily. But I have no doubt that he has followed me here, and that he is watching us from some point of vantage at this very moment. That is why I have explained the incident of to-day."

"I understand."

"It has nothing to do with my request to see you."

"You will explain that in good time."

"When I spoke to you this morning, I was on my way to

meet—our friend. It was my intention, when I did see him, to urge him to meet us both somewhere this evening. My plans miscarried. He had gone when I arrived."

"I understand, then, that you knew where to find him this morning—or thought you did?"

"I have known exactly where he was for three weeks and more. He had met with an accident. His ankle was injured, but he now has entirely recovered. I was notified of his intention to leave the place—and, also, of the two principal reasons he had for going at once. You, Mr. Clancy, are thoroughly his friend, are you not?"

"I am. Thoroughly so. To the last ditch, Miss Maxwell."

"One more question, please. You do not believe him guilty of that theft at the Centropolis Bank?"

"No more than I am, or than you are."

"Then I may speak frankly."

"You may—as I shall, when it comes my turn; and I have some very intimate and direct things to say to you, Miss Maxwell."

"All the better. I should have said that he had three reasons, instead of two, for leaving the home of the doctor where he was staying when he did so; but the third one is the natural consequence of the other two. I will mention it first in order to be rid of it."

"Very well."

"It was a desire to avoid an interview with me."

Clancy was silent.

"The other two reasons were"—she bent nearer to him—"first, to find Rushton, and to—to—I cannot use the word. It is all too horrible."

"To kill him," Clancy said quietly. "I know about that, and about the other reason, too. After he has settled with Rushton he means to go away—very far away—never to return."

"Then you know already?"

"Yes. I have known for more than three weeks; nearly four. He was at my house a part of the night and all of the day following his return from a short trip through the West. I think it must have been the night after that when he injured his ankle. We talked a great deal then. I am coming to that presently. But he told me of his intentions toward Rushton, and of his purpose to leave the country afterward—and of some other things that concerned him, also."

"I will conclude what I had to say, Mr. Clancy, and then hear what you have to tell me."

"Very well."

"It may all be summed up in one statement. He has purposely avoided me. It is his fixed intention to go away without seeing me again. He will do that if he can. But I think, I believe, that he will seek one more interview with you before he goes." Again she bent over the table, nearer to Clancy. "I want you to promise me, if it is possible for you to do so, that you will arrange matters so that I may have an opportunity to see him and speak with him just once more before he goes away. Will you try to do that, if it is possible, Mr. Clancy?"

"Yes. Unqualifiedly, yes. If it can be done."

"Thank you." Katherine leaned back in her chair for a moment.

"Only I am of the opinion that he will avoid me as well as you. You must not bank too heavily upon this proposition, Miss Maxwell. You may be disappointed."

"I know. Whatever arrangements you may have an opportunity to make must be made without his knowledge. If he should suppose that you were making an attempt to bring us together he would not consent to it."

"I know. I understand. Now, how shall I find you at any moment of the day or night when I might want to summon you, Miss Maxwell? Is such an arrangement possible?"

"Yes. I thought that out while I was on my way down here. I will register and engage a suite of rooms here at this hotel—"

"Pardon me. Instead of doing that, go over to the Mammoth. I know them over there very well indeed. We will be facilitated at that hotel if we have need to be." He took a card from one of his pockets and wrote hastily upon the back of it. "Ask for Mr. Horton, the manager, Miss Maxwell. Give him that card. Now, after you are accommodated, what then?"

"I will remain in my suite of rooms, and not leave them at all until I hear from you, Mr. Clancy."

"Excellent. Leave everything else to me. If I find Bing, or if he seeks me, you may be assured that I will bring you together. I may be obliged, at the last moment, to give you your instructions over the telephone. I ask only that you will follow them out to the letter if I should do so."

"I will. To the letter, Mr. Clancy."

"And now, Miss Maxwell, that is all fixed. In making the arrangement you have, unwittingly, replied to every intimate question that I meant to ask you. You have assured me, unknowingly, of all that I desired to know. I am no longer in doubt concerning you or your state of mind regarding our friend. You alone among all others in this wide world can save him from— from the thing that threatens. But you can do it, and you will do it."

She lowered her eyes while he was speaking. Perceiving it he turned his own glance toward the window and through it.

With an exclamation of surprise, Clancy started to his feet.

"Do things precisely as agreed," he said hurriedly and was gone. Katherine looked after his departing figure in amazement. The dinner was not half consumed and Clancy had forgotten in his haste to pay the check. But she did not think of that. She realized that only something extraordinary would have called him away so suddenly.

Had she but known it, Clancy had seen Bingham Harvard pass the window.

CHAPTER XXVIII

CLANCY'S STRATEGY

CLANCY HURRIED AROUND the corner and down the street along which he had seen Bingham Harvard pass.

He forgot that he was himself a shadowed man. He forgot, for the moment, that men were outside that hotel who were engaged in watching him, and the lady who had been dining with him as well. He forgot that he might be followed as he hurried through the street to overtake his friend, and that he might betray him whom he desired most to spare.

But fortune favors the reckless and it favored Thomas Clancy then.

The very fact that he went away from the table so abruptly and left his companion seated there argued, to those who were watching and waiting, that he would be absent but a moment or two and would return. Thus, for no other reason than mere good luck, he escaped from the hotel unnoticed, unseen, unwatched.

But for that incidents that happened after it might have been interrupted. As it was, the very boldness of the arrangement of them made them possible and kept them from the knowledge of the police.

Down the street, a hundred feet around the corner, Clancy came upon the man he sought.

Had he not been seeking him and glancing sharply into every nook and cranny and doorway that he passed, he might not have discovered him; for Harvard was withdrawn, as far as possible, into a convenient hallway, while he still maintained a more or less perfect view of the street toward Broadway.

The recognition was mutual and instant.

Clancy halted, then darted into the hallway beside his friend.

"Good!" he exclaimed, with relief. "I saw you passing a window of the hotel. I was inside, dining. What in thunder do you mean, Bing, by being in the streets at this hour of the day when you are almost sure to be seen and recognized?"

Harvard, who after the first glance at Clancy kept his eyes directed up the street, replied without turning his head:

"Rushton is yonder. I am watching him and waiting for him," he said.

"Well, I'll tell you one thing. You're not going to stay here to watch him; not if I know it. You are just plain foolhardy to think of it."

"Oh, no, I'm not. Anyhow, I'm going to do it. Go away, Tom, and leave me. You only make it worse by staying."

"I won't, and that settles it. You can find Rushton at any time you want him. It is not of the slightest use for you to risk everything by staying here."

"I shall stay just the same. Besides, I have no place to go. As well here as elsewhere."

"Not on your life it isn't. Say, Bing, I've got an idea. Will you follow it out, just to please me?"

"I'll hear what it is first."

"You can wait till night, can't you, to hunt up Rushton?"

"Yes; if I had a place to wait."

"Then I'll find you a place. Listen. I'll get a taxi. I'll bring it to this doorway. You will get into it. You will hold your handkerchief over your face as if you were using it diligently while you do that. Then I'll drive you around to the Hotel Mammoth. We'll go to that door in the alley at the back of it. You will sit in the cab while I go inside. Horton, the manager, is a mighty good friend of mine. I'll get a whole suite of rooms, if necessary, and without registering. He will let me have the keys. Then I'll go outside, after you, and you'll blow yourself into the hotel beside me, covering your face as before. We'll go to those rooms and you can remain there perfectly secure till after dark. After that you can go wherever you please, and I promise faithfully not to put out a ringer to detain you. Is that a bargain?"

"Yes—if you will have it so," Harvard replied, after a moment of hesitation.

"Will you promise me to remain here where you are until I return with a taxi?"

"Yes; unless I am discovered in the mean time and have to light out."

Clancy did not wait for a further assurance. He ran. Not toward the hotel, but away from it, for he remembered then all that he had forgotten before about the men who were on the watch.

But he knew where to find a taxi.

The plan worked perfectly as he had outlined it. Harvard entered the cab, and a little later got out of it again without discovery. He followed his friend in silence to the rooms that had been secured.

Clancy had taken one of the larger suites of the hotel—and while he was arranging for it with his manager-friend, he mentioned the card that he had given to a certain Miss Maxwell, who would presently apply for accommodations. More than that, he indicated what particular suite he would like her to have. Still more, he wished to be notified in his own rooms at the moment of her arrival.

Everything, fortunately, was arranged entirely to his satisfaction.

Bingham Harvard and Thomas Clancy were presently secure from interruption in what was probably the safest place to hide in all New York City; a great hotel which they had not been seen to enter.

Harvard threw himself upon a couch. Clancy stood at one of the windows of the large and sumptuously furnished parlor.

"Where have you been?" he asked, presently.

"Laying up and getting well. I met with a slight accident," Harvard replied.

"Then you haven't heard the latest, eh?"

"I hear nothing. What is it?"

"The lady whom you wished me to save from herself has resigned from the police department. She no longer belongs to it."

"What? Is that true, Tom?"

"Yes."

"How do you know?"

"I happened to be down there when she did it."

"Did you speak to her?"

"Yes, for a moment. Then she went away. Don't you think, Bing, that you ought to try to see her again?"

"No."

"By the way, old man, I left word with Horton that, if a certain party came in, I wish to be notified. It is somebody I want to see. So, if the telephone bell should ring, don't be startled. It will be for me."

Twenty minutes later it did ring.

Over at the other hotel, Katherine, mindful of all that Clancy had said to her, and being certain that he would not return to the table where they had been dining together, lost as little time as possible in carrying out the directions that had been given her.

At the Mammoth she found Mr. Horton, who quickly assigned her to the suite that Clancy had selected for her, and she went to it, filled with expectancy of what might—of what she prayed would—happen.

And so, when the bell of the telephone rang in the room where the two men were talking together, only a partition separated Katherine Maxwell and Bingham Harvard. Both of them were, however, ignorant of that interesting fact.

Clancy answered the telephone.

The burden of his replies was, "All right. All right. All right."

Then he hung up the receiver.

"Excuse me a minute, Bing," he said, and went out.

But he did not go far. He passed along the corridor a short distance, and tapped gently against the door of the suite which adjoined the one he had taken for Harvard and himself. At the first moment of entering it he had rearranged the fastenings of the door that communicated between the two. Now he had only to unlock the opposite side of the same door.

Katherine was expecting him at any moment. She opened the door at once when he tapped upon it.

"I'm awfully sorry that I had to leave you so abruptly," he said to her. "I left the check for you to settle, too, didn't I? Fact is, I saw a man that I very much wanted to have a word with. I chased him."

He paid no attention to what she murmured in reply. His mind was upon other things.

He crossed the room directly to that communicating door. In a moment he spoke to her again, over his shoulder. There had not been time enough for her to think his actions strange or unusual. He had gone directly about the business in hand, well knowing that Katherine's natural astuteness would very quickly see through any subterfuge that he might undertake.

"Please come here a moment, Miss Maxwell," he said.

Wonderingly she complied. He seemed to be very busy about something connected with that door. She had no idea what it was. She approached him quickly, as he had requested her to do. When she was beside him—he waited until that instant— he pulled the door open quickly, stepped to one side, forced her gently across the threshold before she was aware of his intention, closed the door again, seized his hat, which he had left upon a chair, and, without so much as a glance backward, passed out of the suite into the hotel corridor.

CHAPTER XXIX

WHEN LEAST EXPECTED

KATHARINE HEARD THE latch of the door click behind her. Startled by what she saw directly in front of her, she paid no heed to it. But she leaned against it, clasping her hands behind her, for the moment benumbed.

Harvard had started to his feet with the first sound of the opening door, so he stood, facing her, beside the couch at the opposite side of the room.

"You?" he exclaimed unbelievingly. Then he moved toward her as far as the table in the middle of the room, and stopped, staring at her, still hardly believing that it was not an apparition that he saw.

As for Katherine, this had been too much to expect, to hope for, or even to pray for so soon. She unclasped her hands, brought one of them forward, and pressed it against her bosom, as if to still the wild throbbing of her heart. She could not have spoken words at that moment had she tried.

"Is it really you, Katherine?" Harvard asked incredulously, after a moment "How did you get here? Did you know that *I* was here?"

"No," she answered, in a low voice, replying only to his last question. Then: "I—I am very glad indeed that you *are* here."

She recovered her natural poise while she was speaking; but she remained where she was, near the door.

For yet another interval Harvard continued to stare at her, devouring her with his eyes. His impulse was to leap past that small barrier which the center-table made between them, to seize her, to tell her how greatly he had need of her; to tell her of his great and overpowering love for her.

But he caught himself in time. He straightened himself and stepped backward, away from the table, and folded his arms across his chest. He remembered what he was—an outlaw; worse, an outcast, a thing hunted.

"How does it happen that you are here?" he asked again; but the character of his tone had changed. Memory of all that stood between him and the beautiful creature who faced him had brought him back harshly to a full realization of the suppressed agony that this interview must, perforce, mean to him. Then, before she could reply, the answer to the seeming puzzle presented itself. "Clancy!" he added.

Katherine bowed her head in the affirmative.

"You were dining with him when he saw me pass that window?" he demanded, and he spoke coldly that time.

Again she inclined her head.

"Then you knew that he came after me? That he induced me to come here, in order that this meeting might be forced upon me, without my knowledge or consent?" He was harsh in his manner then.

"No," she replied quickly. "I did not know that.

I did not know that he had seen you pass the window. He left the table very suddenly, without warning. He said nothing of where he was going. I had no idea that he had seen you. If I had thought that—" She paused.

"Well? If you had thought that, what then?"

"I believe that I would have followed him from the dining-room, in the hope of overtaking you, also," she replied, and the flicker of a smile softened the expression of her eyes wondrously.

Harvard made a half-gesture of impatience.

"You know, you must know, how utterly futile and meaningless this interview between you and me must be," he said. Then:

"How did it happen that you were there, dining with Tom Clancy? I did not know that you two were acquainted."

"I—I telephoned to him, first at his office, then at his house, this afternoon, after I returned from New Jersey, where I had gone to seek you," she replied. "You were no longer there. I felt that L must see you again. Why—why did you go away from there without waiting to see me?"

"You should know the answer to that question as well as I," he replied, with slow emphasis. "I came away from there as I did because I wished, to avoid you; because I did not wish to see you< again—because I believed that I ought not to see you again. I suspected that the doctor would find a way to communicate with you after he parted' with me this morning. I desired, with all the strength there is in me, to avoid the possibility of another meeting with you."

She was looking at him with unfeigned sorrow in her eyes while he spoke those words, and his own fell before them in spite of himself.

Inwardly she refused to heed what he had said. She remembered then all that she had intended to say to him and why she wished to plead with him. She recalled that she believed it was more for the purpose of arguing him out of his resolve to commit a crime than for any other reason that she had so longed for the chance to see him once more.

"Why did you come to New York at all? Why did you not remain where you were in safety, at least until nightfall?" she asked him.

"I have already told you the principal reason," he answered.

"But what was the errand that could have brought you to New York at midday?" she insisted. She wished to force him to confess to her his intentions concerning Lieutenant Rushton.

But Harvard dodged the question again. He repeated, once more, the words that hurt her so cruelly, the words that he must know hurt her. Evidently he intended them so.

But Katherine Maxwell was brave, and she was fighting with

all her strength of will. Harvard repeated, with almost cruel emphasis on each word he uttered:

"I have already told you that. I wished to avoid you. Otherwise I would have stayed on there till night."

Katherine disregarded the repetition.

"That was not the only reason you had for leaving when you did," she said.

"No."

"What was the other one?"

"I prefer not to discuss it—just now."

"You must discuss it—now—with me."

"Must?"

"Yes. I have earned—I have won the right to know. Answer me."

"I had some small preparations to make before going away—very far away this time."

"That reply is a mere subterfuge."

He shrugged his shoulders and made no comment.

"Tell me," she said, "what small preparations you were required to make before you go away—very far away?"

"There was a duty which I felt—no, there *is* a duty which I know I must perform before I go. And"—a seemingly happy thought occurred to him—"also there are several sums of money that I have hidden in different locations and which I will have need of."

"Oh!" she said, and was silent.

"It is my—" he began, and stopped. The inference that might be derived from what he had said was plain. He would not explain. He believed that she already thought him guilty. Let it go at that.

"You did not complete what you were about to say," she told him.

"No. It is unnecessary."

"What is the duty that you feel you must perform before you

go?" she asked him, determined that she would force him to confess it to her, although she already knew what it was.

"It is an act of justice," he evaded her.

She left her position near the door and moved nearer to him, so that she stood at the opposite end of the table.

"Shall I tell you what it is?" she said, looking straight into his eyes.

He did not reply. His own eyes fell before hers. Then he raised them again and stood straight and tall and determined before her.

"No," he said, with slow emphasis. "I will tell *you*, since you must know."

"Well?" she asked, when he paused.

He took a step backward; then he passed partly around the table and faced her. He stretched out his arms and opened and closed his fingers, clenching and unclenching them spasmodically. The expression of his face changed. His eyes burned. His nostrils dilated. His features hardened.

"I am going to kill Rushton—with these hands," he said.

His voice was not raised. If anything, it was pitched a tone lower than before. But the utterance was final. It was the closing of a chapter. The end of an argument. The ultimatum of days and weeks of thought.

"I knew it," she said. Her voice was hardly above a breath.

"Well, then, why did you make me tell it?"

"Because, although I did know it, I would not permit myself to believe it—of you."

"Why not of me? Am I not entirely justified?"

"Perhaps—if you are really guilty of theft."

"If I *am* guilty!" He laughed aloud. "No. You are not justified in committing such an act!" she said. "Nothing could justify it. It is not Bingham Harvard who utters that insane threat. It is the Night Wind who speaks."

"Aye. It is the Night Wind, the felon, the outcast, the hunted.

The so-called thief. But, more than all else, it is the wronged man."

She did not reply.

He stepped forward and grasped her by the arm, hurting her, although he did not know or intend it.

"Listen to me," he said, tensely. All the devil in him was roused then, and the sight of her there before him, with all her matchless charms, roused it. The belief that she still thought him a thief added to it. "Think of what that man has done to me—and to you, also. But think first of what he has done to me."

He paused, lifting his skin and pulling at his collar, as if the swelling muscles of his neck made it choke him. Katherine was silent. He continued:

"I was happy. I was contented. I was at peace with the world and with myself. I had accumulated sufficient funds of my own to lift me above the strife for mere wealth. In the beginning I was a foundling.

"God alone knows who I was. But a man, a good man, found me. I was a stranger, and he took me in. I was naked, and he clothed me. Homeless, fatherless, motherless, friendless, and he gave me a home, became a father and a mother and a friend to me. He gave me still more than all that, for he gave me the greatest thing in the world—*love*.

"I do not know what the real child-love for a parent may be like, for I have never known a real parent; but if it can be any greater or higher or deeper or more profound than the affection I bestowed upon my benefactor, it must be marvelous indeed.

"He educated me. He sent me to college. He took me into his bank. He gave me his trust, his confidence, his respect. All the world was bright and fair and filled with joy.

"Then—then came the snake. Through a crevice made by some hapless person who took what did not belong to him there crawled a human snake. He coiled himself and watched and waited; and when the moment came he struck his poisoned fangs into *my* flesh—mine! Into my life. Into my heart's blood.

"In one moment my whole world was shattered. It fell about me in crumbling ruins that buried me so deep that I could not even gasp for air to breathe. Do you wonder I went mad?

"I was innocent of that charge he made. You do not believe that, and you need not. But *I know* it. Every last item of evidence and clues that were brought to bear against me by that man were manufactured by him for the purpose.

"I know that because such evidence could not have been found otherwise. Why did he do it? you might ask. Don't ask. Was it enmity against me? No; for he did not know me. It was the natural consequence of his own depravity and of that awful form of egotism which must win its own petty af fairs at any cost. Rushton needed a victim. He happened to select me.

"Do you know how he made the charge against me? You were not inside of the house at the time it was made, but you were even then a part of the system that made it possible, and you should know.

"Was I given any chance? Not one. Carefully, before he brought me face to face with the accusation against me, that human snake poisoned the mind of my benefactor, my more than father. Then he flung the accusation at me. He heaped insults upon me and upon my unknown mother. She was my mother, whatever else she may have been. Do you wonder that I went mad? that I seized that man and broke him as I would have broken a dry twig with my hands?

"Even then I would have waited and faced the charge had the man who loved me as a son kept his faith in me. All the insults which Rushton cast at me were as nothing to that greatest of all the wrongs: That he had succeeded already in so poisoning the mind of Mr. Chester that my loved benefactor believed in my guilt.

"I hurt those men who were there to arrest me—Rushton,

and the two who were with him. I meant to hurt them. It is a wonder, as I look back upon that scene, that I didn't kill them."

Harvard paused, turned about, and strode twice the length of the room. Katherine remained as she was, tense, expectant, for she knew not what, absorbed by the one big hope that at the end of it all she would save him.

"I knew when I went out of that house that I had broken the law, indeed," he said, returning. "I had been guilty of interfering with an officer in the discharge of his duty. Well, what did it matter? As well be killed for the old sheep as for the lamb.

"Fortunately—at least in one particular—I was well provided with cash against the extremity and the emergency I had to face. I had closed a sale that day after banking hours of a considerable property that I had purchased a year previously as a speculation. It had been a cash transaction. The cash was in my pocket, in an envelope. It does not matter how much. It was sufficient, and I have enough of it left for my needs. So much for that part of it. Will you be seated?"

"No," Katherine replied. "I prefer to remain as I am."

After a moment he resumed:

"When I went to the house that night *I met you*. If I had guessed then what I now know, I would have passed on and no lure that you could have thrown out would have called me back.

"When I helped you on the car and came away, something about you clung to me.

"Don't ask me what it was. I don't know. It wasn't tangible. It wasn't anything at all more than a faint memory; and whether it was your voice, or your eyes, or the glow in your hair, your smile, or the easy grace with which you walked beside me—or all of them combined—I have no idea. The memory of you remained with me in some indefinite way.

"When I saw you again I was compelled against my will to speak to you, and I followed and did speak. You know what happened then. Rushton again—and the partial betrayal of your occupation was also one of the consequences of that meeting.

"I had succeeded in dismissing the idea from my mind that you were a spy upon me, that you had been sent out purposely to ensnare me, and ultimately to effect my capture, until that night when Rushton followed you home and forced his way in; until that night when I was to take my leave of you.

"Julius very nearly restored all my faith in you that night, afterward, by the faithful and fearless manner in which he served me. We will pass all that. Shall I tell you exactly what I think of you now? Answer me, please."

Katherine nodded. Her lips moved in the formation of the word yes. But there was no sound.

"This, then: You are Lady-Kate-of-the-Police. You are a regularly appointed officer of the police. You were assigned by the powers at headquarters to lure me into a trap. You were expected to make use of your many charms, of your beauty, and your attractions, to ensnare me and to effect my capture. You set out to do all that—although I find it difficult, even now, to believe that you could do it. But you did." He had forgotten, or he did not credit, what Tom Clancy had told him concerning her resignation.

He paused and passed one hand wearily across his eyes. Then he turned his back squarely toward Katherine, as if he dared not face her with what he still had to say, and continued in an even tone that was all the more precise because of its evenness:

"You have found something in me—I do not know what it is—that attracts you. For that reason you have been led into treachery to your employers and your chosen associates. You have assisted me, befriended me, warned me, aided me, when it was your duty to do exactly the opposite. You have betrayed your employers, you have betrayed yourself! And—"

He wheeled upon her, his arms raised, his hands clenched, and, without raising his voice above what it had been all along, seemed almost to shout at her:

"Your spell, that you sought to cast upon me, has succeeded only too well. Your lure has worked. You have added, ten million times, to the agony that Rushton's act has forced me to endure. You have made me love you—and hate you with all the heart and soul there is in me, while I love you. Can you wonder that I shall kill that human snake, Rushton, with these two hands of mine, when I tell you that? Can you wonder? Can you?"

He brushed her aside and sent her reeling backward against an armchair, to which she clung. He sprang to the door into the corridor, and grasped the knob. He was going.

She leaped after him, crying out as she did so:

"Wait! *Wait! Wait,* I tell you! Don't go. For God's sake do not go! There are men down there, waiting. They followed me here. Oh, don't go, I beseech you. Don't leave me now so, with those bitter words, the last I shall hear you speak."

Harvard had hesitated at her first call. She gained his side and clung to him. But her strength was no match for his.

Gently, but firmly, he disengaged her clinging hands and put her from him.

CHAPTER XXX

GATHERING UP THE ENDS

KATHARINE DID THE only thing then that could or would have restrained the Night Wind from his determination to go away at once. She wept.

Had she pursued him, had she called after him, or begged and pleaded with him to remain—had she, indeed, shown anything other than the utter despair she felt at his going—he could not have turned back again.

Nor did she weep as other women might have wept—hysterically, spasmodically, distractedly.

When the Night Wind put her away from him—and he did it very gently indeed, although with unmistakable firmness— she did not so much as turn her face toward him again. Instead, she leaned her lithe and supple body against the casing of one of the windows, and she covered her eyes with her two hands and wept quietly, without sound.

So quiet was she after that one outburst of emotion that it is doubtful if he would have seen her in that position, or have known that she was weeping, had not his innate courtesy forced him to turn half around for one last word of farewell before he passed outside.

He could not avoid seeing her then.

The utter and complete dejection of her attitude, the entire abandonment of her position against the window-casing, the hopelessness of it all stopped him.

He hesitated, then returned to her.

Tentatively he touched her arm with the tips of his fingers, and she started.

Gently he took a firmer hold upon her, this time by both arms. He pulled her away from the casing and drew her tenderly, but firmly, to the middle of the room. Then he seated her upon a chair, forcing her very gently down upon it, and stepped backward away from her.

"Katherine," he said quietly, "you must not do that. You must not weep, least of all for me. You must not give way. It is not like you. It is not a part of the Katherine Maxwell whom I have known."

She did not reply. She did not take her hands from her eyes or show by any sign that she heard what he had said.

"I think I understand you," he went on softly. "I think I comprehend at last. I thought I did before, but I was mistaken."

He hesitated yet another moment, then continued in a lower, but more vibrant, tone, still maintaining his position at some distance from her:

"This is no time or place for egotism. You will not accuse me of it, or misunderstand me, when I tell you that I *do* understand—at last."

Again a short silence.

"Oh, the pity of it, Katherine; the pity of it. *I* can bear the pain of it, but it is not just that you should be made to do so. I know there is no fault of mine in this condition, Katherine. It is, I suppose, the working out of the higher law, which no human soul has yet learned to comprehend. Won't you raise your eyes to mine and look at me?"

She shook her head slowly and kept her face buried in her hands.

"What I have to say now," he went on gently, "is very hard indeed to say—but in justice to us both it must be said. Will you listen to me calmly, and try to understand me, and all that I will say, and will you forgive me, also, for the words I shall utter?"

"Yes," she faltered. It was the first word she had uttered. She did not look at him when she spoke it.

Had he done so she would have seen that he was suddenly white to the lips. She would have discovered that he was controlling himself only by a great effort, and that he was maintaining that respectful distance between them solely by sheer will power. Within him there was a condition of fear such as he had never known in meeting with the actual dangers that he had faced.

"I have told you that I love you," he said slowly. "I told you, also, that I hated you *while* I loved you. That latter statement was untrue, although I did not think it was when I said it."

She shook her head, as if she had known all along that it was not true.

"I think, I believe, now that the seed of my love for you was planted in my soul at the moment when I first looked into your eyes and heard the sound of your voice—I believe that it found fruitful soil, that it took root, and sprouted, and grew, and grew, and grew—without my knowledge."

Again she bowed her head affirmatively, as if she thoroughly understood.

"Sometimes I realized, in part, that there was a new and strange development going on inside of me, but inevitably pulled down a mental curtain between it and me, and shut it away forcibly, perhaps, from my clearer vision.

"You see, Katherine, I must have realized all the time how utterly impossible it was that such a thing could be—and—until I started to leave you, a moment ago, it never even remotely occurred to me that *you* cared.

"But then, like a tidal wave, that rises and swells, unexpected and unseen until it is upon you, and sweeps everything before it, I saw and I understood. I knew. And now I must go far away from you; and I must carry with me the added pain of knowing that, even though unwittingly, I have called down suffering upon your gentle heart.

"Help me to be brave, Katherine. For I am not brave in the face of such a thing as this. Help me to be brave, for I am a coward when I face this extremity. Yet I am only stronger than most men. Help me to play the man. Won't you?"

She started to her feet. Her hands fell from before her eyes. She stood beside the chair, with one hand resting upon the back of it, steadfastly facing him.

There were traces of tears still in evidence, but her eyes were clear and they shone like stars upon him.

He kept his distance with an effort, for he saw then in her eyes that greatest of all truths which no man ever sees more than once in a lifetime and which few men ever discover at all.

"It is love, Katherine," he said simply. "We both know it. Why need we deny it, even though it may not be fulfilled?" Then his whole manner changed to sternness, and he added bitterly: "And to think that but for Rushton and the system it might have been."

"Bingham," she spoke his name in a tone so low that it barely reached him, "have you thought that if it had not been for Lieutenant Rushton and the system that made him what he is we might never have seen and known each other at all?"

"I don't believe that," he answered her. "We would have been brought together somehow. Nothing could have kept up apart always."

"Nothing should keep us apart—now—should there?" she faltered; and lowered her eyes, while the quick red blood mounted to her cheeks and brow.

For a moment he stared at her speechlessly; and in that moment the knowledge of all that he would be compelled to face in the future rushed over him.

Again his manner changed to sternness. Again the frown gathered upon his brow, the softness forsook his voice, the muscles flexed beneath his skin.

"Something does keep us apart," he asserted, bitterly. "Rushton does. The lie that he manufactured does. The false evidence that he created does. And Rushton is responsible for it all. Rushton! Always Rushton! Don't you see"—he bent forward toward her—"that I have got to kill him?"

"Then, indeed, when you have done that, Bingham, something will keep us apart, forever and ever; in this world and in the world to come—for all time, and all eternity. Then, then indeed, we will be kept apart."

"Well"—he straightened his tall form again—"is there any recourse? Is there any other way for us to follow save that one of facing the bare facts? Is there? Can you think of one?"

She shook her head slowly.

Dejection fell upon Harvard again. Once more the fierceness went out of him.

"You are a wonderful woman, Katherine," he said, with slow' emphasis. "All women are wonderful when they really love, I suppose, but it seems now to me that you are the greatest wonder of all."

"Why?" she gazed steadfastly into his eyes.

"Because you do love me. Because I believe that you would marry me, become my wife, the consort of an outcast, the sharer of a criminal's future, the partner of a felon's life, if I should ask it of you—if I would permit it."

Katherine's hand tightened upon the back of the chair where she grasped it, and she bowed her head in silent assent.

"How could you?" he cried. "If it were otherwise, between just ourselves, it might be different—though even then it would still be impossible."

"What do you mean?" she demanded.

"You would consent to be my wife. You would marry me. You would go away with me, and live with me, and share all my vicissitudes and misfortunes until the long arm of the law reached out and claimed me. You would permit yourself to become the wife of a thief just because it so happens that you cannot help loving him."

"A thief?" she gasped.

"*You believe that I am one.* You believed it from the first. You have always believed it. Deep down in your heart and soul you believe it now. And yet—"

"It is a lie—*a lie*—*a lie*. I do not believe it. I never have believed it. You have no right to say such a thing to me or to wrong yourself. But you wrong me most of all when you do say it. You know you do."

He stared at her incredulously. He could not bring himself to believe that he had heard correctly.

She bent toward him, but without approaching him, her eyes alight with something that was very nearly akin to anger.

"Do you know me so little as that?" she asked him tensely. "Am I a woman who could love a thief? Am I the sort of creature who would accept, or so much as touch with my hands, a man who had dishonored himself? Could you have brought to life within me this great and overmastering love if you were not *you*? If I did not *know* that you are *you*?"

"Katherine!" he cried out.

A wonderful light leaped into his eyes. A wonderful vibrance sounded in his voice. A great calm, still more wonderful, came over him.

"Katherine!" he repeated. Then slowly he extended his arms toward her. "You do not believe—you never have believed—that I am guilty?"

There was no need for her to reply in words.

She went to him swiftly. Her eyes looked up into his that were gazing down into her own. His arms encircled her. He drew her close against him. Her face was raised to his, and he bent his own down to it.

Then the great curtain of forgetfulness of all things else than themselves and their great love dropped down upon them and around them, and hid from them for the moment every trouble, every pain, every sorrow, every misgiving.

Rushton and his machinations had indeed been overcome, but in a different and a better way than the Night Wind had intended.

Thus was Rodney Rushton slain.

CHAPTER XXXI

THE NIGHT WIND GOES AWAY

ONE OF THE busiest of the North River piers in New York presented a hustling view of life one morning, nearly two weeks after Lieutenant Rodney Rushton and his frame-up had been slain, in all but physical fact.

Just how and in what manner Bingham Harvard and Katherine Maxwell had made their escape from the Hotel Mammoth within a few hours after the stirring interview between them does not matter. It is quite sufficient that they did so and that their going was so secret, so perfectly planned and executed, that not one of the men who watched below guessed it or imagined it.

The ingenuity of Thomas Clancy, with the competent assistance of his friend of the hotel management, accomplished with little difficulty that which had seemed to present the impossible.

The Night Wind had not been recognized in the streets of the city that day. Three weeks and more had elapsed since he had been seen and recognized. Clancy had succeeded in avoiding Rushton's eagle eyes when he left that table in the dining-room so abruptly. Later, when Rushton followed Katherine to the Mammoth and found that she had taken rooms there, he was content to wait below for her reappearance.

But she did not reappear. That was all there was to that.

Then two weeks followed upon the three-and-more during which nothing was seen or heard of the Night Wind by the police, and down at headquarters his non-appearance was generally believed to be the result of one or two possibilities. Either he had in despair made away with himself, or—and this was the more generally accepted idea—he had taken himself off to some other part of the world.

It is a fact worth recording that there was not a uniformed officer or a plain-clothes man in all the greater city who was not perfectly well satisfied that it should be so.

So confident had the police department become of this view of the "Alias the Night Wind Affair" that the watch was taken off of Thomas Clancy—after it had been established that he went daily about his business precisely as he had always done in the past.

The disappearance of Lady Kate, as well as of the Night Wind, was, of course, commented upon. But the police inevitably discover a method of explaining circumstances which they do not in the least comprehend; and so it was generally conceded that not only had the Night Wind gone away, but that he had succeeded in taking her with him. And, if he had done that, it was not likely that he would return.

Where were they during those two weeks? you would ask.

Thomas Clancy owned a home in the country—in Connecticut, where the formality of a marriage license and other betraying incidents were not required. And Thomas Clancy saw to it that they got there safely and that they were well guarded and protected while they remained there.

So much for that.

Then the morning of that busy scene at the North! River pier arrived.

The great steamship *Golgotha,* giant and monarch of the entire Atlantic fleet, was to steam away that morning, and her going was slightly of more than ordinary interest by reason of the fact that a large delegation to a Woman's Congress, to be held in Sweden, was departing with her.

The delegation was followed to the pier by hundreds of others who were not to sail, but who insisted upon "seeing them off," and so it happened, naturally, that the ordinary quota of police-men were there to see that all things went quite smoothly and well.

The regular detail for such occasions was increased, and, in addition, there were plain-clothes men from the central office standing about, watching things. Pickpockets might consider the sailing of that delegation a good opportunity for their ac-tivities.

All things have an ending. The time of waiting for the de-parture of the great ship was rapidly approaching. Five minutes remained before the heavy gangway was to be drawn out upon the dock. Then three minutes. Then two.

Two of the policemen in uniform stood beside two of the plain-clothes men from the central office, half-way down the pier. Their present duties were about over. In a moment more the ship would steam away and they could depart. They were gazing at the throng of moving people indifferently; they were exchanging comments upon the occasion haphazardly. Then:

One of the men in uniform seized the other one by both arms, whirled him around suddenly, pointed over his shoulder excitedly, and half gasped in his ear:

"F'r the love of Pete, look there!" he exclaimed.

The pointing finger was directed through the moving throng of people who were leaving the pier, toward the figures of two persons who were walking rapidly down it, toward the spot where waiting longshoremen were already gathered in readiness to haul the gangway from the vessel's side.

A man and a woman were hurrying along, side by side, toward the ship that was on the point of departure.

The woman held a closed parasol partly across her shoulder, but in such a position that it half concealed her features. The man, who grasped her by one arm and seemed to endeavor to hasten her steps, half covered his own face with a large hand-kerchief which he held in the other hand.

The officer who discovered them, and who so excitedly called the other policeman's attention to the fact, was Compton—and Officer Compton had not forgotten a memorable night, many weeks before that day, at the corner of Seventy-second Street and Amsterdam Avenue. That had been the only time he had ever seen the Night Wind, but he had not forgotten it—or the man.

It happened, too—both of them had been transferred more than once since their unfortunate experiences—that the other policeman was Casey—he of the Elevated-steps incident.

His recognition of the man who was passing so rapidly down the pier beside the woman was as complete as Compton's; but he merely stared, open mouthed, and said not a word.

The two plain-clothes men who had been talking with them, perceiving something out of the ordinary had occurred, turned their eyes also in the direction indicated.

"Who is it? What are you two guys rubberin' at?" one of them demanded.

The man and woman were hurrying with all speed toward the gangway. Compton saw that in another half-dozen seconds they would reach it. He wanted them to get it, and so he purposely delayed his reply to the question.

But the plain-clothes man demanded again, and surlily:

"Who is it, I say? What's up, Compton?"

Casey answered: "It's the Night Wind, that's who it is!" he said.

"He's goin' away—on the ship," said Compton.

"An' he's got his girrul wid him," said Casey.

"By jingo, if it ain't Lady Kate!" the second plain-clothes man cried out; and he started to dash forward toward them.

But he had not taken a full step before Policeman Compton grabbed him by the arm and held him.

"For the love of Patrick, don't do that!" he cried excitedly. "You can't stop him now. He's too far gone. And, anyhow, do you think for a minute that he'd *let* you stop him?"

"Let go of me, you—" He did not finish the sentence. Casey seized him by the other arm.

"You sha'n't go afther him if I git broke for holdin' ye!" he exclaimed. "You're me superior officer, I know, but I don't give a whoop if ye are. Can't ye see he's goin' away, you fool? Hold onto that other guy, Compton."

"I don't need any holding. Not me," the other guy replied, grinning. "I never saw the man in my life. I haven't seen him now. I don't want to see him. Let him go in peace, can't you? Lady Kate has got him under her wing. He won't come back. She won't let him. We're well rid of him, believe *me!*"

"Sure; we are that," said Casey.

"Betcher-life!" echoed Compton.

"I'll slape aisyer in me bed *this* night," said Casey.

"It's too late now, anyhow," Compton joined in. "There they go, up the gangplank."

"An' they're the last ones up, at that," Casey responded. "Sure, the men are afther haulin' it out. Heave-o, ye spalpeens! The saints be praised! They're on the ship, an'—*there* you go, me hearties! Haul away, men!" Casey almost shouted the last words. Then he wheeled upon the others.

"Ye can't git him now if ye want to," he said, grinning broadly. "The Night Wind has gone away."

"*Who* has?" Compton demanded in mock surprise.

"Divil a wan of us saw him at all, at all," Casey replied, catching on. "Sure, we'll forgit it; all of us. What's the answer?"

Compton and the two plain-clothes men nodded their heads solemnly.

The passenger gangway from the pier to the deck of the great ship fell with a resounding slap upon the planking of the pier. The hoarse siren of the huge vessel sounded its note of warning to the craft on the river. The mammoth liner forged slowly ahead.

The throng on the pier waved handkerchiefs and hats. People who were gathered along the rails of the ocean greyhound responded. A void, gradually growing wider, separated ship and shore. Casey ran to the edge of the pier and waved his cap in one last farewell. Compton followed him and did likewise.

The two plain-clothes men, as if by common consent, put toothpicks into their mouths and chewed them—and were silent.

The Night Wind had really gone away.

Those four men knew it. Nobody else was aware of it. And those four men had agreed among themselves that they would not tell of it. But they breathed easier for knowing the fact.

"Would he ever return?"

Each of them asked himself that question, silently, knowing that there was no answer.

The Night Wind had gone away.

ABOUT THE AUTHOR

Frederic Van Rensselaer Dey, who wrote a thousand "Nick Carter" detective stories, aggregating more than fifty million words. The first was written in 1890; and during a period of years he averaged one complete book of about 33,000 words each week. In addition to his "Nick Carter" stories he has written others under the signatures Ross Beekman, Dirk Van Doren, Varick Vanardy, and also under his true name, Frederic Van Rensselaer Dey.

Mr. Dey was born in 1865, in New York City. He now lives at Nyack, on the Hudson. His article is a human document of extraordinary interest.

THIS IS NOT a "detective story." It is an autobiographical sketch of a Detective of Fiction in the making and in the development. In this writing I confess to egoism; but I ask acquittal of egotism. I refer to the second definition of each word in the *Century Dictionary.* The true tale cannot be told without the emphasized *I.* Modesty is shut out. Such is the Editor's *sine qua non.* " 'Go to it,' sez 'e." I go.

Nick Carter came into "being" at a luncheon table, in a downtown club. Figuratively, he sat down beside us. We were three, at the table: O.G. and G.C. Smith, of the firm of Street & Smith, publishers, and I—until Nick made a fourth.

He became "real" to me at that moment. From that moment I chummed with him, lived with him day and night (with few and short hiatuses) for nearly a quarter of a century.

Boiled down to one sentence the proposition made to me, was: "Can you write an acceptable thirty-three-thousand-word story a week around one character, and keep it up indefinitely?"

I replied that I could. And I did it. One can always do a thing if one *thinks* of it as an accomplished fact. It is not enough to believe that one can do it, and to try to do it under such restriction. One must think of it as already done.

Frederic Van Rensselaer Dey

"Prove it by writing ten of them in ten weeks," said S&S.

I sent the firm a list of ten titles (for advance advertising) within a day or so. I wrote and delivered four of the stories within three weeks. It was then decided to reduce the length to twenty thousand words. So I cut those four to that length, and wrote and delivered the remaining six, all within seven weeks from the start. I did not use a typewriter, then. I wrote with a short-handled stub gold pen. I should say, here, that the Nick Carter stories were kept at twenty thousand words only a short time. They were presently lengthened to thirty thousand, and subsequently restored to the original length—thirty-three thousand.

I do not now recall the exact number of Nick Carter stories I have written—call it approximately a thousand—and don't run off with the notion that I wrote all of the published Nick Carters. One of my early stunts was to train other writers to do them, so that I could also supply Nick Carter serials (eighty thousand words and up) for the *New York Weekly,* a story paper. It was the regular thing to begin publication of these serials before I had completed the writing. And it was a common incident (while a story was running in the *Weekly*) to receive instruction like this from the firm: "Don't end 'Tracked Across the Atlantic' with the fifteenth installment. Keep it going till further orders." (Installments were six thousand words each. One serial installment a week, in addition to a *Nick Carter Library,* which was then the name of the regular Nick Carter publication.)

You can see why it became necessary to "train" additional writers for the regulars. I did all of the serials until Frederick W. Davis was discovered. Ultimately he relieved me of them. I take off my hat to him. He was (and is) as good as I at it. Sometimes (I thought) better, although he never worked as fast. And there were Tozer, and Hooke, and Derby, and Phillips, and others, who wrote few, or many.

Let me hark back to that luncheon: An important thing to consider was the selection of a name for our detective. Mr. O.G. Smith had already made that selection, tentatively—provided it appealed to me, who was to write the stories. One of their writers, John R. Coryell by name, had written two stories for the firm in which he had named one of his characters Nick Carter, a son and pupil of Seth Carter, an "old detective." The name pleased Mr. Smith, and I fell for it.

To that extent, Coryell created Nick Carter. But, I took him when he was a kid, educated him, developed him, brought him up, made a man of him, directed his destiny through many millions of printed and circulated copies of the stories about him, and carried him into a dozen languages in translation.

The first actual Nick Carter story published was entitled "Nick Carter, Detective; by A Celebrated Author." I wrote it. The firm chose the "Celebrated Author" moniker; not I. Possibly S&S had, then, a prophetic vision of Nick's future celebrity.

Anyhow, I *am* the author of Nick Carter. I have written millions of words about him. But I never wrote one that could not have been read aloud to a Bible class without shocking it. I never permitted him to lie, nor to condone a lie. I made it a point with him always to seek the good qualities in men and women, and to overlook the distorted ones when possible and consistent. He never (in my writing) made use of a profane or vulgar word, nor permitted it if he could stop it. He discovered, among the byways of life, Chick, and Patsy, and Ten-ichi, and Peter, and Joseph, and Ida Jones, and Adelina, and Mrs. Peters, and made upright, God-fearing men and women of them. He always kept his word. He never touched liquor, nor permitted his assistants to do so. He respected all womankind under all conditions, in reverence for the memory of his mother.

I made Nick Carter *my* ideal of all that is good and right and truthful and honorable and upright and just, in ideal manhood. All writers, I think, in their heroes visualize and oralize an impossible but ideal self.

UNDERSTAND, first, that Nick is much more real to me than are a majority of the persons who actually exist within my environment. Any casual acquaintance, whilom friend, or whimsical associate, is more fictitious than he is—to me. I have lived with him, slept with him, eaten with him, dwelt with him constantly through many years of comprehension and under-standing. He has been ever a harsh, unbending mentor and critic, never a sympathizer. Sympathy from a friend, and self-pity from the ego, are character's deadliest poisons.

I had only an introduction to him that day at luncheon. He came away from it with me. I was eight days writing the first story; we were getting acquainted. I wrote the second one in five days; the third, in four; the fourth, in three. Thirty-three thousand words (by column measure) each. Then, I cut the four to twenty thousand and wrote the fifth, in a week. After that, I rarely took more than three days to a story, and I wrote very many of them (while they continued at twenty-thousand-word length) in two days, always with my little stub gold pen. (I have it yet.) When they were lengthened again to thirty and thirty-three thousand, I worked three, sometimes four, days in the week, and played (sailed, and rowed, and fished at Sunapee

Lake, New Hampshire) the other three. When the serials began, it added six thousand words a week to my stunt. I did it for a while, and then shouted for help! Not so much because of the extra words, as because it meant keeping the serial going (one story) while eight, ten, twelve, or more, *distinctly different* stories were being written at the same time. But I never did get mixed, and I have never been charged with repeating or plagiarizing myself.... More ego! But it's true.

How did I do it? Well, let's see. There were a lot of things which had to do with the doing.

First, I loved the work, enjoyed it. Aside from the mere labor involved, I had quite as good a time writing the story as John Doe found in reading it. Nobody does anything well without experiencing joy in the doing. I never plotted a story in advance in my life. I knew no more than the reader what Nick was going to do in the next chapter. So, I got fun out of it, recreation with the application. You've got to go at what you have to do with a whole heart, a clear vision, and with clean mentality. I never thought about my work from the moment I put it aside until I took it up again the following day. I rarely returned to it later in the day, and I *never* worked at night.

Second, I systematized the work, and I rarely permitted anything to interfere with the system. I got up at dawn. I do so still, every day, with rare exceptions. I ate a hearty breakfast. Newspapers or letters I did not look at. If a telegram came, it was opened and read for me. Unless it was imperative, I did not know of its arrival till later. I went at my work as soon after daylight as possible. I called eight hours of writing a day's work.

Sometimes I wrote six or seven hours; sometimes I wrote nine. The length of the day depended upon the facility of the story, and please observe that I attach the word "facility" to the story, not to myself. An express train is often late, a hot-box or an obstruction on the track has delayed it. But it has to arrive to finish its work—and I had to write a certain number of words to finish mine.

Third, I was well equipped for that kind of writing—detective stories, so called. I was a lawyer, and had practiced law with some success. In the beginning when paying clients were rare, I applied to the judges in the criminal courts and requested "assignments," which means that when a person charged with crime has no lawyer and no money to retain one the Court assigns a lawyer for the defense. One has to call at the Tombs, and Raymond Street jail and other places of detention, to consult with that class of clients. If you treat such a man "white," and particularly if you are successful in his defense, he passes the information along; but it is treating him "white" and being strictly on the level with him that wins his everlasting regard, more than getting him clear, for very often he hasn't a shadow of defense, and knows it. Before I realized it, I had a paying criminal practice—and I knew as many crooks as a headquarters operative.

AGAIN, I had traveled nearly all over the world. I had met, and known, all kinds and classes and conditions of men and women, and wherever I went I made it a point to meet and know them, and to make them like me. I had worked on newspapers as police reporter, general reporter, special correspondent, and at differing editorial desks, and had acquired, thus, another angle of cosmopolitan education. I was Washington correspondent through parts of two administrations, and I had not let that opportunity for assuaging my insatiable thirst for general information get past me without mopping it up. I got to know, personally, and often intimately, so many senators and congressmen and officials and public men generally that when I glance back at my old notebooks it amazes me.

My appetite for superficial knowledge was always voracious. Whenever I struck a new town I sought the streets, and the purlieus, rather than the parks and churches, boulevards and museums, libraries and art galleries. The only public buildings I cared to investigate were the courthouse and the jail. I was never a gambler, for greed, or for excitement, but I had a passion for visiting gambling houses and knowing gamblers. I have known scores of them from the Atlantic to the Pacific, and there was never a time when I couldn't "get in," even when "the lid was down," notwithstanding the fact that they knew I didn't play—not what they call "play." As a matter of fact, they liked me the better because I did not.

Also, I developed a passion for being "taken through" all sorts of factories, and talking with the workers: rolling mills at Pittsburgh, thread mills at Willimantic, lead-pencils, saws, files, paper mills, knitting mills, woolen mills, shoe factories, machine shops, dairy products, stock yards, packing houses, ship yards.... You would see me headed for such goals pretty soon after I hit a new burg—places where they made things! And yet I have no mechanical gift or taste. I know about as much about mechanics as a hog knows about skating. It was the worker I wanted to see and to know. The men and women and boys and girls who toiled in such places; and I would not swap some of the friends I've made in that manner for all the high-brows on earth.

THAT brings me directly to the gist of this whole subject. If you want a rule to go by for producing (whether it's writing thirty-three thousand words or more a week about Nick Carter, or selling wares, or putting up a proposition, or succeeding in anything you undertake to do) I can give it to you in two words. Here it is: *Know* PEOPLE... *all* people! *every kind* of people! *all sorts and conditions* of people! Know them in the street, in the workshop, in the drawing-room, on the tail-end of surface cars, and straddling between platforms of subway or L cars. Play pool with them in fire-houses; chat with them behind the hotel desk, across a counter, punching tickets, making the ferryboat fast in the slip. They are all human, intensely human, and that is what you need to know—*humanity*.

I have mentioned only men, but I mean women, too. They are just as well worth knowing, and just as easy to know. And they will not resent your knowing them if there is nothing in the back of your own mind to make them resentful. That is up to you. And you can't put it across if there *is* anything of the sort in the back of your mind. You can't hide it if it is really there. In getting acquainted with Humanity it is essential to know women as well as men. Every man works to help some woman; every woman works to help some man—mother, father, sister, brother, wife, husband, sweetheart, offspring. It may not always be in dollars and cents, but it *is* always help, in one form or another. You must absorb superficial knowledge of both viewpoints in order to attain to excellence in any calling. Put that into your pipe and smoke it!

In the days when a string of truck-gardeners' wagons en route to Washington and Fulton Markets plodded down Fulton Street, Brooklyn, from East New York to the ferries, between 1:00 A.M. and daylight, I loved to ride with the drivers, and chat with them. And I mean *chat*. Don't ask prying questions. Begin by telling something. Tell a story about a child, or a mother; better still, tell one about your own mother. Abjure profanity. Vulgar and profane words never get you anywhere in anything. Don't talk much. Venture a bit of information observed by you in another community or country upon the business that he is engaged in; then shut up.

When making sea voyages I always seek the assistant engineers—and I see that vessel from stem to stern, and from keelson to upper deck, and talk with the men in every part of it, before port is made. I have ridden in locomotive cabs on nearly every railroad in the United States and Mexico, and many in South America, at one time and another. I have spent days at a time in the coal mines at Scranton and Wilkes-Barre, in the silver mines of Nevada, in the gold mines of Colorado, and I have gone through sulphur mines in Mexico. That wasn't pleasant! I went to the top of Popocatapetl as the guest of a Mexican governmental engineering outfit (eighteen thousand feet) and sat in the sling and was lowered thirty meters down into the crater over the water that covered the deposit of sulphur at the bottom of it, several hundred feet beneath me. That wasn't pleasant, either; but I wrote a Nick Carter with that scene in it, later.

I rode several miles down a lumber chute in a V-shaped "boat" in Nevada, once. I wouldn't do it again for Mister Croesus's bank account. I went down to the bottom of the North River in Professor Tuck's submarine called *The Peacemaker* in 1880-something. We did not go anywhere else. We just stayed there three quarters of an hour, and—Tuck had proved that it could be done. The sub was a little thing, and looked like a "punkin-seed" fish, save for the coloring.

I NEVER visited a factory or a mill or an engine-room or a stokehole or a harness shop or any industrial center, however big or little, to observe any part of the technic; I visited them to *know the people who worked in them,* and to acquire a superficial marginal knowledge of their work and their mental attitude toward it, and toward the rest of the world. I'd rather sit at the end of a river pier and whittle and chat with a longshoreman than to listen to the best platform lecture ever delivered. I make it a point, to this day, to stop and chat with "the cop at the corner" when he isn't busy, and looks to be in a chatty mood; and I remember him and his name thereafter, and he remembers me and mine. I love to go out with the harbor police on their rounds. I have been made honorary member of three companies of the fire department. I never let a G.A.R. man get past me if I can help it.

Postmen are the most entertaining chaps you can imagine. Truck drivers and white-wings have families and homes and children and lares and penates, which they like to talk about— but you've got to be one with them (not of them) before they'll open up. I visited "Beggars' Paradise" in Hoboken once, years ago, and passed a night there studying panhandling as a tine art, and acquiring the slang. Talk about richness of expression! My, oh, my! The place was not over-clean, but I enjoyed it. I have been cod- and halibut-fishing with crews from Cape Cod, and I have picked cranberries down there, too. I've been swordfishing from Martha's Vineyard. I have never been up in a balloon or an aëroplane—but I'm longing for an opportunity. (Aviators, please take notice!) I cannot give the entire list. It would be endless, because it means everybody in every walk of life where I have had opportunity to penetrate. (I was going to interpolate "high or low," but there are no such things in everyday life, save as they exist in your own mental attitude; and if you have that attitude, you won't get to the inside of things.)

I HAVE been called a good "mixer," but mixer isn't the word. One must be "it" for the time being. If you are dressed better than the guy you talk to, you must make him "not see your clothes." You must not use Harvard talk; you must talk his language. Jockey talk in the paddock, longshore talk at the river front, old-timer talk to the cop, because that's what he wants to hear; and so on. Tom Byrnes, Alick Williams, George Mc-Clusky, George Titus, Steve O'Brien, and men in uniform unnumbered have been my personal friends. It has been the same with the firemen. I have made many friends in crookdom, and I have visited them, and done small favors for them, when they were "doing stretches."

Any person, no matter who or what he or she may be, will like you and trust you when sure that you are not a double-crosser. George Cohan in a recent issue of this magazine gave a pretty good definition of being "on the level." But he didn't go far enough. On the level means *being* to the other fellow precisely what you would want him to be to you under the same circumstances. When he finds out that you are doing exactly that thing, you can go as far as you like. The sky and the center of the earth are the limits, and all space is the boundary.

Nick Carter was a detective because he loved to right wrongs, and to foresee and prevent them. He taught the principle that one must *love* one's work. If you can't love the thing you are doing, then love what the doing accomplishes. If there is no real joy in the actual labor, find joy in the consequences of it.

If you are asked if you can *do* a thing, say "Yes," and do it.

You can accomplish it through others if you cannot actually saw the boards and fit the pieces and drive the nails. Every man and woman and boy and girl and worker and idler and lawmaker and lawbreaker whom I had seen and talked to and hobnobbed with helped me to write the Nick Carters. Every one of them performed part of that work for me, but under my direction—in the abstract.

Are you behind a counter, or in front of a steam hammer; or a trained nurse, or doing millinery? Are you a stenog, or a forewoman, or what-not? All right. Who pays you? How did they attain to the positions from whence they could pay you? Find that out. Take heed of the system. Three times out of five their beginnings were smaller than your own. Compel every human with whom you come into contact to like you, and to respect you—to recognize your eagerness to accomplish; willingness is not enough; you must be eager.

When you go to your room at night, after you have prepared for bed and are ready to extinguish the light, do this: Go to the mirror. Stand before it. Look upon the reflection within it. If you can nod your head and smile and say, "I have been square with you all day," you're all right. You will sleep well. You will do better work to-morrow. Don't regret yesterday; that won't get you anywhere. Don't anticipate tomorrow; that won't produce results.

Get busy when you wake up. Above all, get out of bed the instant you do wake up—and go to that same mirror and nod and smile, and say, "I'm going to be strictly on the level with you all day." Divorce yourself from alarm clocks. You can wake up at the right time if you want to do it. At breakfast, remember that gentlemen never willingly speak of disagreeable subjects. Make people around you smile; not at funny things, but because of pleasing ones.

I USED to get thousands of letters from all over the world, from all sorts of people who sought suggestion for some form of betterment. I got one from Russia that was addressed to

"Nick Carter, America." There was rarely a letter which could not have been answered with the five words: "Know people, and be kind."

With these few remarks—

No. There is one more point: The ego.

You've got to keep the ego in the mind's eye all the time. Never let it get away from you nor dodge you—but don't cram it down people's throats. And always respect the other fellow's ego. The hardest work on earth to do is to do nothing. The rich man who retires from active business to a life of idleness does not as a rule live long afterward. A Jewish friend of mine, a very old man, was once asked, in my presence, why he did not retire. His reply was very much to the point. He said:

"Because I don't want to go to my own funeral."

Here is the old Nick Carter signature:

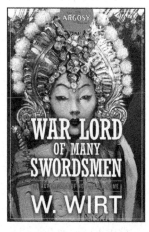

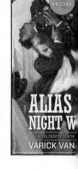

THE ARGOSY LIBRARY ™

SERIES 3 INCLUDES:

* BURROUGHS * ZAGAT * MERRITT *

* BRAND * KLINE *

* BEYER * HENDRYX *

* WIRT * VANARDY *

* WORTS *

THE BEST FICTION
FROM THE FRANK
A. MUNSEY LINE

Made in the USA
Las Vegas, NV
03 January 2023

64750205R00149